The stranger in her bed . . .

Wedded and bedded, Lucy is devastated when she's abandoned by her new husband the very next day. Though it was a marriage of convenience, their heated wedding night gave her hope that it would turn into something more. But she refuses to be the demure bride left behind on a country estate while the stranger she married goes gallivanting about London—even if she has to create a scandal of her own!

Simon, the Earl of Devingham, would prefer his exquisite young bride remain at home where he left her. Instead, she follows him to London . . . seducing him with her fiery kisses, enchanting him with her scorching touches, and awakening in him an insatiable hunger. His duty to the Crown demands that he remain in town, but Lucy has entered a most perilous game—and she will not forfeit without Simon's total surrender.

By Debra Mullins

TWO WEEKS WITH A STRANGER
SCANDAL OF THE BLACK ROSE • JUST ONE TOUCH
THREE NIGHTS . . . • A NECESSARY BRIDE
A NECESSARY HUSBAND • THE LAWMAN'S SURRENDER
DONOVAN'S BED • ONCE A MISTRESS

If You've Enjoyed This Book,
Be Sure to Read These Other
AVON ROMANTIC TREASURES

AUTUMN IN SCOTLAND *by Karen Ranney*
A DUKE OF HER OWN *by Lorraine Heath*
HIS MISTRESS BY MORNING *by Elizabeth Boyle*
HOW TO SEDUCE A DUKE *by Kathryn Caskie*
SURRENDER TO A SCOUNDREL *by Julianne MacLean*

Coming Soon

AND THEN HE KISSED HER *by Laura Lee Guhrke*

Debra Mullins

Two Weeks with a Stranger

An Avon Romantic Treasure

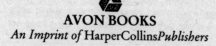

AVON BOOKS
An Imprint of HarperCollinsPublishers

AVON BOOKS
An Imprint of HarperCollins*Publishers*
10 East 53rd Street
New York, New York 10022-5299

Copyright © 2007 by Debra Mullins Welch
ISBN: 978-0-06-079924-3
ISBN-10: 0-06-079924-2
www.avonromance.com

First Avon Books paperback printing: February 2007

Avon Trademark Reg. U.S. Pat. Off. and in Other Countries, Marca Registrada, Hecho en U.S.A.
HarperCollins® is a registered trademark of HarperCollins Publishers.

Printed in the U.S.A.

10 9 8 7 6 5 4 3 2 1

For Gail Freeman,
who saved my life with Alphie.

Prologue

Devingham Park
The night of the wedding

The marriage had been well and truly con-summated.

Simon, Lord Devingham, propped himself on one elbow and watched his bride as she slumbered beside him, her dark brown hair a fan of silk across the pillows. Never had he imagined when he'd offered for the squire's daughter that she would prove so pleasing in the marriage bed. He was more satisfied than he'd been in his life, and all because of the curvaceous young woman who now bore his name.

He'd chosen her for practical reasons. She had been raised mere miles from his estate by her widowed father, Squire Heathpot, so he knew she would understand Devingham and its people well. She had no desire to go to London and be part of Society, which suited him perfectly. He wanted a wife who would stay in the country, look after the estate, and raise their children.

Not one who would interfere in his London affairs.

Lucy Heathpot—no, Severton now—had enjoyed his poetry. She'd made him laugh and brought sunshine to his dark and duty-bound world. She wasn't the most beautiful woman in the county, and some had even referred to her sweetly rounded figure as plump, but her playful spirit had captured him and made him realize within an hour of their first meeting that he wanted this woman to be his bride.

But even with all that, he still hadn't expected this. Hadn't expected her to give herself to him so sweetly, to embrace her sensual side with such abandon. A man expected such things from a mistress, not a wife. He was lucky indeed.

The mere memory of the previous hours had him hard and hungry again in minutes. He watched the rise and fall of her chest, tempted to wake her, but the gentleman in him hesitated. Then she sighed and turned, the sheets slipping aside to reveal one plump breast. Gentleman be damned.

He reached for her.

Lucy came awake slowly, dimly conscious of a large hand warming her cooling flesh. Her eyelids drifted open.

Meeting Simon's hazel eyes brought the previous day back in a rush. The wedding, the breakfast that followed, and lastly, the world of sensual intimacy revealed to her in her husband's arms last night.

"Is it morning?" she murmured, curling into the caress of his hand.

"No." He bent down to brush his lips against her sleep-softened mouth.

She gave a little gasp as his thumb brushed her nipple, and he swallowed the sound with a deeper kiss that sent her head spinning. She fought her hands free of the covers to cling to his shoulders.

He tossed the blankets aside with one hard yank, sliding his hand along her hip to pull her fully across his naked body until she lay atop him. Startled, Lucy broke the kiss, balancing herself on her hands to meet his hungry gaze.

"It's all right," he murmured. "Let me show you more."

Hard male flesh pressed against her with silent demand, but she no longer feared that part of him. She had given him her maidenhood, and he had already demonstrated the pleasure to be found between man and woman. She leaned down and kissed him, his hand cupping the back of her head, her hair falling around them and transporting them into a private paradise.

Heat curled in her belly, and she shifted against him, craving more. He guided her, hands sliding over her flesh, showing her what he wanted, what he liked. She kissed him as he'd taught her, loving the taste of him, teasing his tongue with hers. How could she have known when she'd agreed to marry sober, bookish Simon that such a world of delights awaited her?

"Try this." He cupped her hips and rubbed her lower body against his loins. When she copied the movement, his eyes slitted as he arched his head back with a hiss of pleasure.

His reaction encouraged her. She rubbed her body against his, conscious of the solid length of him pressing against her belly. The more he groaned with pleasure, the more she moved, improvised, urged onward by the delicious taste of feminine power.

"I want to be inside you," he rasped near her ear.

"Not yet." Encouraged by her own boldness, she trailed her mouth down the side of his throat, rocking her hips against his. He gripped her with desperate fingers, pulling her tighter against his demanding flesh.

"Simon," she whispered against his collarbone, then touched him there with the tip of her tongue.

"Temptress." He wrapped his hand in her hair and tugged her mouth to his for a long, unrelenting kiss that heated her insides and sent rational thought swirling away. He rolled her beneath him and nudged her legs apart with one hand. Just his fingers between her thighs made her tremble, and the skill of his caresses overwhelmed her senses. Holding her in place, he slid inside her with a strong, decisive stroke that sent her nerve endings singing with pleasure.

"You're mine," he muttered, and dragged her up for another kiss.

She clung to him, swept along by the passion burning its way through her blood. She was clay in his hands, molded by a master artist into a greedy creature yearning for completion. His hand lingered between her legs, his thumb rubbing that one spot that had sent her winging to the stars mere hours ago, his hips jerking in a fast, relentless rhythm that left her gasping.

Moments later it came, that sudden explosion of pleasure that arched her back and ripped a high, keening sound from her throat. She dropped limp and gasping against the pillows. He continued his movements, longer, slower. Then suddenly he froze, and his whole body tensed and shuddered as a moan tore from him. She held on to him as he reached his own satisfaction, glorying in his evident enjoyment.

Quiet settled over the room, broken only by their gasping breaths. Long moments passed before he shifted one arm to tug the blankets back over them. She started to slide from beneath him, but he caught her and rolled over, draping her over him. Then he tucked the covers around her.

"I'm too heavy," she murmured, exhaustion already creeping up on her.

"You're a mere feather," he said with a yawn.

She shifted to get more comfortable. "What if you want to return to your own bed?"

He gave her an appreciative pat on her bottom that startled a tiny yelp from her. "I won't," he said with a chuckle. "All I want is here."

Her heart warmed at his words, and she smiled, her eyes already closed. She had thought that marriage to a nobleman might be a cold arrangement, with separate beds and mutual convenience. Though they did not yet know each other well, it was a relief to realize that he believed in building an affectionate, trusting relationship with a wife.

"I like having you here," she whispered. "I will do my best to be a good and loving wife to you, Simon."

"You're already doing a fine job of it." He dropped a kiss on the top of her head. "Go to sleep, wife. We'll talk more tomorrow."

Her lips curled again as sleep washed over her.

Lucy slept late into the morning. When she finally woke, the sun was streaming in through the windows. She rolled onto her back, shading her eyes against the brilliant light, confused for a moment by the muscle aches that were making themselves felt. Then she remembered.

She turned to look at Simon . . . and discovered she was alone in the bed.

Well, of course. It was clearly late in the day. No doubt he'd let her sleep.

She shifted into a sitting position, leaning back against the pillows. How sweet he was, this husband of hers. So considerate. He'd known how exhausted she would be this morning—how could he not, since he was the cause? Her cheeks burned as she remembered the events of her wedding night. Her aunt Hazel had been mistaken in what she'd hastily confided to Lucy the night before the wedding. Men weren't beasts, and her wifely duties were in no way unpleasant. In fact, she now looked forward to them.

She glanced down at the gold band on her finger. The ring gleamed bright in the morning light, and she touched it reverently. She was well and truly married now. She was Lucy Elizabeth Severton, Countess of Devingham.

As the daughter of a country squire, she had never imagined that she would wed an earl, much less the grandest local landholder in the district. The arrangement suited her to the bone. Not only had her marriage elevated her social status to a level that would allow her to arrange sound matches for her younger sisters, but Devingham Park was located mere miles from her childhood home. She would be able to visit with her father and sisters whenever she liked.

All her life she had seen Simon from afar, never quite traveling in the same circles for an introduction. She still could not believe that he had offered for her when he could have chosen anyone to be his bride.

Because of her father's failing health, their courtship had been a short one. Yet ever since Simon had approached her at the Thursday night social, pressing Aunt Hazel, her chaperone, for an introduction, she had been captivated by this self-contained man with the mantle of obligation so heavy on his shoulders.

She had been driven to crack that shell of unrelenting responsibility. Simon's late father had also been a man well-known for his great self-control and duty, but Lucy was a firm believer that too much work and not enough laughter was bad for the soul.

The first time Simon had come to call on her formally, her puppy, Lancelot, had taken it into his head to chase her sister Charity's kitten throughout the house. The pursuit had led straight into the morning room, where Lucy sat awkwardly with Simon beneath Aunt Hazel's watchful eyes. The kitten had sped by, upending Lucy's embroidery basket with its passing, and Aunt Hazel's gasp of horror got lost in the puppy's frantic yapping.

With a masterful sweep of his hand, Simon had scooped up Lancelot and held the squirming animal while the kitten made its escape. He'd raised one brow, wicked amusement lighting his hazel eyes, and asked, "Is this reprobate yours, Miss Heathpot?"

Right then and there, she had known this was a man she could come to love.

Their courtship had rapidly progressed from that moment, and each time she succeeded in making him laugh, her heart leaped with joy. He needed her, this too-solemn earl, needed her to lighten his spirit as he dealt with his many responsibilities.

She remembered the first time he'd presented her with one of his poems. He'd seemed almost nervous. As he'd handed her the sheet of paper, a flash of emotion had crossed his face, warning her that his poetry was something special and private he had chosen to share with her. She had accepted the verse with genuine pleasure, assuring him that she would keep the lively retelling of Lancelot's pursuit of the kitten in a special place.

More verses had followed that, along with walks in the gardens, where she had discovered his passion for botany. He had offered for her there in the rose garden, after a mere fortnight of courtship, and he had kissed her there for the first time, a sweet pledge to seal his promise.

The wedding had followed quickly after that to accommodate her father's fragile health. Before the month was out, she was walking down the aisle in the church where she had been baptized, her sisters attending her and a posy of Devingham roses in her hand as she approached Simon to say her vows and become his bride.

Had that been only yesterday?

No matter how hastily the deed had been undertaken, it was her fondest wish that she and Simon would be able to build the sort of deep and loving unity her parents had shared. No marriage of convenience for her, where both parties sought other lovers after the children were born. She would be blessed with a real marriage, one of faithfulness and trust and, hopefully, love.

A knock came at the door, and it opened to reveal a maid with a breakfast tray. The older woman was the same cheerful, blue-eyed servant who had assisted her with undressing the night before. "Good morning, my lady."

Lucy started, not used to the title. "Good morning . . . Molly, isn't it?"

"Yes, my lady. I've been checking every hour or so to see if you were awake yet." She set the tray on the bed. "You'll be wanting a wrapper before your breakfast, I imagine."

Suddenly aware of her nudity beneath the covers, Lucy nodded. "Yes, please. What time is it?"

The maid bustled to the wardrobe. "About half past twelve. You tell me if that chocolate has gone cold, my lady, and I'll have them send another pot right away."

Lucy glanced at the tray containing the pot of

hot chocolate along with fresh bread and jam. An envelope stuck out from beneath the plate of food. "What's this?" she mused, pulling it out.

"From his lordship, I expect." Molly bustled back with a lacy wrapper in her hands.

A note? Uneasiness made her stomach quiver. Oblivious to the maid, who stood ready to assist her into the garment, she ripped open the envelope. The two lines on the paper inside dashed all her fanciful hopes into sharp, jagged pieces that tore her heart.

Have returned to London.

Yours, Simon

Chapter 1

How female mystery lures the mind of man
And shatters logic as no other can . . .

The journals of Simon, Lord Devingham,
on the subject of women

London
Two months later

Simon fingered the pale pink, scented stationery. The elaborate script of Isabella's latest
note flirted with him as seductively as the lady
herself. If all went well at Creston's ball this evening, he might well be on his way to uncovering
the signorina's most intimate secrets.

If all went well.

He tossed the letter on the desk with a snap of
his wrist, then leaned back in his chair, folded his
hands over his abdomen, and studied the femi-

12

nine scrap of paper with a frown. Isabella Montelucci was a woman coveted by most men. The dark-haired, dark-eyed temptress moved with a sensuality that naturally drew the male eye. She was an accomplished coquette with a husky voice that hinted of unspoken pleasures, and her seductive laugh caught the attention of every man within hearing distance.

She was female sexuality personified, and it was his job to seduce her.

The mere thought of the task tensed his shoulders and started the vein throbbing at his temple. What were his superiors thinking, charging him with such an undertaking?

Never in his life had he been the sort of man for whom women pined. Oh, he was attractive enough, he supposed, though personally he believed that his past romantic attachments had more to do with his title and fortune than his physical form.

Weapons, he knew—how to care for them and how to fire them, swiftly and with deadly accuracy. He had killed men in the course of duty and walked away without a backward glance. He spoke four languages, and he could slip past Napoleon's army into Paris, pass as a Frenchman, then return to England undetected with the information he gathered.

He enjoyed a good game of chess or a quiet night composing poetry for his own amusement, and he had spent season after season breeding just the right shade of pink for his soon-to-be-famous hybrid rose, the Devingham Star.

He was too private to be a flirt, too tongue-tied around females to be a rake, and too damned bookish to engage in empty prattle. Charming women had always been Fox's forte.

Fox. Guilt swelled, seizing with black, churning power. He clenched his jaw and closed his eyes, holding steady against the daily struggle. Three years had passed. What was done, was done. His world had changed, as had John Foxworth's. They could only go forward from here.

He opened his eyes again and focused on the familiar sight of his desk. The note from Isabella, pale pink against the dark mahogany wood. The inkwell. His poetry journal, set aside when Dobbins had brought the post. And, on top of the stack of correspondence, a letter bearing the neat, curving slant of his wife's handwriting.

He straightened, lifting the communiqué from the pile. Ah, Lucy. Someone who did not inspire anxiety or despair. He traced a finger along his name, written in her hand. Never had he expected that anything in his work might harm her. But this business with Isabella could, if rumors reached Devingham.

Had that prattlebox, Mrs. Colfax, carried tales home with her after she had seen him flirting with Isabella at the theater last month? What damnable luck that the biggest gossip he knew lived but a stone's throw from his ancestral home, and that she had chosen to visit relatives in London at so inopportune a time. He had considered the possibility that she had gone straight to Lucy with her rumors and innuendos, but the tone of his wife's letters remained unchanged, suggesting that his countess suspected nothing.

That uncomfortable itch between his shoulder blades pricked him yet again. Was it the discomfort of having to portray himself as a rake—as far-fetched as it appeared to him—or was it guilt? Charming Isabella was a necessary evil for the good of all England. Should his wife hear the gossip, she would no doubt be stung by those sharp tongues, but he would think of an explanation that she would accept.

He hoped.

The heaviness in his chest eased somewhat, and he turned his attention to her note. No doubt her missive included the usual chatter about Devingham. Perhaps Lucy's newly betrothed sister, Alice, had set a date for her nuptials. Or maybe the vicar's wife had given birth to her child, or the new groom his steward had hired last month had proven unreliable. He wouldn't know until he read the letter.

As he went to tear through the seal, a familiar scent teased him. He stopped and lifted the missive to his nose. The flowery fragrance of lavender greeted him, and he closed his eyes, inhaling deeply. Instantly, he was transported to Devingham. To Lucy and their one night together. To the welcoming sheets of her bed, as soft and warm as her pliant, passionate body, and the sweet smell of lavender flooding his senses as they mated.

He would never again associate that scent with anything but the delicious release to be found in his wife's eager arms. He hadn't wanted to leave her, but the urgent summons from Sir Adrian, his superior, had brooked no argument. He had intended to return to his new bride within a matter of days, but instead, business had kept him tied here to London for the past several weeks. As much as he wanted her company, he had no intention of inviting her to join him, as he couldn't allow Lucy to become embroiled in his affairs here in the city.

When he'd decided to wed, he had deliberately searched out a soothing country miss who would be content to remain at Devingham and raise their children while he tended to important matters in London. A woman whom he didn't feel obliged to impress with clever social chatter or sly *on dits.* Country-bred Lucy had fit the bill, and her playful spirit had made living up to this particular obligation less onerous than he had expected.

He had gone a-courting with some trepidation, since he knew nothing about the business of marriage. His own parents' union had been an arranged match geared toward ensuring the family line. After the birth of Simon and his younger brother, Roderick, his parents had quietly turned to separate interests. His mother had left the care of the children to nursemaids while his father routinely instilled the Severton sense of duty into his offspring. By age seven, Simon had already understood the great responsibility that awaited him as heir, and he had quietly assumed that duty upon the death of his father.

He had seen marriage as yet another duty to be fulfilled, and the timing had proven practical and necessary with all the matchmaking mamas in London throwing their virgin daughters at his head. Yet Lucy made him realize that their union did not necessarily have to be a cool business arrangement. There could be affection and even laughter in their future.

Once this newest assignment was completed, perhaps he would take his bride on a wedding trip so they could get to know each other better. They had chosen to delay their travel because of Lucy's concern over her father's failing health, but his wife's last letter had reported an improvement in the squire's state.

The idea of getting her alone for several long days had a greater appeal than he would have imagined.

A footstep in the hall shook him from his reverie, and he realized he was smoothing his fingers

over the letter as if it were a precious pet. He
dropped it like a pickpocket caught with his hand
on someone's purse. What was he doing, acting
like a schoolboy with his first infatuation?

He frowned down at the familiar seal. He wasn't
certain when it had happened, but somehow his
wife's weekly correspondence had become vital
to his sanity in a very short time. Perhaps it was
because she brought news of Devingham into his
otherwise solitary life. Devingham, his home.
The one place in all the world where he could
truly find moments of peace amid the darkness in
which he was forced to live.

A knock came at his study door, and he pushed
aside the unopened letter. "Come."

The door eased open, and Dobbins, his very
correct London butler, entered the room. "A message from Mr. Foxworth, milord."

"Indeed?" Simon rose from his chair and met
the butler halfway, taking the newly arrived note
from his hand. He tore it open and scanned the
brief message, then said, "Have Socrates brought
around. I will be going out."

"Very good, milord." Dobbins bowed out of the
room.

Simon turned away and strode back toward his
desk, ripping the note in half as he went. He went
directly to the fireplace, where a low fire burned
to offset the chill of the dreary gray weather that
had plagued them for days. He tossed the scraps

into the flames and watched as the communication rapidly blackened and curled into ash.

When nothing remained but charred remnants of what had once been very expensive stationery, he turned back toward the desk. Fox had summoned him, and Simon had promised long ago that he would make himself available at a moment's notice should his friend require his assistance. He owed John Foxworth more than he could ever repay, and so he had never yet broken that vow.

His glance fell on his wife's unread letter. With a brief twinge of regret, he strode from the room. Duty before family. Fox was waiting, and Lucy's letter would still be there upon his return.

Fox stood near the window, one bare hand gripping his cane for balance as he raised his whiskey to his lips with the other, gloved hand. Every window of the study had its curtains drawn except this one, overlooking the street—though the few inches he allowed between the two drapes might not be considered "open" by most standards.

But he could see out, and no one could see in, and that was the way he liked it.

He sipped again at the whiskey, savoring the smooth bitterness, and wondered how long it would take Simon to arrive.

Almost as the thought formed, his friend came into view and reined in his mount in front of Fox's town house. A young groom ran out to take the horse's reins as Simon dismounted with easy dexterity. His long stride took him quickly to the front door with the same sort of grace he himself had once taken for granted.

The rapping of the knocker echoed through the house. Fox tossed back the last of the whiskey and tamped down the embers of anger that still smoldered after three years. He glanced again at Simon's horse, being led away by the groom, then stiffly turned from the window, leaning heavily on the cane as his damnable leg proved uncooperative yet again.

Once upon a time he, too, had ridden like Satan on horseback and walked with a straight and painless stride.

He'd made it to his desk by the time his butler, Peters, scratched at the library door. He set the empty tumbler down and called, "Come."

Peters peered inside, his manner hesitant, as if he feared his master would hurl the whiskey decanter at his head. Fox sighed. He'd only done that once, for pity's sake.

"What is it, Peters?" he asked, when the servant continued to hover behind the door.

"Lord Devingham to see you, sir."

"Show him in, blast you. I sent for him, didn't I?"

The butler paled and mumbled an apology, then abruptly disappeared. Simon pushed open the door himself, glancing behind him at the fleeing butler. "Dreadfully skittish servants you have, Fox."

"He came with the house." Fox made his way to his chair, his cursed knee aching like the devil. "Come in, then."

Simon nearly winced himself as Fox leaned the cane against the desk and gingerly lowered himself into the heavy leather chair. He wanted to assist, to hold the cane while Fox went through the clearly painful process of lifting his leg with both hands and easing it into place beneath the desk. But Simon had tried to help him in the past, only to have curses heaped on his head by the very one he sought to aid. The day that Fox had treated him to an elbow in the gut had been the last he'd tried to help the man against his will.

Now Simon stood silently, waiting as Fox arranged his disobliging body, every hiss of pain like a sharp, slender blade slicing into his chest. Guilt rose like thick, black ichor. He clenched his fists at his sides, powerless against the stark truth of the situation.

Fox would still be whole and healthy if not for Simon.

"That's better." Breathing a bit harder than normal, Fox gestured at a chair with his gloved hand. "Sit down, Dev, and let me tell you what the bloody French have been up to."

Simon sat, shoving aside his roiling emotions to focus on work as Fox opened a drawer and pulled out a sheet of paper.

"This was intercepted on a French smuggling

ship three days ago," Fox said. "It mentions Isabella."

"Indeed?" His attention caught, Simon leaned forward.

"I've spent the past twenty-four hours decoding it." Fox's small smile of satisfaction held a hint of the scoundrel he'd once been. "It is as we surmised," he continued. "This Isabella Montelucci is the same woman rumored to be the lover of the assassin, Antoine LaRue."

"LaRue was reported dead months ago." Simon tapped his fingers on the arm of his chair. "I've been wondering what his mistress would be doing in England."

"Apparently she intends to reap the rewards of LaRue's demise. According to this letter, she claims to have a list of informers loyal to England, which she intends to sell to the highest bidder."

"Bloody hell! When? How?"

"That's all the letter says." Fox set aside his translation. "Your part in this now becomes critical, my friend. You must charm the details of the sale from this woman and obtain that list before it falls into the possession of our enemies."

"It would be so much easier to sneak into her house when she is not at home and pilfer the thing."

"We tried that. Even you could not locate a single piece of evidence that connected Isabella to LaRue."

"Until this moment, we were not even certain that this Isabella was indeed LaRue's mistress," Simon muttered.

"Now that fact is confirmed, so we can proceed with our only option. Our usual network of informers knows nothing about this woman, so the last choice—our only choice—is to get close to her on a personal level."

"I know, I know." Simon clenched his fingers around the arms of the chair.

"It shouldn't be difficult. She's a stunning woman. You're an attractive fellow. Enchant her."

Simon snorted. "I'm not an enchanting sort of man, Fox. That was always your arena."

"But no longer."

The words hung like dripping icicles in the sudden silence.

"I didn't mean that." His gut twisting, Simon rose to his feet, holding his friend's gaze. "It's just . . . blast it, Fox, but seduction has never been my forte! I've always been the shadow in the dark, the thief, sometimes even the assassin."

"Calm yourself, Dev." A brief grin curved Fox's lips, but there was no humor in it. "I will be happy to share my vast knowledge on the subject." He shrugged. "I shall certainly not be using it."

"Damn it." Simon clenched his jaw, his hands, struggling to keep his own painful emotions in check. "Do you think that I don't remember that your life was destroyed to save mine?"

"I know that you're whole and hearty, and I can no longer dance the minuet." Fox leaned back in his chair, a steely glitter in his eyes. "But the choice was mine. I could have let them kill you, I suppose."

"We might have both been better off."

"Now, Dev." Clucking his tongue, Fox shook his head. "You're a valuable asset to England. And my friend. How could I let any harm come to you?"

"Are we still friends, Fox?" Simon asked quietly. "Or did our friendship die on that wretched day?"

A long moment stretched into eternity before Fox replied with a careless shrug. "Of course you are. And that's one of the reasons I shall impart to you some of my secrets on seducing the fair sex."

Sensing the defensive barrier, Simon allowed the subject to change. "I'm glad to hear that, because I feel I will need as much help as you can give me."

Fox chuckled, genuinely this time. "It's a miracle you were able to woo your own wife, my friend."

"Lucy is an uncomplicated woman. A country squire's daughter doesn't require much in the way of posies and sonnets, merely a substantial marriage settlement presented to her father." Simon let out a sigh as he again recalled the sweetness to be found in his pretty wife's arms. "Would that all females were as easy to please."

"Practical, eh? Well, consider yourself lucky in that regard, my friend. Most women require all manner of folderol and flummery, and I fear this Isabella is no exception."

"You do not cheer me with this observation, Fox."

"Come now, man. It's not as bad as all that. Half a dozen fellows would envy you this assignment. All you need do is bed the woman and entice her secrets from her with sweet words and kisses."

His stomach gave a lurch. "Good God."

Fox barked with laughter. "What's this? Do you worry about your reputation?"

"I would be a fool not to. Affairs are supposed to be discreet."

"Ah, so you fear that your new bride will hear of the affair and come racing to London to ring a peal over your head."

"Lucy would do no such thing, even if such tales made their way to Devingham. I imagine she would either write or wait until I returned to the country, if she brought up the subject at all." Simon flexed his suddenly tense shoulders. "Women cause difficulties, Fox. I prefer focusing on business without sex confusing the issue."

"But in this case, your business *is* sex."

"Not if I can help it." Simon sat down, stretching out his legs and forcing his clenched muscles to relax. "I'll whisper the sweet words and perhaps steal kisses in the dark, but I'd prefer not to bed the woman unless absolutely necessary. I refuse to bring shame upon my wife that way."

Fox arched his brows. "And if it becomes necessary?"

"Then I shall do my duty, of course. But perhaps gifts and compliments will be enough. It's important that I remain clearheaded." He met Fox's gaze and held it. "You of all people know how women can tangle a situation."

"I do."

The tension mounted again until Simon broke it by glancing away. "I believe my target plans to attend Creston's ball tonight. I shall approach her there."

"An excellent notion."

Simon narrowed his eyes at the wicked amusement that Fox made no effort to hide. "I'm glad to see that you can still laugh. Begin talking, my friend, and tell me the best way to make myself irresistible to Isabella Montelucci."

By the time he descended the stairs of his town home dressed in evening clothes for Creston's ball, Simon had begun to worry that his brain would explode from the wealth of worldly knowledge Fox had imparted to him that afternoon. How did the man keep everything straight? And how was it that completely opposing suggestions could each of them work on the same female? The lack of logic baffled him.

Roses were so much simpler. Water, sun, manure, and you beheld a beautiful blossom.

He thought longingly of the greenhouse attached to the back of his town house, of the quiet and tranquillity to be found amongst the lush leaves of his prize rosebushes. Even being scarred by thorns would be more welcome than the task he had to perform tonight.

But this was business. Isabella Montelucci posed a serious threat to the safety of both England and their loyal agents abroad. He needed to push aside his own discomfort with the assignment and just do what needed to be done to protect his country. Even if that meant a wild fling with a cold and calculating woman.

The thought of Lucy flickered through his mind, and he banished the image with a twinge of guilt. A wife had no place in business. He must concentrate on his target.

Isabella had been flirting with him ever since she had arrived in England, his title and fortune a potent allure. Tonight's ball would prove the setting for his active pursuit of her. He would dance and engage in pointless social chatter and do his damnedest to persuade the woman into dark corners for soft whispers and furtive caresses. He'd extracted information from the unwary before—only in this case he would have to do so under the guise of seduction.

Fox had made it sound fairly easy to entice a

woman to give up her intimate secrets. Perhaps he was overthinking matters. How complicated could it really be?

He reached the foyer just in time to see Dobbins open the front door. Two footmen staggered in, weighted down with baggage and hatboxes. Following them came Molly, his wife's maid. Which meant. . .

"Hello, Simon." Lucy swept into the house, her warm, welcoming smile blowing all of his carefully laid plans to the farthest corners of hell.

Chapter 2

A man's best plans so well and soundly laid
By woman's games are often then unmade.

The journals of Simon, Lord Devingham,
on the subject of best laid plans

Lucy set down her reticule on the foyer table
and smiled calmly, even as her pounding
heart threatened to explode from her chest. Her
husband stood poised on the staircase, looking
completely shocked at her arrival.

Shocked? Or guilty?

"I see you are on your way out," she said, hand-
ing her reticule to her maid. It took everything
she had to keep her fingers from shaking. "I do
hope I will not delay you."

Simon said nothing, just looked at her with something akin to dismay, and his continued silence
shook her fragile composure. She glanced away to-

29

ward the bustling servants so that he wouldn't see how pitiable she was. How the mere sight of him in stark black evening attire made her knees weak.

It was an awful thing to be so attracted to one's husband, especially when rumor had it that he was interested in someone else.

"Lucy, what a surprise." His words made her look back at him. Some flicker of emotion cast a shadow over his features, and for one instant he looked like a cool, distant stranger.

Then in the blink of an eye, he was her Simon again, a fond smile curving his lips as he descended the stairs.

She couldn't tear her eyes away from him. His straight dark hair echoed the shade of his evening clothes completely, and the wicked slash of his eyebrows emphasized the sharp planes of his face, lending a fierceness to his expression even at rest. But it was his mouth that drew her attention in a wanton manner that made her blush just to think of it. That full-lipped, mobile mouth brought back memories of scandalous things done in the night hours, sinful things done in private between husband and wife. It was all she could do to maintain a serene demeanor as he took her hand and pressed a quick kiss to it.

"Surprise?" Tugging her hand gently away, Lucy untied her bonnet and handed it to a waiting servant. "I wrote to tell you I was coming, Simon. Didn't you get my letter?"

His dark brows lowered in a puzzled frown. "Not one that told of your arrival."

"Well, that's neither here nor there, I suppose. I'm certain it won't take the housekeeper long to prepare my rooms." She turned away before he could voice the protest she sensed coming, and started walking. "Perhaps we could continue this conversation somewhere besides the foyer?"

"Of course. You must be weary from traveling. Perhaps—"

"I imagine there is a fire laid in your study. The rain was positively dreadful, and I am chilled to the bone."

"I was going to suggest the blue salon," he said, a hint of command in his voice that stopped her in her tracks.

She glanced back at him, and the flinty light in his hazel eyes nearly melted her courage altogether. But this was a small battle, and as long as she could count on Simon to be a gentleman, it was a battle she could win.

"The blue salon?" she repeated with raised eyebrows. "Unless you have been receiving callers this afternoon, I vow that room will be cold as a tomb." She rubbed her hands along her chilled arms and gave him a cajoling little smile. "Your study is bound to be warmer, for if I know you at all, I would wager you have spent the day in there attending to business."

Some of the formality melted from his expression. "I have indeed," he admitted ruefully. "Very well, let us adjourn to the study."

"Excellent notion." Lucy hurried toward the room in question, the low murmur of her husband's instructions to the staff following after her.

She opened the door to the study and slipped inside. As expected, the warmth embraced her like a welcome lover, and she hurried closer to the fireplace. As she passed Simon's desk, the rush of her movement blew a letter to the floor. She reached down to pick it up.

Pink, scented paper. Feminine writing.

My dearest Simon,

I am moved to express my gratitude for your kindness to a lost and lonely visitor in your country. . .

She dropped the letter as if it had singed her fingers. It floated down to the desk even as Simon's footsteps sounded in the hallway. She backed away, coldness curling in her belly despite the warmth of the fire. That coldness solidified into icy dread as she spotted her own letter, unopened on the pile of post.

Her husband had read another woman's letter before hers.

Her stomach clenched into a knot as a shard of pain pierced her vulnerable heart.

Dear God, the rumors were true.

Trembling, she turned toward the fire, seeking some hint of warmth, some inkling of life to combat the deadness that had settled inside her.

Simon entered the room behind her, shutting the door. They were alone, the three of them—she and Simon, and the seething secret that hissed from the shadows like a cornered snake.

Panic flared as his carpet-muffled footsteps approached. He must not guess. He must not know. His pity would rip asunder the fragile threads of her pride. And if that happened, there was nothing she could ever do to make him fall in love with her and be the husband she so desired.

Simon laid a hand at the small of her back, a gesture so sweet that it nearly brought her to tears. "Lucy, you're shaking."

"It's chilly outside." She managed to flash him a half smile, but didn't dare let her gaze linger on his beloved face lest her true feelings betray her. "The fire is helping."

"I've sent for tea, but you should really go upstairs and change out of your traveling clothes. I imagine you're tired."

"Not really." She gathered her churning emotions and held them tightly within the firm grip of dignity. "I cannot believe you did not receive my letter. I sent it days before I left Devingham."

"I did receive a missive from you just this morning, but I have not yet read it." Simon glanced at the desk. She felt him stiffen, saw the trace of alarm chase across his face. Then he casually stepped over to the pile of post and rummaged through the letters.

She knew hers was on top, but said nothing. Had she not been watching for it, she would have missed the swift twist of his wrist that slid that dreadful pink piece of paper out of sight, beneath the pile.

And with that subtle motion, the ice in her heart melted and steamed beneath the burning force of red-hot anger. Did he think her a simpleton? She was not a woman to be set aside mere hours after the vows were spoken, while her husband dallied with another!

He stepped away from the desk, her own letter in his hand and an innocent smile on his lips. "Here it is. I assume this is the note you sent to tell me that you were coming to London."

"More than likely." She dug her fingers into her arms and looked into the fire. She had to play this game and play it well if she wanted to keep her husband from another woman's bed. "The last few days have been difficult. I don't even remember what I wrote."

"What's happened?" He took her by the shoulders and turned her to face him. The concern in his eyes seemed genuine, though how could she judge? "Is everyone well?"

She managed to remain calm, though his casual touch made her want more. "Mrs. Wolcott has died, Simon. Just last week."

"Good Lord." He dropped his hands, his expression dull with shock. "I'm terribly sorry to hear that. My steward usually writes to inform me about the death of a tenant."

"I wrote to you myself." She glanced at the unopened letter. "I used to visit Arminda before you and I were even betrothed. I met her at the Thursday night social, and we became fast friends." Just like that, grief swelled, and she fought it back. Not here. Not now. Not with her shaky emotions barely under control.

"I didn't know her well, but I can see that you did." He stroked a hand over her shoulder. "She was getting on in years, and I know she was feeling poorly these past few months. Please accept my condolences, Lucy, on the loss of your friend."

His compassion was more than she could bear. Soft, hiccuping sobs bubbled up from deep inside her. Tears burned her eyes, then slid slowly down her cheeks as the bleak reality of Arminda's passing crashed over her.

With her mother long dead, and unable to talk of intimate matters with her unwed sisters, Lucy had found in Arminda Wolcott a friend and confidante. The loss of that lady at this crucial time crippled her resolve when she needed to be strong to save her marriage.

Simon caught her to him as her knees weakened

beneath her sorrow, and he held her securely in his strong arms, her face buried in the hollow beneath his shoulder as she wept out her raw grief. He murmured comforting words, his embrace sheltering her in her moment of vulnerability.

Her heart squeezed in her chest. He treated her like she mattered, but how could she believe that, knowing what she did?

"Hush now," he whispered, and brushed a kiss to her temple.

I dare not love you. The thought nearly broke her.

"Is this why you came?" His voice rumbled in his chest, close to her cheek, as he stroked a hand down her back. "To be away from the painful memories?"

"Partly." She sniffled, bringing her emotions under control, and found his handkerchief pressed into her hand. With a murmured thanks, she began tidying the effects of her unexpected outburst even as the flame of wifely outrage simmered anew.

She well remembered why she had come, and her late friend's last appeal was only the half of it.

"Arminda made a request of me, husband, and I must see it through." She handed his handkerchief back to him.

"What sort of request?" he asked, tucking the scrap of linen away.

"She wished me to bring a family heirloom to

her daughter, Mrs. Nelson, who lives in London. It's a jewelry chest of some sort, just a small thing that has been passed from mother to daughter for several generations."

"A simple enough task." He smiled and brushed a tear from her cheek. "You are a good and loyal friend, Lucy."

She took a deep breath, once more undone by his touch. Shameless. She was utterly shameless and weak in her husband's hands. "I don't believe the errand will take too long. I expect I shall return to Devingham in a matter of days."

He gave her a slow, lopsided smile that stopped the breath in her chest. "I am glad to see you, Lucy."

"Oh." A nervous laugh escaped her lips. "Even though I have interrupted your plans this evening?"

"What plans?"

She indicated his evening attire. "Clearly you are going out."

"Oh, yes. Lord Creston's ball."

"A ball? How exciting!" She clasped her hands together and turned hopeful eyes on her husband. "If you will wait for me, I will go and change right now. It will be our first public appearance in society since our wedding."

She saw the refusal in his expression and laid her hand on his arm before the words could leave his lips. "It will do me good to forget for a while."

Her soft plea had the desired effect. The negative response never came. Instead he nodded. "Very well. I will wait for you."

"I will hurry." She pressed a swift, wifely kiss to his cheek.

"Perhaps I shall pass the time by reading your letter," he said with a grin.

She smiled back at him, but the curve faded from her lips as she turned away and headed for the door. She knew with every fiber of her being that Simon had intended to see the author of the pink, perfumed note tonight. But she was his wife, and she'd shave her head bald and run naked in the streets of London before she would let anyone forget that fact.

Arminda would be proud.

Simon crept out to the hallway and watched from the shadows as his wife climbed the stairs to the second floor. Once she had disappeared from sight, he hurried back to his study, his mind racing to decide the best course of action.

Gad, what a coil. He'd no sooner accepted his part in this mad game than his wife arrived in London! He'd intended for her to remain in the country until he was able to visit her there. During the times he resided in London, he focused completely on business, secure in the knowledge that no inquisitive females would get in the way of his duty to his country. That had remained his hard and fast rule, completely unshakable, ever since Georgina.

Blast it all! Why had Lucy come *now*?

He paced his study, haunted by memories of the past and the realities of the present. Georgina and her petty jealousies had nearly gotten both him and Fox killed three years ago, and now Lucy had arrived on the scene, a very attractive blockade to his clever plans for the evening.

There was no way on Earth he'd feel comfortable wooing another woman with his new bride attending the same social event. He'd feel like the worst kind of cad, and it would humiliate Lucy. Yet he'd not had the heart to deny his wife her request to accompany him, not when she was so clearly distraught by the death of her friend.

But at the same time, he dared not allow Isabella to turn her interests elsewhere. He could barely manage to charm one woman, much less two. He needed help.

He grabbed a piece of stationery and scribbled a quick note, then sanded and sealed it firmly. His determination solidified as he wrote the name of the intended recipient on the outside.

Fox would help, he thought grimly as he summoned a footman, or else the entire plan would be lost.

The Creston ball proved to be a huge crush as expected. Lucy gaped at the cream of the *haute ton*, garbed in shimmering silk and covered in sparkling jewels.

Her evening dress wasn't too terribly out of fashion, but she could tell from the glances of the other women that it wasn't all the crack either. Next to all these slender, swanlike beauties, she felt like a plump little partridge, fresh from the fields. She smoothed a hand down the skirt of the blue silk and comforted herself with the knowledge that she wore the perfectly matched Devingham pearls at her throat and ears. Simon had presented them to her the day before their wedding. Nothing could compare with them, and they were the badge that branded her unequivocally as Simon's wife.

She fingered her dress again, and Simon leaned down to whisper, "You look lovely."

She glanced up into his face, startled and pleased at the sensual warmth lingering in his hazel eyes. Heat spread through her body at his admiration. The last time he'd looked at her like that had been on their wedding night.

Her body tingled at the very thought.

"Shall I fetch you some punch?" he asked with a gallant smile.

"Yes." The word came out on a breathy sigh. "Thank you."

He led her to the edge of the room where the dowagers sat exchanging gossip, then gave a little bow and began to make his way through the crowd to the punch bowl.

She watched him as long as she was able, until the crowd swallowed him up. Her blood pumped with excitement. He was so charming, so attentive. Certainly, he could not be indifferent to her? Hope swelled.

Two gentlemen staggered by, obviously sotted, and she stepped aside a few paces to avoid being trampled. She returned her attention to the area of the punch bowl just as the crowd parted.

And Simon handed a glass of punch to an exotically beautiful woman.

Her heart nearly stopped in her chest. The woman's jet-black hair fell over her nearly bare shoulders in attractive disarray. Her impressive bosom challenged the very rules of propriety, her bodice cut so low that every breath promised to be the one that would expose her assets completely. Her figure was the one that every female longed for—curving or slender in all the right places.

Every inch of the dark-haired beauty spoke of sensuality, her every gesture an invitation. Simon lingered by the punch bowl, leaning in to talk to her, smiling as if he treasured her every word.

When the woman placed her fingers lightly on Simon's sleeve, Lucy's breath seized in her chest.

This, then, must be Isabella Montelucci.

Simon gently removed the Italian woman's fingers from his arm.

Isabella pouted. "Do you not wish my company, Lord Devingham?"

He smiled and gazed deep into her eyes as Fox had advised him to do. "You are the most enchanting of companions, Mrs. Montelucci."

"Then why do you leave?" She tapped his arm with her fan. "Stay and talk to me, my lord."

"Alas, duty calls. My wife has just arrived in London."

"Ah." She licked her full lips, a motion designed to arouse a man. "Perhaps you will dance with me later, then?"

He remained immune to her obvious charms, but played the game. "If any dance remains unclaimed, I would be honored."

"A waltz." She leaned closer to him, her big dark eyes brimming with barely controlled passion. "I will save it for you, Lord Devingham. Only for you."

He blinked, suddenly aware she was not referring to the dance. Playing his part, he dipped his head in agreement and smiled at her. "I look forward to it. If you will excuse me—" He took up another glass of punch and swiftly left.

The farther away he got from Isabella, the easier it became to breathe. The Italian woman exuded sex, but he found himself repelled rather than enticed. He much preferred subtlety in his females, much like his wife.

He reached Lucy's side, where she stood conversing with their hostess. The barest whiff of lavender touched him, tossing to the surface all manner of arousing memories of their marriage bed. Where did that scent linger? In her hair? Did she drop it into her bathwater? Or spray it on her person after dressing?

"Is that for me?" Lucy's quiet voice shook him from his imaginings.

"It is indeed." He handed Lucy her punch and smiled at Lady Creston, who regarded him with amusement. "I fear you have both caught me woolgathering."

"No doubt you are distracted with the arrival of your lovely bride," her ladyship teased.

"Quite so." He caught and held Lucy's gaze as she sipped at her punch, not bothering to hide his admiration. Her cheeks pinkened, and she glanced away, lowering her glass to continue her conversation with Lady Creston.

He hadn't lied when he'd said she looked lovely. Her dark brown hair was arranged in an upswept style with curls and ringlets, but he much preferred it loose and falling over her shoulders. He remembered burying his face in her hair while sated from their love play.

She was small of stature, and some might consider her plump, but her lush, womanly body lured him. He preferred his women with curves, not sticks with breasts like many of the debutantes. He rather favored her round, lavish bottom and enjoyed feeling it snuggled against him as they curled together in her bed after sex.

He'd missed her, rather badly actually. It occurred to him just then that she was staying the night in Town, and he'd have an unexpected opportunity to make love to her tonight. The thought excited him to the point where it stirred him physically, and he turned his attention away, scanning the room for any kind of distraction.

He found it in the scowling face of Fox as his friend limped into the ballroom.

"My word, is that Mr. Foxworth?" Lady Creston gasped.

"It is." He gave the ladies a brief bow. "If you ladies will excuse me, I must speak with him."

Lucy watched her husband make his way across the ballroom, emotions churning like an unleashed storm within her. Had Lady Creston not chosen that moment for a conversation, she couldn't have guaranteed what her reaction would have been once her husband returned from the punch bowl. Something extremely unladylike and physical came to mind. Only their hostess's presence had lent her the restraint to resist causing a scandal.

But it had been a very near thing.

She took a deep breath to calm her racing heart. The rumors about Simon and Isabella had merely raised speculation and dismay that her husband might be having an affair. Now that she had actually seen Simon flirting with the Italian beauty, she had no doubts at all that the woman was a threat to her marriage.

"I can hardly believe Mr. Foxworth chose to attend!" Lady Creston's excited whisper broke Lucy's train of thought. "He has been quite the hermit for the past three years and *never* accepts invitations."

"I didn't know that." Willing to be distracted by the lady's enthusiasm, Lucy peered through the crowd, but her petite stature prevented her from seeing Mr. Foxworth.

"My ball will be the talk of London!" Lady Creston crushed her fan between her fingers. "You must introduce me."

"I cannot, Lady Creston, as I myself have never met the man."

"What?" Lady Creston gaped in shock. "Mr. Foxworth is your husband's dearest friend, Lady Devingham. I can hardly credit that you have never made his acquaintance."

"Still, it is true. You said it yourself that he does not attend many functions."

"I shall press your husband for an introduction."

"So will I," Lucy murmured, and wondered what else her husband kept secret from her.

Chapter 3

A study of the cuttings cultivated in London and replanted in the gardens at Devingham reveals a much hardier bloom with surprisingly strong thorns buried beneath tender leaves.

Scientific notations on roses
by Simon, Lord Devingham

Fox glared at the few members of the *ton* who looked like they might approach him and, without a word to any of them, followed as Simon cleared a path through the crowd. "I cannot believe that you have brought me here," Fox muttered. "I do not go about in Society anymore."

"I need you." Simon cast smiles as he made his way past the curiosity seekers. "I cannot manage tonight without you, Fox."

"If your wife is the problem, send her home."

"I can't." Simon stopped and faced his friend.

"I know what this is costing you," he whispered. "I do, truly, understand. But think of the cause. *I need your help.*"

Fox looked like a hound with a sore paw. "I'm here, am I not? Just don't expect me to like it."

"Fair enough. Just help me through tonight. Lucy should be on her way back to Devingham in a day or so." Simon turned away and pushed through the throng.

"See that she is," Fox grumbled.

"Be charming," Simon advised in a low voice as they approached the ladies.

As Simon returned to them, Lucy studied Mr. Foxworth with some curiosity. Simon had mentioned him in letters and casual conversation, and she also remembered that her husband had been disappointed that this man had been unable to attend their wedding. She had been under the impression that Mr. Foxworth was simply a business associate.

But as she watched them together, she could clearly see there was something more.

John Foxworth was nearly as tall as her husband. He was a handsome man, though the lines around his mouth implied someone of disapproving disposition. Hair the shade of cherrywood curled unfashionably over his forehead and ears, and his evening clothes appeared a shade out of date. He bore an elegant silver-topped cane that clearly functioned as more than an ornament, given the man's pronounced limp. He wore white evening gloves, but when he shifted his grip on the cane, she caught a glimpse of scarred, puckered skin just above his wrist. She jerked her eyes to his face and met his hard, blue-eyed stare.

"Lucy, may I present to you Mr. Foxworth? Fox, my wife, Lucy, Lady Devingham."

Fox dipped his head in a brief semblance of a bow. "A pleasure, Lady Devingham."

"Mr. Foxworth," she acknowledged, chilled. His emotionless tone belied his proper words that this meeting was a pleasure.

Simon turned to introduce Fox to their hostess. "Lady Creston, I believe you know Mr. Foxworth."

Lady Creston nearly simpered as Fox bent over her hand. "I am so pleased you could attend this evening, Mr. Foxworth."

Fox gave his hostess a brilliant, captivating smile that made him look like another man entirely. "Word of your wonderful hospitality reached my ears, Lady Creston, and I could not stay away."

"My goodness!" Lady Creston pressed her folded fan to her bosom as a blush of pleasure tinted her cheeks.

"I am full of admiration over your event, your ladyship, and I would beg a dance of you, save for this." He tapped his leg with his cane.

Their hostess giggled like a schoolgirl. "You are truly a charmer, Mr. Foxworth."

"Perhaps Lord Devingham would do the honors for me?" Fox arched a brow at Simon.

"It would be my pleasure if Lady Creston would take a turn around the floor with me," Simon replied with a bow.

"How lovely!" Lady Creston extended her hand. "Be warned, Lord Devingham, I shall ask you innumerable questions about Mr. Foxworth."

"I accept the risk," Simon said, guiding the lady's hand to his arm. "Fox, I trust you to take care of my wife until I return."

"Of course."

Lady Creston and Simon went off to the dance floor, leaving Fox and Lucy standing alone together. Lucy glanced over and was startled to find Fox's attention completely focused on her. When their gazes met, he smiled with a warmth that made her feel like the only woman in the room.

She snapped open her fan and waved it to cool her suddenly hot cheeks. When he chose to, John Foxworth could steal a woman's breath with that smile. Why would he waste it on the wife of his best friend?

He halted a passing servant. "Would you care for champagne, Lady Devingham?"

"No, thank you." She placed her empty glass on the servant's tray, then waved him along. Turning back to the utterly magnetic man beside her, she caught a glimpse of something in his eyes that immediately put her on her guard—a flash of calculation that seemed at odds with his amiable demeanor. "Mr. Foxworth, how long have you known my husband?"

"Several years, madam. Since we were school-boys."

"You did not come to the wedding." Lucy frowned as she caught a glimpse of Lady Creston dancing with an elderly admiral. Where was Simon?

"I was indisposed."

"He was disappointed." Lucy began searching the crowd on the other side of the ballroom for some sign of her husband. "He wanted you to stand up with him."

"I don't believe I could stand at all that day."

The quip startled her. She turned to him in sincere apology, compassion softening her voice. "How clumsy of me. I apologize. I should have realized." She glanced at his cane, then back to his face.

His smile tightened just a hint along the edges. "You have only just met me, Lady Devingham. You could not be expected to know my history."

"I should not have assumed. I was just . . ." She frowned, jerking her attention back to the dance floor as she realized that the social faux pas had distracted her from her search for her husband.

Fox stepped into her line of vision. "Do not distress yourself. After all this time, my feelings are not so fragile."

The hint of suspicion niggling at her grew into

full-blown doubt. Watching him carefully, she said, "Mr. Foxworth, perhaps your greater height will allow you to see Simon in the crowd."

He scanned the throng. "He is still dancing with our hostess." His angelic smile was in place when he turned back to her. "Are you certain I cannot fetch you some refreshment?"

She narrowed her eyes at him. "How odd that you should mistake that elderly gentleman promenading with Lady Creston for Simon. Perhaps you need spectacles, sir."

He stiffened and whipped his head around again to search the crowd just as Lady Creston passed by with her new partner. He muttered a curse.

Lucy closed her fan with a snap. "What is your game, Mr. Foxworth?"

The charm evaporated from his expression, and she found herself facing what she suspected was the real John Foxworth, his blue eyes glittering with ruthless cunning. "You are new to being a wife, Lady Devingham, and country-bred to boot. You cannot be expected to understand the nuances of Society. I was only trying to protect you from your own naïveté."

She flinched. "How unfortunate you could not attend our wedding, Mr. Foxworth. You might have voiced your objection to Simon's bride at the ceremony." Swallowing hard, she turned away. Where was her husband?

She caught a glimpse of him then, near the terrace doors at the other side of the room. She took a step forward, intending to rid herself of Fox's conniving company and seek her husband's. Then she halted, struck dumb with astonishment as Isabella Montelucci placed her hand on Simon's arm. The two strolled out onto the terrace.

"I tried to spare you that."

She jerked around to face Fox, and one glance at his pitying expression told the tale. Tears of humiliation misted her eyes, despite her resolve. "I see your game now," she managed with her last dregs of dignity. "I shudder to think how far you might have taken it."

Unwilling to hear whatever biting reply he intended, she gathered her tattered pride around her and walked away, well aware that her rapid pace prevented him from following.

Her lack of acquaintances served her well in her escape. She hurried away from the crowd, looking for a moment of privacy to compose herself. Had Simon asked Mr. Foxworth to divert her attention while he sought a moment with his lover? Her husband's earlier attentions had seemed so genuine. Or was she a fool? Just a country bumpkin who thought married couples should be faithful?

A whispered inquiry of a servant sent her to the hallway where there were rooms set aside for ladies to refresh themselves. But voices from that direction sent her the opposite way. She ducked into a nearby alcove off that same hallway and dug through her reticule for a handkerchief.

She should have expected this. Clenching the snowy lace in her fist, Lucy leaned back against the wall of the alcove, took a deep breath, and closed her eyes. She had heard that the *ton* considered marriage to be a convenience designed for merging estates and creating children. That men could take mistresses while their wives were to turn the other cheek and be grateful for the security of their lives.

But she wasn't born a member of the Polite World. She was the daughter of a country squire. Her parents had married for love, and after her mother's death when Lucy was twelve, her father had never remarried. He still loved his wife, still missed her every day.

That was how she believed marriage ought to be. And when Simon had come to her father with his marriage proposal in hand, she had thought that's what he believed as well. He had spoken earnestly of his love for Devingham and its people. He had talked of shared lives and children and growing old together in comfort and companionship.

And then he had left her the morning after the wedding.

Had he lied when he'd made his offer, or had she merely misunderstood his intentions? Was it just that he didn't know her well enough yet to love her? After all, they were strangers—married strangers.

She opened her eyes and stared at the carved marble detail on the wall of the alcove. She had been so thrilled to receive a proposal of marriage from an earl! It had taken the burden off her father to find husbands for four daughters. With Lucy's new social status, she could marry all three of her sisters off to men of means.

The fact that she had watched Simon from a distance all her life, knew him to be a good and honorable man, only sweetened the offer. His tenderness toward her on their wedding night had left her hoping that their relationship was developing into one of mutual caring.

But apparently not. Clearly, she was the only one who had felt that way.

Foolish, naïve girl.

According to the rules of Society, she should turn a blind eye to Simon's affair with the Italian woman and return meekly home to Devingham to await his convenience. Or she could turn him from her bed in righteous anger and deny him his husbandly rights.

Neither option appealed to her.

Arminda had suggested that she seduce her husband away from his mistress. But having seen Isabella Montelucci in the flesh, she had her doubts that a mere wife could accomplish such a thing. After all, wasn't she here, weeping like a schoolgirl, while that Italian woman strolled the gardens with Simon?

But then again, hiding in an alcove would accomplish nothing. It was about time she crept out to the garden and saw the truth for herself.

Lucy wiped the lingering tears from her eyes and stuffed the handkerchief in her reticule. There were doors leading to the terrace at the end of the hallway. She would slip out that way and see if she could find her husband.

She stepped out of the alcove and started down the hallway, determination fueling her steps. Isabella Montelucci had best turn her covetous eyes elsewhere. Lucy had no intention of meekly allowing the other woman to seduce her husband away from her.

Just as she neared the terrace, a door opened a few feet in front of her, and two young ladies stepped out. Both were young, beautiful, and dressed to attract suitors. Lucy continued on her way with apparent disinterest, hoping they would pass her without having to exchange social niceties.

"Can you imagine being seen like that?" the petite blonde asked, linking her arm through her friend's as they strolled closer to Lucy. "To attend a function such as this with *spectacles* on one's face!"

"I can hardly credit it, Minerva," replied the Junoesque brunette. "Spectacles *and* freckles! Why, my mother would never let me leave my room at Pelshaven in such a state, much less attend an event in London."

As they spoke, a tall, slim woman with ginger-colored hair, freckles, and spectacles came out of the room behind them. The unfortunate lady wore a white dress with ruffles and lace that did not become her in the slightest, and she stopped short upon noticing the other girls walking away from her. However, the debutantes were too caught up in their conversation to notice her presence—or to lower their voices.

"It is bad enough the poor thing is so dreadfully tall and has a figure like a boy's," the blond Minerva continued, her giggling tones carrying along the hallway. "But she is an American, too, Helen, and her every word sounds dreadful to the civilized ear."

The newcomer's eyes narrowed. "I suppose that depends on what you consider civilized," she said with a distinctly American accent. "To me, you all sound like a bunch of hoity-toity snobs."

The two girls whirled around to face the taller woman, who folded her arms across her chest and stared them down, unintimidated. Lucy slowed her pace, hoping not to draw attention to herself as she focused on the terrace doors just beyond them.

The blond pixie was the first to respond. "How dare you intrude on a private conversation?"

"It's not so private if you have it in the middle of the hallway."

Smothering a chuckle, Lucy paused, fascinated despite herself. How many times had she played the mediator when her sisters had engaged in such battles?

"We were trying to spare your feelings," Helen said with a haughty sniff. "It is certainly not our fault if you overheard something not meant for your ears."

"Do you think I care at all that you don't like my spectacles or my freckles or my accent?"

"You should care." Helen, the taller of the two, took a step forward, her eyes narrowed. "You are in England now, not America. Minerva and I could ruin you with just a word."

"Is that so?"

"Helen is the daughter of Lord Pelshaven," Minerva informed her. "And my own father is Viscount Barhampton. Others listen to what we say."

"Society includes whom we want included," Helen said, "and *excludes* those we want excluded. All your American dollars cannot buy your acceptance, Miss Matthews."

Lucy shook her head at the blatant lie. These girls had no more social power than Lady Strye's little white dog.

The American woman looked up suddenly and met Lucy's gaze. "Imagine that. My fortune can't buy me the popularity these two ladies can provide on just their say-so."

Admiration for this Miss Matthews spurred her to step forward. "Oh? I shall have to remember that." As Lucy came to link her arm with the American's, the two debutantes nearly knocked heads in their haste to move away from their target.

"Who are—" Minerva began.

"Lady Devingham," Helen interrupted, gaping like a freshly caught trout. "I heard her announced," she whispered to Minerva.

"My dear Miss Matthews," Lucy said, as if the other girls hadn't spoken, "I had wondered where you'd gone. We were discussing our trip to Bond Street in the morning."

"Yes, Bond Street." The American nodded, clearly willing to play along.

"Lady Devingham, I believe we have met before. Perhaps you do not remember me . . ." Helen said.

Lucy flicked her a glance. "No, I do not."

Helen blinked in shock, then snapped her mouth closed.

"I am Viscount Barhampton's daughter," Minerva interrupted, pushing in front of Helen. "I believe my father knows your husband."

Lucy took in the girl from head to toe. "Barhampton. Oh, yes. I believe my husband purchased some very inferior horseflesh from your father to fund your debut." To Miss Matthews she stage-whispered, "Financial difficulties."

Minerva flushed beet red and looked away.

A clock chimed somewhere in the hall, and Lucy smiled at her tall companion. "Come, Miss Matthews. You were going to give me some ideas for the ball I intend to host. It is about time I opened the ballroom at Severton House."

Helen gasped. "There has not been a ball at Severton House in nearly twenty years!"

Lucy smiled. "How lovely that you know the family history, Hester."

"Helen."

"And you are right, there has not been a ball at Severton House in way too long. Of course, now that I am Lady Devingham, that will all change. Good evening to you." She turned away and began to walk toward the terrace doors, the American woman forced to come along because of their linked arms. "Of course my ball must be very special and very exclusive. And I think you, Miss Matthews, can help me put just the right intimate touches on the event . . ."

Lucy kept up a stream of inane chatter until she and her companion reached the doors. She opened them and led her new friend outside as the ill-mannered debutantes marched off down the hallway in the opposite direction. "I must apologize for my fellow Englishwomen, Miss Matthews," she said, shutting the doors carefully. "I'm afraid many of them are quite . . . how did you put it?"

"Hoity-toity."

"Yes." Lucy smiled. "Hoity-toity. Exactly."

"But you aren't. Even though you're Lady Somebody. I'm sorry, I didn't catch the name."

"My name is Lucy. I mean, Lady Devingham."

"You want to tell me what we're doing outside?" Miss Matthews watched her patiently, intelligent green eyes behind the spectacles holding a question.

Lucy hesitated, torn between a desire to confide in another female and caution about revealing secrets to a stranger. "I wanted some air."

"Too stuffy in there?"

"Exactly. Come, let's walk along the terrace to the ballroom."

Miss Matthews didn't move. "Why do I think there's something you're not telling me?"

"Please call me Lucy. My friends do."

The American woman blinked in surprise. "You want to be friends? With me?"

"Why not?"

"Well, because I speak my mind too much, and I think too much for a woman, or so my godmother tells me."

"I find truthfulness refreshing."

"You may be sick of it before long." She seemed to be waiting for Lucy to agree, then shrugged when she didn't. "Let's try this out for a day or two. If you get tired of my plain speaking, I won't take it amiss if you decide we can't be friends."

"I could use a friend." Lucy glanced out at the darkened gardens. "I really don't know anyone in London."

"I don't know anyone in London either."

"You do now, Miss Matthews."

"Gin." She grinned, and a little dimple appeared in her cheek. "I'm Virginia Matthews from Philadelphia."

"I am pleased to make your acquaintance. Now, would you care to accompany me back to the ballroom—the long way?"

Gin chuckled. "I sure would."

As they made their way along the terrace toward the open ballroom doors, the smile faded from Lucy's face as she gazed at the garden with its winding paths and dark corners. Were they still out there together? What would she do if she found them?

"Are you all right?" Gin asked.

Lucy jerked her attention back to her companion and managed a wan smile. "Of course."

Gin narrowed her eyes. "You don't look all right. You're pale."

"It's nothing." Lucy wandered along with one hand on the balustrade, searching the shifting shadows of the garden for someone resembling Simon. Gin trailed along, then nearly crashed into her when Lucy stopped abruptly.

"What's the . . . matter?" The last word faded as Gin followed Lucy's gaze to where Simon and

Mrs. Montelucci were emerging from a shadowed path. They climbed the steps to reenter the ballroom. "Who's that?"

"My husband," Lucy whispered.

"Oh." Gin said nothing more, but Lucy could almost feel the questions hovering in the air.

The couple split up just outside the entryway. Simon allowed the Italian woman to enter first. Once inside, the lady turned right, and Simon stepped through the doorway and turned in the opposite direction.

She had thought she was strong enough to endure this. She had planned to arrive in London a force to be reckoned with, but instead she found herself in the role of scorned wife. Pitiful. Pathetic.

Humiliating.

"Let's go after them," Gin suggested.

Lucy leaned against the cool marble balustrade and rubbed her pulsing temple. "No. Perhaps I should just go home."

"You're not going to run away, are you?"

"Not run away. It is just . . . I traveled all day, and it was foolish of me to attend a ball when I was so fatigued."

"But if you quit, then she'll win."

Gin's words brought Lucy's head up. "This is not a game."

"Yes, it is," Gin said, her gaze steady. "And you can still win it."

"What?"

"All right, let me say it straight out. We don't know each other much at all, but you helped me back there, so I want to return the favor." Gin glanced at the open ballroom doors, lips pursed and eyes narrowed. "It looks to me that your husband is flirting with another woman, and where I'm from, you just don't look away and accept it. You fight back."

"I thought I could fight." Lucy gazed at the doorway to the ballroom, bright lights and musical gaiety spilling out onto the cool, gray stone. "But that was when she was just a name in a rumor. Now that I've seen her . . ."

"You forget something," Gin interrupted. "*You* are his wife. *You* are the one who shares his name and his home. That's your advantage."

Lucy gave a disbelieving laugh. "This is London, Gin. A wife doesn't have much influence over her husband. We marry to gain security, to have children. Husbands can do what they want, and a wife is supposed to pretend she knows nothing about his activities."

Gin gave a snort. "He's a man, isn't he? And you're the woman who lives under his roof. Seems to me that your course of action is obvious."

"Maybe to you."

"To every woman." Gin gave her a mischievous grin. "Seduce him."

"Gracious, but you are blunt." Even as her face

warmed, she couldn't deny the tingle of excitement that spread over her as she contemplated the idea.

"Seems to me a man won't go looking for another woman if he has what he wants at home."

"I suppose not. I would not know, as we have not been married for very long."

"All the more reason," Gin said with a decisive nod. "Now let's get back in there and see what your husband's up to."

"Good idea."

As they headed toward the doors to the ballroom, Lucy couldn't get Gin's candidly stated idea out of her head. *Seduce him.* She could almost hear dear Arminda's shout of agreement from the heavens.

The instant they stepped back into the ballroom, Fox appeared from the depths of the crowd.

"Where have you been, Lady Devingham? Your husband is looking for you."

Lucy stiffened at the hint of accusation in his tone. "I merely took a breath of air with a friend, Mr. Foxworth."

"A friend?" he drawled. "And you newly arrived in London? How quickly you make acquaintances."

His implication was clear. How could this cynical man be Simon's best friend?

"I don't care for your tone or your insinuation, Mr. Foxworth," Lucy said.

"Neither do I," Gin spoke up, not even bothering to hide her dislike.

"And who might you be?" Fox swept his gaze over her from tip to toes.

"Not that it's any of your affair, Mr. Foxworth," Lucy informed him in a low voice, "but this is my friend, Miss Matthews. Gin, this is Mr. Foxworth."

"I would say it's a pleasure," Gin replied, "but it's not."

Fox narrowed his eyes. "American, eh? I do hope that blunt tongue of yours does not land you in trouble, Miss Matthews."

"I imagine I can handle any unpleasantness that comes along." Gin gave him a cheeky grin. "After all, they haven't ejected you from the ballroom yet, so I figure no one will even notice my plain speaking."

Fox blinked with surprise, then his expression turned thunderous. "A wrong word uttered in polite company could be the ruination of a young woman in search of a husband," he warned.

Gin laughed. "What would I want with one of those?"

"Marriage is a woman's natural state."

Gin raised her eyebrows. "Maybe in England, that's true." She turned away from Fox to face Lucy, her body language indicating her dismissal of the man. "I see my godmother waving to me, so I'd better join her."

"I will pay a call on you tomorrow, if it's agreeable," Lucy said.

"That sounds lovely. My godmother is Lady Wexford, and I'm staying with her." She glanced over to meet Fox's fuming gaze. "Good evening, Mr. Foxworth."

"Miss Matthews," he said icily, and gave a brief bow, conveying his disapproval of her with his stiff posture.

Gin glanced back at Lucy as she took her leave. "Remember what I told you."

"I remember."

As the American made her way across the room, Fox curled his lip. "Lady Devingham, I must question your taste in friends."

"How strange, Mr. Foxworth, as I was just questioning my husband's."

His blue eyes flared with temper, but he pressed his lips together in a firm line and turned his attention to the couples promenading along the dance floor, clearly unwilling to draw any further attention with an argument.

Lucy faced the dance floor as well, but she didn't really take note of the dancers. Her mind had turned to her current problem—Simon's lover. Perhaps Gin was right. There was only one recourse.

She would have to seduce her husband.

Chapter 4

The thrill anew past sheltered sweet reward,
Whence two begin to chime a brand-new chord.

The journals of Simon, Lord Devingham,
on achieving aspirations

Seduce her.

Two simple words that constituted his directive from his superiors. Seduce Isabella Montelucci and save England.

Alone in his bedchamber, Simon stared down into his snifter of brandy and watched the flicker of the hearth flames reflect off the amber liquid. The Italian woman possessed a stark, passionate hunger that had startled him, and their flirtation in the garden had clearly whetted her appetite for more. Had he been any other man, he would have had her naked and panting right there behind the statue of Venus.

Fox would have done it that way. Simon sipped at his brandy, contemplating the fire without really seeing it. Fox would have seduced the woman and stolen the secrets in less time than it took to smoke a good cigar.

Instead of wheedling his way into her bed, Simon had wooed the woman with words and poetry, then convinced her to return to the ballroom before even a single kiss was exchanged. She had been hungry for him, taking liberties with her hands in a way that left him in no doubt of her desire, but the thought of a hurried coupling with that lusty creature under the stone gaze of a Roman goddess left him cold.

Fox should have been out in the garden with the eager widow while he, Simon, watched over his own wife.

He rested his head back against the chair. When Simon had finally located Fox and Lucy after his assignation with Isabella, he had found his wife and his best friend watching the dancers in simmering silence. He assumed Fox's bad temperament had made an appearance. His patience with Society tended to wear down rather quickly since the accident.

The ride home had been equally quiet. If not for Fox's presence tonight, he would have suspected that Lucy had seen him with Isabella. However, Lucy claimed fatigue from her journey as the cause of her exhaustion, effectively quelling any lingering thoughts he had about attending her in bed that night. He wanted her badly, but he wasn't a cad.

Or was he? Some might consider a man wooing a woman other than his wife to be a cad, however reluctant.

He heard a movement from his wife's room next door, a gentle swish of material. What was she doing right now? Undressing? Or had she done that already and was slipping between the sheets, wearing nothing but a thin nightrail?

He imagined her hair spilling over the pillow like warm chocolate, that lavender scent clinging to the sheets as she shifted to get comfortable.

He loved her hair, the way it fell down her back and curled at the ends. He wanted to wrap his hands in it and hold her fast as he buried himself inside her. He set the snifter on the table and stretched his stockinged feet to the fire, closing his eyes and reveling in his imagination.

He heard another sound, a soft click. Had the maid left? Did his wife now lie alone in her bed, naked beneath that bit of satin and lace that served as nightclothes?

Did she think of him?

He shifted his hips, hard at just the thought.

Another swish of material, then the scent of lavender teased him as a small, feminine hand touched his shoulder.

"Simon," she whispered, "are you awake?"

His eyes jerked open, and he stared at his wife.

Reflections from the red-gold flames danced across the white cotton of her nightdress. Her hair spilled over her shoulders, loose and freshly brushed. Her eyes looked dark and luminous as she knelt beside his chair.

"I didn't mean to wake you," she murmured.

Dear God. He reached out and stroked a hand over her hair, his fingers drifting through the silky locks. She was here. She was real.

"Lucy." He sighed, still half-convinced he was dreaming.

"I thought . . ." She glanced away, the firelight throwing her cheekbones into sharp relief as she modestly lowered her eyes. "You haven't been home in weeks."

He sucked in a sharp breath. "Did you come here to share my bed, sweet wife?"

"Yes." She met his gaze, a playful smile curving her lips. "Or you could share mine. They're both quite big."

A hoarse bark of laughter escaped him, and he reached for her, tugging her halfway into his lap as he kissed her.

Her taste exploded through his system. He cupped her head in one hand, his other clenching in the material at the small of her back while he dragged her closer, demanding more of her. She parted her lips as he'd taught her, and he took shameless advantage, trying to fill himself with the essence of her.

Her hands stroked over his shoulders, his cheek. Her gorgeous hair spread around them like a blanket, the scent of lavender filling his nose and lungs and sending his blood pounding.

She squirmed in his arms, and he loosened his hold, expecting her to move away. Instead, she shifted upward to straddle him.

He forgot to breathe as desire roared through him. Her secretive smile enticed him as she lifted one of his hands and placed it on her breast. "Touch me, Simon. I've missed you."

He'd forgotten how uninhibited she could be and how quickly she had picked up on the nuances of lovemaking. He fondled her sumptuous flesh through the silk gown, rubbing his thumb against the hardening nipple that sprang to life. Her eyes slid closed to near slits, her lips parting as a moan escaped.

"Do you like that?" He lifted his other hand to her other breast and gave it the same attention.

"Yes." She opened her eyes and looked at him, her dark gaze brimming with desire. "Don't stop touching me."

A rough laugh broke from him. "Never fear that."

She arched her back, pressing herself into his palms. He slid an arm behind her to pull her closer as he cupped one breast and brought it to his mouth.

She gave a cry as his lips closed over the nipple

right through the cotton. He tugged gently, then teased the bud with his teeth. She gripped his shoulders, digging her fingernails into him, and gently rocked her hips against him.

God, she made him hard. He switched to the other breast, tonguing and nibbling that nipple until she was panting. He slid his hand up her back to the nape of her neck and pulled her down for a kiss.

Her head spun. She had started as the seducer but now found herself seduced.

Her breasts ached for his touch, the tips sensitive from the cooling cotton. She longed for the warmth of his mouth there again, but his kiss tasted too delicious to give up. He took control of the situation, answering her own hunger with his own, masterfully turning her body into a burning, melting tangle of yearning.

She wanted to maintain control, but it was impossible. He was too skilled, and she not experienced enough.

He slid his hand beneath the hem of her nightgown, caressing her thigh and hip possessively. Beneath his eager touch, the material bunched at her waist, leaving her lower half bare to his gaze.

"You're so lovely." He combed his fingers through the hair of her mound, watching the movements of his hand in the flickering light.

"I'm glad you think so." She caught his gaze with hers and held it. "Make me yours, husband."

He chuckled. "So eager, my bride?"

She laid a hand on his cheek. "I've been a bride for two months now and only known my husband for a single night. Of course I am eager."

Something hot flared in his eyes. "Well then," he growled, "let me teach you more, my sweet." He shifted her in his lap, and when she meant to stand up, he stopped her. "Where are you going?"

"To the bed." Flustered, she gave a little wave toward the piece of furniture in question.

"We need no bed." He reached down and unfastened his pantaloons, freeing himself to her shocked gaze. "Do you ride, my dear?"

She let out a little yelp, shocked despite herself. "I . . . do I ride?"

Some of the fierceness left his face. "I'm sorry, Lucy. I forget that you are yet an innocent."

"No, I can . . ."

"Come, let's be comfortable on the bed." He tucked himself away, then rose from the chair and took her hand, leading her to the magnificent four-poster as if she were a child to be tucked in for the night.

He threw back the covers, and she looked at him with dismay. "Perhaps we should return to the chair," she said.

"Do not fret, my dear wife. I forgot that you are young and gently reared." He took her by the shoulders and kissed her cheek. "Let's get this nightrail out of our way so we can both find our pleasure, shall we?"

He tugged at the garment, and she raised her arms obediently, allowing him to sweep it over her head. He tossed the nightgown aside, and it pooled on the floor in a soft pile. Then he cupped her naked breasts in both hands, stirring her passions all over again.

But something was wrong. She attempted to slide his coat away, but he caught her hands, kissing her while he held her fingers trapped against his strong chest. His kiss was softer, sweeter, than before.

What had happened to the ardent impatience that had possessed him only minutes ago?

"Into the bed," he murmured, kissing her temple. He assisted her up onto the high mattress, and when she sat back against the pillows, he shed his coat.

"Simon, I'm not a child."

"No, you're not." With a glance as simmering and hungry as before, he laid his coat on a nearby chair and started working on his shirt. "You're a woman. Of that, there is no doubt."

"Then why . . ."

"You're a lady. I understand about your sensibilities." His shirt joined the coat, and he began unfastening his pantaloons again. "A man makes love to his wife like the lady she is. I forgot that." He stripped the garment off his legs and tossed it aside, standing naked and erect before her.

"But—"

"Hush." He knelt on the bed and brushed his mouth across hers. "Lie back, my sweet. I'm afraid I want you rather badly."

Hope stirred. "Do you really, Simon?"

"Of course." He scooped one arm beneath her and edged her along the mattress until she could lay down flat. "You're a beautiful woman, Lucy. I'm mad to make love to you."

"Oh, Simon," she breathed, as he stretched out on top of her and parted her thighs. "I want to make love to you, too."

"Then we shall do well together." His hardness nudged her thigh, and then he was centered between her legs, sliding into her welcoming body.

"Dear Lord." She shivered, pleasure dancing along her skin like flames as he filled her.

"Yes," he whispered near her ear. "Give yourself to me, sweet wife."

He began to move, and rational thought drifted away. She knew there was something she wanted to remember, something that bothered her, but she could concentrate on nothing but the passion flaring between them. His panting breaths echoed her own as he plunged into her, and she bent her knees to give him more access to her body.

He made a sound of approval, then took her leg and wrapped it around his waist. She followed suit with the other leg and locked her ankles together, and soon they both raced toward the same summit, wrapped around each other and desperate for release.

When it came, the climax grabbed her by the throat and shook her like a wet kitten, leaving her trembling and gasping beneath him.

He slowed his thrusts, his eyes closed and jaw tight with concentration. Minutes later he gave one last, deep plunge and held there, shuddering as satisfaction rolled over him. Then he dropped down on her like a discarded rag doll, harsh breaths echoing in her ear. Gradually, those breaths eased into gentle snores.

After a moment, she worked her way out from beneath his heavy weight by pushing against his shoulder and wiggling to the side. She managed to get out from under him and would have returned to her own room, but his arm came up and curved around her waist, trapping her in the bed.

What had just happened here?

She turned her head to look at Simon, and her heart softened at the sight of his slumbering features and tousled hair. He looked so content, so peaceful. He had clearly enjoyed their lovemaking.

Why, then, did he turn to Isabella Montelucci?

She turned her gaze to the green-and-gold-trimmed bed hangings. Perhaps she already had her answer. Hadn't Simon said it himself, that a man did not make love to his wife the way he would a mistress?

Their activities this evening had more than satisfied both of them, and she recognized that Simon was an excellent lover. But if she was going to win his attention away from the Italian woman, she would have to be more than his well-bred wife.

She would have to become his fantasy come true. Creative. Passionate and fearless. She would so thoroughly have to enchant her husband in the marriage bed that he would have no reason to look elsewhere to satisfy his manly desires. But how? How was a motherless country miss to discover the sexual secrets that would keep a man fascinated with his wife above all women?

He was gone when she woke the next morning.

She sat up in the bed, panic flaring before reason took over. The rumpled pillow beside hers proved that the night before had been no dream. She had shared Simon's bed last night, and while he had risen early, there was no reason to believe he had left the city.

He hadn't left her as he had before.

Wrapping the bedclothes around her, she slid from the bed and silently crept across the room and through the connecting door to her own chamber. The latch clicked softly as the door closed behind her, and she let out a long sigh. Now that she was in her own room, she felt foolish for sneaking out like a thief in the night.

But sunlight streamed in through the window, chasing the vestiges of night into the shadows of memory. On the bureau, Arminda's wooden jewel box gleamed like warm honey, reminding her of her other reason for being in London. She had given her friend her word that she would personally see the box delivered to Arminda's daughter, Mrs. Daphne Nelson.

Once the box was delivered, she would have no further reason to linger in London.

Perhaps she could talk to Simon about taking their delayed wedding trip. After all, their lack of one was certain to be commented upon, and the gossip alone might spur him to agree. Then, when she had him away from the influence of Isabella Montelucci, she would be able to show him what a good wife she could be. They could begin building a true, caring marriage.

She leaned back against the door, the mere thought buoying her spirits. After her task was complete, she would be able to focus her energies on winning her husband's affection.

He would miss her when she was gone.

Simon cut his sausage into neat slices, then stabbed a piece with his fork and ate it, chewing slowly as he contemplated the previous night. Lucy had been as welcoming and sensual as he remembered, and this morning when he'd awakened, he'd contemplated lingering in bed for another bout. But duty (in the form of Fox's voice in his head) had nagged at him.

Once she had delivered this box to its rightful owner, she needed to return to Devingham so he could get on with his assignment.

As if the mere thought had summoned her, Lucy appeared in the doorway of the breakfast room, wearing a pale yellow morning dress that suited her dark coloring. She paused as she saw him. Their gazes locked. Shared memories of the night before linked both of them in a long, silent moment of communication. A hint of pink swept her cheeks, and her eyes softened like warm chocolate before she glanced away at the breakfast spread out on the sideboard.

"Good morning, Simon," she said, hurrying toward the food.

Her shyness charmed him, and he couldn't resist a bit of mischief. In a low, insinuating voice he said, "Did you sleep well, wife?"

She spun around at his sensual tone, and the fat sausage on her plate rolled to the edge and plopped on the floor. Her face reddened even more as she stared down at it. "Oh, botheration!"

He roared with laughter. She glared at him, and before the footman could do so, she snatched the sausage off the floor and threw it at Simon. The chunk of meat bounced off his blue superfine coat.

He stopped laughing even as an expression of horror crossed her face. Both of them stared at the smudge of grease that marred his heretofore pristine garment.

"My goodness." She covered her mouth with her hand, her eyes wide with shock. "I'm so sorry, Simon."

He glanced from his ruined coat to her mortified face, stunned that such a thing had happened in the formal breakfast room of his London town house. Amazed that his sweet, civilized wife had done such a thing.

And warmed to his toes that the woman with whom he would share the rest of his life clearly possessed a strong sense of playfulness.

He gathered his features into a frown. "This was one of Weston's finest."

She shook her head no, her expression growing more distressed.

"He's an excellent tailor but quite expensive. My valet, Plath, regards his garments as cherished treasures."

"I don't know what came over me," she whispered, and set her empty plate down on the sideboard.

"You do realize," he continued, "that you will now have to endure the wrath of Plath."

She blinked and dropped her hand away from her mouth. "The wrath of Plath?"

His own lips twitched, and he found it difficult

to maintain his severe demeanor. "Indeed. Plath's wrath."

A giggle escaped her lips, and her posture relaxed. "You're funning with me, aren't you?"

"Not at all." He gave her a stern look, but allowed the amusement into his tone. "The wrath of Plath is nothing to be trifled with."

Another chuckle spluttered from between her lips, and once she started, she couldn't seem to stop. Soon she was laughing so hard that she had to hold on to the back of a chair to remain upright.

Simon grinned, caught up in the good humor that permeated the room. He glanced at the footman. "George, please get my wife a plate of breakfast, as she is clearly incapable of doing so without ruining my wardrobe."

She howled anew at that wry statement. Simon rose and took her arm with one hand, pulling out the chair with the other. "You'd best sit, my dear, before you fall down and trip George. I should hate for the kippers to smudge my shirt."

Still giggling, she sat, looking up at him with her eyes brimming with laughter. "Or for the eggs to soil your neckcloth."

"Or for the ham to ruin my boots."

She snickered, but managed to utter thanks as George placed a platter of hot breakfast before her. She lifted her fork, and though Simon knew he should return to his own chair, he continued to linger near her. The scent of lavender combined with laughter seduced him as nothing else could. Before he realized what he was doing, he stroked his hand over her long hair, which she wore simply tied back from her face with a ribbon.

She froze with the forkful of eggs halfway to her mouth. The utensil scraped the side of the dish as she set it down and turned her head to look at him.

Her movement brought her face into alignment with his hand, his palm cupping her cheek. He stroked her smooth skin with his thumb, remembering their interlude last night and how much he had wanted her.

How much he still wanted her.

"Simon?"

Her whisper broke the spell and reminded him of what he could not have. What he must do. Turning away from the hopeful interest that lit her face, he went back to his own chair. "Eat your breakfast," he muttered, taking up his fork again.

He didn't look at her as he stabbed another bite of sausage, but every inch of his being was aware of her. He fixed his gaze on his plate, concentrating fiercely on his breakfast, as his body hummed with attentiveness to her every action.

He knew when she picked up her own fork and slowly began eating. He knew when she glanced at him between bites. He knew when her shoulders sagged in defeat.

He wanted to go to her, to hold her and comfort her. But he dared not. He could not encourage her to stay. It was vital to his duty that she return home immediately.

No matter how much he wanted to keep her with him.

Perhaps after all this was done, they could take that wedding trip. He would make amends then.

"I will be going out today," she said, breaking the silence that had until now only been disturbed by the clink of silverware on china.

"Where?" He picked up *The Times* and scanned the first page with apparent absorption.

"To see Mrs. Nelson—Arminda's daughter."

"Ah, yes. Your purpose for being in London." He took a scoop of eggs without looking away from the newspaper. "Be sure to take a footman with you. Or perhaps Molly."

"I will take Molly. Perhaps I will send a note around to my friend Miss Matthews and ask her to accompany me as well."

"Who's Miss Matthews?" He glanced over, one brow lifted in inquiry.

"Someone I met last night at the Creston ball. She's an American."

"Ah. I believe Fox mentioned her."

"I imagine he did. He was quite rude to her."

Simon shrugged and turned his attention back to the headlines. "Fox doesn't go out in Society much anymore. Perhaps he's forgotten how to get on."

"That's hardly an excuse."

He put down the paper this time, chilled by the memory of his own part in Fox's circumstances. "You don't know what he's lived through," he said. "John Foxworth is my friend and none of your affair." He folded up the paper, placed it next to his plate, and stood. "If you will excuse me, I must go change my clothes before I attend to my business today."

"Simon . . ."

He cast her a stern glance that silenced her. "Your obligation is to deliver the inheritance to Mrs. Wolcott's daughter. Then, dear wife, I expect you to leave for Devingham as soon as that task is completed."

Driven by duty and dark memories, he left the room, knowing without looking back that his words had stung. But the pain Lucy felt now paled in comparison to the wounds Fox had suffered three years ago because of Georgina's meddling.

He would be damned if he would let a woman interfere with his assignment ever again. Lucy would go home to Devingham. And he would remain in London, ever dutiful, ever loyal to his cause, clinging to memories of a heady night of passion and the sweet scent of lavender.

Chapter 5

'Tis best to strip the thorns from a rose rather than be pricked by them.

Random scribbling on roses
by Simon, Lord Devingham

While in England, Miss Virginia Matthews was staying with her godmother, Lady Wexford. The widowed dowager had a fashionable Mayfair address not far from Lucy's own, so it didn't take long at all to fetch her friend when she set out in the Devingham carriage that afternoon.

Gin had chosen to wear a charming new dress on their errand. The blue-and-white creation suited her pale complexion and reddish hair rather well, but the flattering effect was spoiled by the ghastly orange flowers on the large straw hat that she wore.

"Gin, what a . . . lovely bonnet."

85

"It's my gardening hat," Gin pronounced, settling into the seat beside Lucy. The coachman commanded the horses to a brisk walk, and as the coach lurched into motion, Gin raised her voice over the jangle of harnesses. "Aunt Beatrice wanted me to wear some silly blue thing with fruit dangling off it. Fruit is for eating, not wearing. But she insisted I wear a hat, so here I am."

A laugh spluttered out before Lucy could stop it. "Good for you, Gin."

"You, of course, look lovely. Yellow is your color." Gin sighed, casting a slightly envious glance over Lucy's dress and matching bonnet with its cluster of daisies. "We really must go shopping together. Aunt Beatrice tells me I am hopeless when it comes to tasteful clothing."

Lucy's cheerful mood faded. "I'm afraid I won't be able to do that. You see, Simon has commanded I return home to Devingham as soon as I have delivered the box to Mrs. Nelson."

"He *commanded* you? Has he been declared king of England without my knowing?"

Lucy sighed. "I know it must seem strange to an American, but here in England, a husband's word is absolute. If Simon insists that I leave, then I must go. He has the law behind him."

"Then make him want you to stay." Gin leaned closer, her green eyes sparkling behind her spectacles as she whispered, "Did you try my suggestion?"

Heat swept through her face. "I did," Lucy murmured back, conscious of her maid half-dozing in the seat across from her. "And this very morning, he demanded that I go home as soon as I delivered the box to Mrs. Nelson."

"What? How are you supposed to make him fall in love with you if you're in the country and he's in London?" Gin sat back and folded her arms, lips pursed in thought. "There must be something you can do."

"I've been searching for an idea all morning, but nothing yet." Lucy swept her hand over the silken material that she'd wrapped around the box to keep the dust from it. "This morning we laughed together and last night—" She sucked in a breath and straightened her spine. "We have been getting along famously, and I had hope for our marriage. But his instructions at breakfast were quite clear."

"If only you had more time," Gin mumbled, staring off in deep contemplation.

"That would be ideal."

The two ladies fell into a contemplative silence as the carriage wended its way through the crowded London streets to the Nelson home.

Mr. and Mrs. John Nelson lived quietly in a respectable section of the city. Their town house was small but tidy, and the steps were kept scrupulously clean, as Lucy noticed when she, Gin, and Molly climbed them to the front door.

Since Lucy was holding the box, Gin stepped forward and rapped the door knocker.

Long moments passed. Gin had just raised her hand to knock again when the door opened to reveal an elderly man, stooped with age. He glared at them from beneath bushy silver brows. "Yes?"

"I am Lady Devingham," Lucy said, stepping forward. She managed to hand him her card, but nearly dropped the box in the process. Gripping the antique more firmly, she continued, "I am here to see Mrs. Nelson."

"Lady Devingham?" The butler held the card close to his face and squinted to read it. "By heavens, she'll be sorry she missed you!"

"She's not home then?" Gin asked.

"I'm afraid not. Mr. and Mrs. Nelson are visiting family in Scotland for a fortnight." He smiled at Lucy. "I'm certain she will regret that she was not here when you called."

Lucy masked her disappointment. "Do you know exactly when she will return?"

"Tuesday. Not the one coming, but the Tuesday after."

"Leave your card," Gin encouraged. "We can visit again when Mrs. Nelson has come home from Scotland."

"All right," Lucy said. "Though I don't know when I shall be able to call again."

With the butler promising to pass her card on to his mistress, the three women descended the stairs and returned to their carriage.

"Isn't this a great piece of luck?" Gin said, grinning from ear to ear as the carriage started down the street.

"Luck?" Lucy replied, failure weighing heavily. "How can you consider this a turn of good luck when I was not able to complete my duty?"

Gin laughed out loud. "My dear Lucy, don't you realize what's happened? You've just been given two more weeks in London!"

"But Simon said I must return home today."

"Not exactly. He said that you had to return home after you gave the box to Mrs. Nelson." Gin nodded toward the box that still rested in Lucy's lap. "Looks to me like you can't do that for two more weeks."

"Two more—" She stopped abruptly as Gin's words sank in. "You're right. He said I must return home after I completed my task."

"And your task is currently incomplete. Looks like you'll be around a bit longer than you thought."

Slowly a smile spread across Lucy's face. "Virginia Matthews, I do believe you are right."

"Is she gone from London yet?" Fox leaned heavily on his cane as he entered the study where Simon awaited him.

Simon sent him a dark look. "She's leaving tomorrow."

"Good." Fox lowered himself into a chair, then set his cane against the arm and rubbed at his bad knee. "The sooner, the better."

Simon bristled, haunted by the look on Lucy's face that morning when he'd ordered her home. "She's my wife, Fox. Do remember that when you speak of her."

Fox merely raised a brow. "You've only been married for a few weeks, and already you're protective."

"I know what my assignment is. Let's leave my wife out of it."

"As you wish." Fox held up a hand in surrender. "How went last night's meeting with the beauteous Isabella?"

Simon gladly tucked away his private turmoil and focused on work. "She's a shrewd woman. One moment she was panting with desire, and the next she was as modest as a debutante. I learned nothing except that women are bloody confusing."

Fox laughed. "A valuable lesson. Though I imagine there was some discomfort for you to flirt with this woman while your wife was nearby. Once Lady Devingham has returned to the country, you will feel more comfortable in the fair Isabella's arms."

"I don't know that I shall." Simon rose from his chair and prowled the room. "I don't know if I am the type of man to seduce women in the garden, Fox."

"Then seduce her in private. Just get the job done."

"Blast it, but it's not as easy for me as it was for you." He gestured at the papers scattered over Fox's desk. "That used to be my job. Cryptography. Thievery. Marksmanship when necessary. I am a man who prefers to work in the background. And alone."

"And I was always the fellow who could win anyone's trust and wheedle out of them the information we needed." Fox's lips curled in disgust. "I have lost that particular gift. It was a dismal failure with your wife."

Simon rubbed the back of his neck. "I wish we had found something to prove Isabella's involvement with LaRue the first time I sneaked into her house. If not for your decoding talents, we would not have confirmation that Isabella is indeed the enemy. At least I am not engaging in an affair on mere speculation."

"It's for your country, Dev. Getting intimate with this woman will put you in a position to obtain firsthand information. When she arranges the auction, you may be able to tell us where and when it will be."

"And then we can stop the sale and recover the list, I know. It's just the damnedest thing to have to stand by and wait for her to make the first move. I am a man of action."

"You are just not used to the challenge of managing two women at once. It will be easier for you to pursue Isabella once Lucy has returned to Devingham."

"This is a challenge I never wanted to face."

"You will handle it well." He flexed his knee and winced. "Blasted leg. Too much standing and walking about last night."

"Perhaps you should attend more social events, exercise it more often."

Fox shook his head. "Bollocks to that! Last night was an aberration, Simon. I don't miss Society, I assure you. They've thrown the doors wide open and let in every cit and shopkeeper's daughter. Why, there was even an American in attendance last night."

"Lucy mentioned something to that effect. Miss Matthews, wasn't it?"

"Ghastly creature. The twang of that awful accent still vibrates in my ears. No manners to speak of, either."

Simon chuckled. "Why, Fox, I do believe this is the first time I've heard of a female you did not charm from the first instant of your meeting."

"I'd sooner charm a snake." Fox gestured to the decanter on the sideboard. "Care for a bit of brandy, Simon?"

"A bit early for me, thank you."

"Well, I could use a glass. This blasted leg is throbbing." He massaged the muscle above his knee.

"Allow me." Simon rose and made his way to the decanter on a nearby table.

"That woman means trouble, I assure you," Fox warned.

"My wife?"

"No, the American. Don't get your hackles up, Dev."

"Just having difficulty keeping up with your thought process." Simon uncorked the decanter and splashed some brandy into a glass.

"Then again, she seemed cozy enough with your bride, Dev. Perhaps she does have ulterior motives."

Simon faced his friend, amusement curving his lips. "Do you suspect her of being a spy for Boney, then?" He lifted the glass in a mock toast.

"One never knows." Fox scowled as Simon walked over and handed him the beverage. "I shall have my resources look into the matter."

Simon shook his head. "She's just a girl, Fox. How dangerous could she be?"

"Dangerous enough," Fox muttered, then tossed back a swallow of liquor and changed the subject.

The carriage containing the dangerous American and the new Countess of Devingham weaved through the crowded streets of London. Lucy worried her bottom lip with her teeth and studied the merchant shops they were passing. "I don't know if I should do this without speaking to Simon first."

"Oh, don't back out on me now. Don't English husbands provide their wives with an allowance or something?"

"Well, of course. Simon is very generous with my pin money."

"Then there should be no problem with your buying some new clothes. You're a countess, aren't you? Shouldn't you be dressed up in all the latest styles? Be a leader of fashion and all that?"

Lucy laughed. "I doubt that I shall ever set any trends, Gin. But if I am to stay in London for the next fortnight, I do believe I will need clothing more fashionable than I currently have. I would not want to embarrass Simon."

"Well, that wouldn't be my motivation, but if it means you will go shopping with me, then so be it." Gin turned and addressed Lucy's maid. "What do you think, Molly? Shouldn't Lady Lucy update her wardrobe while she's here in London?"

Molly looked stunned to be addressed so frankly. "I . . . I would imagine so, miss."

"See?" Gin said with a triumphant grin that lit up her face. "Even Molly agrees with me."

Lucy shook her head, a smile breaking free despite an effort to remain dignified. "You are truly an original."

"Much to the dismay of my parents," Gin declared with a laugh.

"Are your parents here with you in London?"

"No, they're home in Philadelphia. They sent me to stay with my godmother in hopes I would find a husband." Gin rolled her eyes.

"Marriage is not the worst thing that could happen to a girl," Lucy said. "You make it sound like a plague."

"Because I have yet to meet a man who doesn't want to marry me for my money. I'm an heiress, you know."

"No, I didn't," Lucy said, discomfited by her candor.

"Father owns coal mines," Gin said. "They sent me to London after I knocked the governor's son into the pond when he tried to kiss me."

"You didn't!"

"Well, perhaps my idea to protest for miners' rights had more to do with my banishment than that little incident," Gin admitted.

"My word!" Lucy stared at her new friend, uncertain if she felt shock or admiration.

"Stop the carriage," Gin called out. The driver slowed the horses and pulled closer to the curb.

"What are you doing? Madame Dauphine's isn't on this street, and I thought you wanted to purchase a new wardrobe."

"First I want to visit the bookseller. There was a volume on English history there yesterday that I just fell in love with."

The footman hopped down and opened the

door to the carriage, offering his hand to Lucy to help her alight. Gin followed, then Molly, who settled down on the servants' bench outside as Gin and Lucy entered Humbolt's book shop.

Fashionably dressed gentlemen and ladies filled the store near to bursting, many of them doing more gossiping than perusing of titles. Some of the women eyed Gin's hat with disdain as they passed by.

Lucy glanced at the garish orange flowers adorning the American's hat and sighed at the thought of battling the crowd. "We do need to get you a decent bonnet, Gin."

"No fruit," Gin warned, as they worked their way through the crowded establishment. Suddenly Gin stopped with a hiss of warning.

"What is it?" Lucy squeezed up to stand beside Gin. She bit back a gasp of surprise.

Isabella Montelucci stood just ahead, idly studying the volumes lining a bookshelf near the back of the store.

"We don't have to stay here," Gin said, turning concerned eyes on her friend. "We can come back later, when it's not so . . . crowded."

"That's not necessary." Lucy tried to smile, but she couldn't take her eyes off the fashionably dressed woman.

"Really, we can go somewhere else."

"You said you had set your heart on this book. I refuse to disappoint you." Lucy started forward, but Gin held her back with a hand on her arm.

"We don't have to," she said again.

Lucy looked her straight in the eye. "I can't run away every time I see her, Gin." She lowered her voice. "Not if I want to keep what's mine."

Gin hesitated, then gave a nod. "Your decision."

More slowly now, the two women started forward again. Despite herself, Lucy studied every detail of the stunning Mrs. Montelucci as they got closer. What was it that so attracted Simon to her? And did she, Lucy, have enough appeal to win her husband away from this gorgeous creature?

"Cherries on her hat," Gin snorted beneath her breath.

Lucy grinned at the disgust in Gin's voice and found it easier to pass by the Italian woman as if she weren't even there. They stopped to look at a display of volumes on the subject Gin desired, and Lucy surreptitiously watched Isabella as Gin searched for her book.

There was no question that the woman was beautiful. She was also exquisitely dressed and exuded a sensuality that Lucy was certain attracted men like flies. But who was her family? Where did she come from?

Rumor had it that she was from Italy and a widow, but no one really knew anything more, and even that could be pure fabrication. The mystery alone was what kept the woman at the top of every hostess's guest list.

"Stop staring," Gin whispered.

"I'm not." Lucy turned her attention immediately to the history book Gin was examining.

"You are."

"Fine, I am. I can't help it." Lucy darted another glance Isabella's way and grabbed Gin's wrist. "Look. What's she doing?"

Gin sighed. "Shopping for a book, I suppose. I'm surprised she reads at all."

"No, it's more than that."

"What—"

Lucy made a shushing sound and pretended to study a stack of books on poetry.

A young man had come from the back of the shop with a stack of newspapers and paused near Isabella, laying out various issues on the table near the fire. Isabella murmured something to him and did it in such a furtive manner that had Lucy not been watching the woman closely, she would never have noticed the exchange.

The young man gave a subtle nod, then turned and disappeared behind the curtain leading into the back recesses of the store. Moments later, Isabella began a slow but steady migration in the same direction, pausing to peruse various shelves of goods on her way.

"What is she doing?" Lucy murmured, more to herself than Gin.

With a growl of frustration, Gin turned away from the merchandise she was examining. "Lucy,

I understand your distraction with the woman, but she's not doing anything wrong."

"I disagree," Lucy hissed, "she's leaving through the back of the shop!"

As Gin glanced over, Lucy edged past her friend and as surreptitiously as possible, worked her way over to where Isabella had vanished in the young man's wake. With a mutter, Gin abandoned the history display and followed.

Lucy didn't even hesitate. She pushed aside the curtain and slipped through it, aware that Gin was behind her. She found herself in a narrow hallway with doors leading off it. At the end of the hallway was another door. Sunlight streamed through a filthy window next to that door, illuminating the less-than-pristine walls of the hallway.

"She could be anywhere," Gin said, gesturing toward the rest of the doors.

"What is she doing back here?" Lucy mused.

"Aha!" Gin pointed at the door at the end of the hallway. "She's outside. I see cherries."

Lucy choked as she tried to suppress her laugh. "We really must discuss your distrust of fruit sometime. Now follow me."

Lucy slipped down the hallway with Gin behind her. As she got closer, she, too, could see the brim of Isabella's hat through the window, and a sudden thought occurred to her. "She could come back inside at any moment."

"If she does, we'll hide in one of these rooms."

"Good idea." Conscious of her friend's comforting presence behind her, Lucy bent down as she reached the end of the hallway, then crouched beneath the dirt-streaked window, Gin doing the same. She met her friend's gaze. "Ready?"

"Slowly," Gin said.

"Right. One, two, three."

The two women eased up until their noses lined up with the bottom of the window.

"She's not alone," Lucy hissed. "That young man is with her."

"What's she doing?"

"Talking. Looks like she's ordering him to do something from the way she's waving her hands about. Oh!"

"What is it?"

"She just handed him a purse. It's money, I think. He's bouncing it in his hand, like he's weighing it."

"Why would this woman meet a man in a back alley and give him money?" Gin asked. "That's not the sort of thing you English do, is it?"

"She's not English," Lucy reminded her. "But even so, it is a bit beyond the pale."

"I should say so."

"He's coming back in!" Lucy whispered. "Hide!"

The two of them darted toward the nearest door. Luckily, it was unlocked, and they were able to dodge inside what looked to be a storage room and ease the door closed just as the young employee came back inside and strode rapidly down the hallway. Moments later, Isabella followed.

Lucy kept the door open a crack, just enough for her to peer through it with one eye. The young man had disappeared. Isabella strode down the hallway without glancing around at all. Then she slipped past the curtain into the bookshop.

Exchanging a questioning look, Lucy and Gin slipped out of their hiding place and soundlessly followed their quarry back to the public area.

Chapter 6

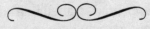

Her scent is sweet, her petals wet with dew,
My lavender's bloom entices me anew.

The journals of Simon, Lord Devingham,
on lavender

Simon arrived home that evening in a black mood.

His meeting with Fox that morning had started out well enough, but it had gotten progressively worse as the day went on. Fox had originally summoned him to discuss another communication pilfered from the French. However, this one had been written in a new code, and Fox had yet to crack it. His frustration with the code and his experiences of last evening had combined to make for a very short-tempered partner. Irritated with Fox's continued mention of Lucy's imminent departure, Simon had finally left his friend snarling over the unreadable French communiqué.

His next visit late that afternoon had been to Isabella's home. After their meeting in the garden last night, he had expected to be welcome in her drawing room. Instead, he had been summarily dismissed by the lady in question. Having just returned home from a shopping expedition, she was piqued that he hadn't spent more time with her, that he had focused on his wife at the Creston affair. Thus he had been asked to leave her presence and not make any other advances unless he apologized for toying with her affections.

He had apologized then and there, though the words had nearly stuck in his throat. And still she had ejected him from her home.

He had returned to his own house, leaving Socrates in the hands of a young stableboy, and made his way to the greenhouse.

The instant he opened the door, inhaled the lush scents of moist soil and fragrant flowers, some of his irritation melted away. His tilting world settled into place, and he roamed through the rows of young plants, checking their progress, verifying they had enough water.

This was his haven, his retreat from the world outside. In here, he was in control.

He came to a table in the back where three pots rested. All contained struggling rosebushes. His hybrids. His creations. The prospective combina-

tions that would eventually produce the Devingham Star.

He verified that each of these potential marvels
had been given the proper care by the servants,
then he stood and just looked at them. Soil, water,
sunlight—and you had a miracle.

Why couldn't the rest of his life be so simple?
He had wealth and power. He had spent years in
service to England, secretly. Even his family had
not been aware of his activities. His father had
been a rigid man, one who often pontificated on
the villainy of England's enemies but considered
serving in the military a betrayal of his duty as
earl. He had expected his heir to share his senti-
ments. That restriction had not applied to Simon's
younger brother, Roderick, who had chosen a
military career as his contribution and currently
served on the Peninsula.

But Simon had wanted to help defend England
against conquerors like Bonaparte. While trained
to respect the consequence of his position, he had
nonetheless wanted to do *something*. When Fox
had approached him about working for a secret
organization, he had happily agreed.

But now the cause was interfering in his personal life. He had married to keep the Society
mamas from thrusting their daughters on him,
to make himself unavailable for pursuit while at
the same time doing his duty to his family line.

He had chosen a woman who preferred the country so a disaster of Georgina proportions would never occur again. It should have all fallen into place, leaving him free to charm Isabella while not dishonoring his wife at the same time. He was a man who thrived on order, and his plan had appeared flawless.

But Lucy had chosen just then to come to London. She had accompanied him to the ball where he was to meet Isabella, and while nothing of a disastrous nature had happened, she had still interfered with his work by her very presence, and now Isabella was put out with him.

Lucy was going home immediately. Tomorrow.

He would miss her. He reached out to stroke the petals of one of his blooming rosebushes, reminded of the softness of her skin. Lucy was a sweet-natured woman with a passionate spirit. She made him laugh, and he could envision many nights of contentment with her at his side. They would conceive children together and create a cordial home life built on affection and respect.

But not right now. Not until this mission was over. Once he'd done his part, he'd take some leave from the organization and get to know his pretty bride.

He'd already ordered her things packed for an early-morning departure for Devingham. At least they would have this one last night together before parting again. Remembering her innocent eagerness to please, he found he looked forward to spending another night in her arms.

And he regretted that after tonight, it would be some time before they would see each other again.

The soft scrape of a shoe and the gentle click of the greenhouse door closing alerted him that he was not alone. He turned away from his creations and frowned as the intruder drew nearer. Who had dared invade his sanctuary? The servants knew better than to interrupt him.

Lucy came around a tall bush of flowering Old Blush, the myriad of dusky pink blooms having hidden her from view. She had changed from her daffodil-colored morning dress into a dinner dress of Bishop's blue. She gazed around at the riot of color created by his carefully bred blossoms, her dark eyes wide with wonder.

"How beautiful," she breathed.

Something inside him loosened and flowed again at her obvious approval. He hadn't realized until just that moment that he had been concerned about her reaction. He rarely shared his creations with anyone, since so few people could appreciate the delicate work involved in breeding a new type of flower.

But Lucy found his private sanctuary beautiful.

"How did you find me?" he asked, approaching her.

"The servants told me."

He raised a brow. "Did they also tell you that I dislike being disturbed when I am in here?"

She bit her lower lip, looking the slightest bit guilty. "It was mentioned."

"Indeed. And yet here you are."

"I wanted to see inside," she admitted.

Her contrite expression soothed some of his irritation. "In the future, please respect my privacy."

She nodded, then turned to leave. Lavender teased his senses with her movement.

"Where are you going?"

She glanced back. "I thought . . ."

"You're already here," he grumbled, his blood thundering after that one teasing whiff. "You might as well stay."

"Not if I'm disturbing you."

"Not at all," he lied.

"Then if you don't mind . . ." She slipped past him, going to each of the different plants and touching their blooms with gentle fingers. He followed her, drawn by the sight and scent of her, his hardening flesh aching as he watched her delicate fingers glide over the petals of his roses.

He wanted her to touch him like that.

"Do you like them?" he asked, hardly aware of what he was saying.

She turned to face him with a whisper of silk and curls. "Very much. Do you breed them yourself?"

"I do."

"Fascinating. You will have to show me some-time. I've always loved roses." She leaned forward to smell one, and her generous breasts swelled forward. He caught his breath, unable to tear his gaze away from the succulent flesh.

She was his. He could touch those breasts when-ever he wanted, bury his face in them.

She looked up just then. Her smile faded as she caught him staring, but he couldn't look away. Couldn't pretend it hadn't happened. Her lips parted, and her eyes grew large in her face.

He wanted to reach out and pull her into his arms, to shove aside the empty pots on the next table and lay her down there and make love to her. But this was his gently bred wife, not a com-mon strumpet. He would have to woo her into his arms with sweet words and caresses.

Damn it. He wasn't certain of his control just now.

"Simon?" Just his name, but he heard the un-spoken question.

"Lucy." He stepped closer, stroked her cheek. "'Tis our last night together." He pressed a kiss to her lips, slowly and gently, resisting the rag-ing desire that demanded he take her hard and fast.

"No," she whispered.

"No?" Shocked, he stepped back from her. "Are you . . . do you refuse my advances?"

"Not at all." She reached for his hand and placed

the palm against her face. "I want your advances, Simon. I want you to teach me what you like."

"Precious wife." He took her face in both hands, tilting her head to receive his hungry kiss. "I will teach you anything you want to know tonight."

Before she could reply, he took her mouth yet again, his hands shaking with the effort to hold back the immense passion that burned within him. He wanted her badly, and it was all he could do to remain civilized.

He stepped back from her with hands on her shoulders, breaking the kiss. "I will miss you, Lucy."

"I'm not leaving." She gave him a brilliant smile. "Mrs. Nelson is in Scotland for the next fortnight. I will wait here in London and deliver the box when she returns."

"What?"

"I said that we have two weeks to spend together. Isn't that wonderful?"

"That wasn't our agreement." He pushed her away, stunned by this news.

And even more stunned that part of him *wanted* her to stay, assignment be damned.

Lucy's bubble of elation burst at his reaction. Given his passionate advances, she had thought that he would be happy to have her remain with him for a time. But then again, how could he pursue his mistress with his wife beside him at every function?

All the more reason to make certain he did *not* send her packing off to Devingham.

"You told me that I would have to return to Devingham after I delivered the box to its owner," she reminded him, hands on her hips. "Well, I can't do that for a fortnight."

"You were supposed to deliver it today."

"I tried to. Mrs. Nelson is out of town." She shook her head. "I've told you this, and frankly, I don't understand your reaction."

"The servants have nearly finished packing for your departure tomorrow."

"Then they can *un*pack. I won't be leaving in the morning."

"Everything is arranged," he snapped, then turned away, rubbing the back of his neck with his hand.

"Then we will simply unarrange it. Really, Simon, I'm your wife, not a leper."

"Leave the box with me," he suggested, whirling back to face her. "I will see it gets delivered to its rightful owner."

"I can't do that!" She gaped at him, aghast at how badly he seemed to want her gone. "I made a promise to a dying woman, Simon, and I will see it through."

"As long as it gets delivered, does it matter by whom?"

"It does to me." She pressed her fist over her heart. "This is a matter of honor. Surely you, who call yourself a gentleman, understand that."

"A woman's sense of honor—"

"A woman's sense of honor is the same as a man's," she interrupted. "And don't you dare say otherwise."

He scowled. "I still don't see the problem with having someone else deliver it, as long as it's done. I'll bring it to her myself, if that makes you feel better."

"It doesn't." She spread her hands in supplication. "Simon, it's more than just seeing an inheritance passed on to its rightful owner. Arminda and her daughter have not spoken in over twenty years."

"I see no reason to make this into a Drury Lane drama, Lucy. If the two weren't even speaking, then I don't see how the manner of delivery makes a difference. How do you know Mrs. Nelson will even accept her inheritance?"

Frustration had her hands clenching into fists. "Because it is my duty to see that she does accept it, Simon. This jewel box has been passed down in Arminda's family from mother to daughter for generations. Once I have convinced Mrs. Nelson to take it into her keeping, then I will know that she has forgiven her mother."

"A very touching tale, but I must insist that you follow our original schedule and leave for Devingham on the morrow."

She folded her arms. "No."

"No?" He took a step toward her. "Do you remember to whom you're speaking, wife? I should hate to cut off your allowance for such a simple matter."

"Simple matter? Simon, you are calling my very integrity into question! And as for my pin money, you can keep it. I'd rather live on the streets than be beholden to a man who thinks so little of honor."

"You bloody well will not live on the streets!" he roared.

She tilted her chin, unintimidated. "We've been married a little over two months, dear husband, and we have yet to take a wedding trip. The gossips are already chewing on that. What will they say to the Countess of Devingham living outside of her husband's beneficence?"

"I don't care what the gossips say. You are my wife, and you will do as I bid you."

"And you don't know me at all if you think I value money over honor!" she snapped back. "I swore on my mother's grave to see this through, Simon, and I will not be dismissed back to Devingham like a child."

He took a deep breath. "You're going home, and that's the end of it."

She narrowed her eyes. "If you force me to leave, Simon, I swear, the last place I will go will be Devingham. I will stay here in London with friends if need be, but I *will* see my duty discharged."

He loomed over her. "When did you get to be so bloody difficult?"

"About the same time you forgot your language in the presence of a lady," she shot back.

She was right. He was losing control, and her nearness didn't help matters. The way she stood up to him without backing down stimulated him in a way he hadn't expected. Her eyes flashed with temper, and a delicate flush swept her cheeks. Her bosom rose and fell, and her scent surrounded him, drowning his senses in lust. He struggled to remember why she had to leave.

"It's only two weeks, Simon." She stepped forward and laid her hand on his chest, her dark eyes still simmering with aroused passions. "I'll stay out of your way. We can live separate lives, attend separate events. I won't interfere with your business. Just please, let me do this."

He barely comprehended her words through the roaring in his ears. She was stroking his chest with her hand, leaning lightly against him, and the warmth of her body distracted him. He saw her lips moving, but all he could think about was what he wanted those lips to be doing to him.

She was saying something else, something about not even knowing she was there. Ha! As if he could overlook each rustle of her skirts or the feminine scent of her in every room of his very masculine abode. He could not ignore her, not when he ached for her so.

She stepped back with a soft sigh, disappointment turning down the corners of her mouth. The absence of her touch hit him like an icy wind, but when she turned away and trailed her fingers along the edge of the table, he couldn't bear it. He stopped her with firm hands on her shoulders.

She turned only her head to look back at him, then laid one hand over his.

Just that.

Just that small touch, and passion roared through him like a beast let loose. He turned her into his arms and kissed her, attempting to comfort even though he was the source of her distress. She wound her arms around his neck, kissing him back eagerly, despite the fact that they'd just had a disagreement.

Her sweet acceptance was his undoing.

He should take her hand and lead her upstairs to his bed. He should whisper sweet words to her and undress her with gentle hands. He should woo her tenderly in the firelit shadows of his bedchamber and coax her between the sheets with compliments and caresses.

But he wanted her too badly. Here in his private paradise, he held her in his arms, her soft body yielding to his, and he couldn't manage a single step. Couldn't utter a single word of flattery, couldn't dig deep beneath the primitive hunger that claimed him to find the slightest pretense of a gentleman.

And she didn't seem to care.

The brief taste of her couldn't sate his hunger.

He swept his hands over her, greedy for the feel of soft flesh. The aromas of roses and lavender swirled in his head, mixing with the loamy fragrance of the soil that surrounded them. The soft sounds she made urged him on, her own hands clutching at him with definitive purpose.

She wanted him just as much as he wanted her.

The idea struck like an aphrodisiac, sending lust thrumming through his veins and shoving sensible thought to the back of his mind. All that mattered was her.

He tugged at her clothing, baring pale flesh. She whimpered with pleasure as he nibbled at her neck, working his way down to lick at her tightening nipples. She arched into him, silently begging him for more.

He lifted her off her feet with one arm around her waist, sliding his other hand beneath her skirt to stroke up her leg. She shivered, whispered his name. He turned with her still in his arms and sat her on the edge of the table.

She lay back with his guidance, her dark hair loosening from its pins and spreading across the surface. She looked like a pagan goddess with her hair all around her and her naked breasts exposed by his hands. A siren.

He stripped off his coat and threw it to the floor, then tugged free his cravat and tossed it aside as well. She crooned his name, and he came to her, bunching her skirts up to caress her calves and thighs. She stretched her arms above her head, her dark eyes heated with wanting, and let him touch her.

The scent of her arousal made his nostrils flare with primitive possession.

Her head spun with need. He stroked his hands higher, his fingers darting between her legs to caress her sensitive flesh. She gasped and held still, allowing him free rein.

"My sweet," he murmured, then crouched down and licked her *there.*

Her hips came up off the table as a cry of surprise burst from her. She flung out her arms to the sides, knocking aside an empty flowerpot.

He didn't appear to notice. He continued to caress her with his mouth, shocking and exciting her both at the same time. She gripped the edge of the table above her head, her eyes closed as her body pulsed with avid hunger.

She had never expected such sensations. Never imagined such feelings were possible. Her flesh trembled with need, and every touch of his lips and tongue only sent her higher.

How could a man's mouth be so soft? How could so simple an act send her body pulsing, her sensibilities reeling?

He slid his hands beneath her bottom, warm skin to warm skin, and held her still as he closed his lips around her sensitive core. Just that slight touch jolted through her body like a lightning strike, and she clenched her fingers harder around the edge of the table as he licked and nuzzled at that responsive little bud. She wanted to move closer. She wanted to pull away. She wanted . . .

The pressure built. Slowly. Steadily.

Then the tension snapped. Her climax ripped through her, tearing a cry from her throat. Tears stung her eyes, and her throat closed up on a gasping breath as satisfaction flooded her system.

She lay there, her body humming, unable to move. Barely able to breathe.

He stood. Clothing rustled. Then his hands guided her legs apart again, and she felt the blunt head of his sex against the entrance to her body. He paused there, flexing his fingers on her lax thighs, rubbing himself against the still-tingling flesh. She opened her eyes to look at him just as he slid inside her.

He groaned, his eyes drifting closed as he stood still, hot and hard inside her, as if relishing the experience. Then he began to move—once, twice—gliding in and out of her with slow, exploratory strokes.

She shifted on the table, lifting her hips toward him. He opened his eyes, still maintaining that deliberate, even pace. Their gazes locked, possessive need glittering in his as they watched each other.

Desire kindled anew. This was a primitive mating, torn from behind the veils of civility. There was something right, something inevitable, about opening to him, allowing him to do what he wanted with her.

He pressed her legs wider apart, his hips pounding against her fevered flesh as he drove himself harder, deeper. His fingers dug into her thighs with a power that made her flinch, but then the brief pain vanished, disappearing into the breathless thrill of his unrestrained lovemaking.

Between one breath and the next, control fell away. She watched the change in him, from disciplined gentleman to untamed male. It was there in the glow of his eyes, the clenching of his jaw, the strength of his grip.

Suddenly he took her ankles and lifted her legs up in the air, parted them wide, and looked down at where their bodies joined, his face taut. A wild rhythm overtook him, pounding into her. So deep. So hard.

The primitive mating shook her, echoing through her feminine core. Another wave of pleasure erupted—smaller, but no less devastating—fogging her brain, making her tremble anew. She melted beneath him like warm pudding, unable to move, utterly content.

He threw back his head and cried out, his features rigid with wrenching climax. His thrusts slowed to gentle rocking.

He stilled. Shuddered. Sucked in a deep breath. Then he opened his eyes and looked at her, astonishment echoing in familiar hazel depths as he released her ankles and leaned heavily on the table, still buried inside her.

Long moments passed. Her body felt liquid, boneless, contentment pulsing through her veins with each heartbeat. She closed her eyes and had almost begun to doze when he moved.

He slid out of her with a soft wet sound. Clothing rustled nearby, and her eyes drifted open. He came back into her line of sight, clad in his coat with his shirt unfastened and his cravat nowhere to be seen. He took out his handkerchief and pressed it between her legs, regret carved into his features.

"I'm sorry," he said.

Sorry? Was this a thing a man said after he'd made love to a woman as if it were their last day on earth? She leaned up on her elbows. "What's wrong, Simon?"

"What's *wrong*? I just took you like a savage. You're my wife, for heaven's sake!" He helped her to sit up and went about arranging her clothing as if she didn't have two good hands to do so herself. "You're a lady," he went on, tugging her bodice back into modesty. "I'm supposed to be a gentleman. I'm supposed to be in control."

He took back his handkerchief, shoved it into his coat pocket, then pulled her skirt down to cover her legs. His quick, jerky movements emphasized his emotional distress.

Clearly he thought he'd hurt her or dishonored her or some silly thing.

She remembered the night before, when she'd come to him and he'd believed her too refined for more adventurous bed sport. How he'd tucked her into his bed as if she were made of glass, then gently made love to her.

This could not go on. He'd just taken her like a barbarian conqueror—treated her like a *woman*—and she was not about to let him continue behaving as if she were made of tissue paper!

"Do you need help with your hair?" He combed his fingers through her dark locks.

She grabbed his wrist. "Simon, look at me."

He did finally, his hazel eyes shadowed with torment.

She brought his hand to her cheek. "I liked what we did."

He blinked with surprise. "But—"

"But what? I'm a lady, so I wouldn't enjoy your attentions? Really, Simon, where do you get your ideas?"

He frowned. "I don't understand."

She sighed. "I'm not a porcelain doll that you should fear breaking. I'm your wife. I'm a woman, flesh and blood. You seem to have some notion in your head that you should not give rein to your passions when we are together."

He straightened, his hand falling away as he continued to struggle with the idea. "I've been taught that ladies don't share a man's ... baser instincts."

His withdrawal hurt, but she knew she needed to make him understand. "I don't have worldly experience, Simon. I can only tell you about myself. I'm your wife, yes. And I would like to learn more about this part of marriage." She leaned forward. "I'd like to learn more about you—what you like. What you need from me as your wife."

He sighed, propping his hands on his hips and staring at his boots for a long moment. Then he looked up. "I suppose your hairpins are somewhere about."

She flinched. "Hairpins? Aren't you listening to me, Simon?"

"I am. I just—" He swept a hand to indicate the table where they'd made love and the broken flower pots on the floor. "This sort of thing is not normal for me."

"For me either."

He grinned at that, though his eyes still reflected hints of inner turmoil. "I should think not. However, since we do need to leave this place sometime tonight, I suggest we look about for your hairpins and set you to rights so the servants have nothing to gossip about."

"Gossip? From the servants of the Earl of Devingham?" She gasped in mock astonishment. "You tolerate such a thing?"

Simon shrugged. "They're human."

"So are you. So am I."

"Indeed." Their gazes met for one intense moment, and then he looked away. "Aha!" He nearly pounced on a hairpin resting on the floor near the table. He snatched it up and presented it to her triumphantly. "I am no ladies' maid, but I imagine I can assist in some way to arrange a suitable hairstyle."

She took the hairpin, sensing that he was finished talking about more intimate things. Very well. Let him mull over what she'd said. Perhaps he would soon realize she could be everything he needed, if he only gave her a chance.

"I am used to doing without a maid," she said. "The one we had was kept busy with my sisters, so I learned at a young age how to arrange my hair. But perhaps you can locate the rest of the missing pins."

He nodded, obviously relieved that the discussion had turned to more practical matters, and set about searching the floor.

She combed her fingers through her hair, finding a couple of more pins that had remained entangled, and watched him. Simon was a kind man, and intelligent, and honorable to a fault. But it was becoming more and more clear to her that he knew nothing about women.

Well, perhaps *nothing* was not the word. He certainly knew how to pleasure one.

She would have to teach him about her. She

would have to overcome her natural modesty and become bolder, to tell him what she liked and find out what he liked as well. She would have to share her thoughts and dreams. She would have to trust him with her heart if they were ever to develop the sort of loving marriage her parents had enjoyed.

And if his wife satisfied all his needs, he would have no more reason to pursue the Italian woman.

Just the thought of Isabella cast a pall over her dreams of a happy marriage. Isabella was not why she was doing this. She wanted to capture her husband's attention, to show him that ladies were not necessarily fragile flowers that could be crushed with one night's passion. She wanted him to be her partner in life, the loving father of her children, her companion and friend when they both grew too old to shatter pots in the greenhouse.

Isabella was a threat only because she could distract Simon from what Lucy was trying to show him. As long as Lucy continued to lure him to their marriage bed night after night, they had a good chance of building a real marriage that would sustain them both for the rest of their lives.

Simon came over, and, with a crooked smile that made her stomach flutter, he extended his hand, displaying the pins he had retrieved from the floor. She scooped her hair back and coiled it at her nape, then took the pins one at a time, sliding them in to anchor her hair.

The intimacy of the moment squeezed at her heart. Never had she performed her toilette in front of a man. It only deepened the connection between them, and she could see by the look on his face that he felt it, too.

When she picked up the last pin, he left his hand extended. She tucked the pin into place, then clasped his hand and allowed him to lead her out of the greenhouse.

Chapter 7

I am a man in control of my fate.

The journals of Simon, Lord Devingham,
underlined quite firmly and written
in uppercase letters

Simon woke to bright sunshine and burgeoning guilt. As the events of the previous night flashed through his mind, he swiped a hand over his face and groaned.

How could he have lost control so completely?

First he had taken Lucy like a madman in the greenhouse. Then he had regained his senses and after dinner, had escorted her to her chamber with all the chivalry of Galahad himself.

Only to end up in her bed that very night, making love to her yet again.

What was wrong with him? He was a man who had quietly defended England for eight years,

125

whether the task involved lying, theft, or even assassination. Why was it that this one young girl could melt his self-control like butter in a hot skillet?

Yesterday he had been determined to send her home. He *should* send her home. It was his duty.

But he didn't want to send her home.

He was a selfish bastard.

He sat up in bed and threw aside the covers, still naked from last night's sexual exploits with his wife. When he'd escorted her to her room after dinner, she'd held out her hand in invitation, and he hadn't been able to resist. Even when he noticed that her trunks had been unpacked, had he commented on her disregard of his orders? No, he'd just rushed her back to bed like a lad with his first woman.

He should have his footmen stuff her into his traveling coach and escort her back to Devingham—with the points of their pistols, if it came to that. But just the thought of it made him feel like a blackguard. He wanted his wife to like him—maybe even love him, damn it all—and such an extreme measure would win him her enmity for certain.

And he wanted her too much to take that chance. Their conversation in the greenhouse prodded at him with as much insistence as his morning erection. Could it be that what he had been taught about gently born ladies had been in error? That they might actually enjoy a rousing bout of bed play, despite their delicate sensibilities? This certainly seemed to be the case with Lucy.

His father had drummed it into his head that a man copulated with his wife in a civilized manner in order to beget children. Once his heirs were born, it was courteous for him not to force his attentions on his lady wife any longer. His parents had certainly led by example, the two of them conducting separate social lives once the nursery was full.

He had been taught that more adventurous pleasures were reserved for mistresses and doxies. That these sorts of women were lacking in the delicate sensibilities of gently reared ladies and so were more amenable to accommodating a man's baser needs. He had intended to follow his father's example and eventually find a discreet mistress once Lucy had produced the requisite sons, thinking he was doing the gentlemanly thing. Yet now his unpredictable wife was starting to make him believe that his idea of marriage was completely wrong.

Damn it all, he should send her home.

He leaned his elbows on his thighs and rested his head in his hands. Already the woman had him so befuddled, he couldn't think straight. The thought that a wife could be a lively bed partner grabbed him by his privates and would not let go. Just the knowledge that he could let loose his passion with her and not repulse her, that she might enjoy it as much as he did—

His loins hardened to near pain. Hell, the things he could *teach* her. . .

But only if she stayed in London.

The idea captured him like an insect in the leaves of a Venus flytrap.

She had said they could live separate lives, attend separate social events. Maybe such a plan would work, leaving him alone to pursue his assignment while still granting him access to his wife's bed at night.

He would try it. Surely he could keep Fox at bay for just a day or two, until he was certain the arrangement would work out to his expectations.

A knock came at the door, but before he could respond, Plath entered of his own accord. Simon yanked the covers across his lap—not that such an act could truly hide the insistent results of his musings about his wife. Closing the door behind him, Plath frowned at his master's nudity but said nothing about his painfully obvious state. "I beg your pardon, my lord, but it is nearly one o'clock. You are due at Gentleman Jackson's rooms at three o'clock."

"Blast it, I overslept." Simon stood, hauling the coverlet with him. "Why did you not wake me, Plath?"

The manservant barely blinked. "I just did, my lord."

Simon sent him a suspicious frown, uncertain as to whether or not the inscrutable Plath was being facetious. "Has my wife awakened yet?"

"Some hours ago. She has gone on an outing with Miss Matthews."

"Oh. Good." He squelched the twinge of disappointment. Separate lives. He should be glad she was off amusing herself so he could get on with his own affairs.

"Shall I prepare your bath, my lord?"

"Yes." He shook off his gloom. "And have a tray sent up. I'm starved."

"Very good." Plath withdrew, leaving Simon alone in the huge master's suite.

Had his house always been so quiet? Disturbed by a sense of isolation, he went to fetch his journal to keep himself occupied until Plath's return.

Lady Wexford was a short, plump lady with steel gray hair and a sunny disposition. She led Lucy and Gin through the museum with the authority of a general, pointing out both artifacts and People of Interest with equal fervor. This afternoon, People of Interest seemed to be comprised mostly of eligible bachelors.

"Ah, look there, Virginia. That gentleman with the puce waistcoat by the Egyptian sarcophagus. That is Mr. Jeremy Goodfellow. He is quite plump in the pocket, and rumor has it he has decided to cast about for a wife this Season."

Gin followed her aunt's direction and winced. "He looks to be plump in more than his pocket, Aunt Beatrice."

"The Goodfellows have ever been of large build, Virginia," Lady Wexford scolded. "What matters is that his fortune nearly matches yours, and he is not so high in the instep as to overlook an American for a bride. You would do well to catch his interest."

She proceeded to lead them into the next room. Gin gave a little shudder as they passed the pasty-faced gentleman who filled out his waistcoat as much as the stitching would allow.

Lucy patted her friend's arm. "He would not be my first choice either," she whispered.

"I don't want to get married," Gin hissed in the same low voice. "But my parents have instructed my godmother to find me a husband. They think I'll stay out of trouble with a man to look after me."

"I am certain they want the best for you."

Gin snorted. "They want me to stop protesting for miners' rights and a woman's right to vote."

Gin's vehemence startled her. "Surely they want you to be happy."

"My parents and I have different definitions of happy." Noticing that her godmother had stopped to chat with an acquaintance, Gin took Lucy's arm and guided her toward a display of pottery across the room. "Did you know that women were allowed to vote in the state of New Jersey until just last year? Then they changed the law and took it away. Do you think that's fair?"

"I suppose not."

"Of course it's not. And neither is the lot of the

miners. Their working conditions are abominable."

"I would not know . . ."

"Well, I do. And I protested loudly about it. Mother and Papa own a lot of coal mines, and my causes were embarrassing them, so they sent me here. I'm not allowed to return home without a husband." Her voice broke ever so slightly at the last, and Lucy realized that her brash American friend disguised some genuine wounds with her bold manner.

"I am sorry, Gin." Lucy patted her arm. "In England, a girl's dream is to marry well rather than remain a spinster dependent on one's relations. It's hard for me to imagine a woman wanting anything else."

"Well, at least one of us has gotten what she wanted," Gin said, straightening her spine. "You're positively glowing today."

Heat flooded Lucy's cheeks as memories of the previous night's sexual adventures raced through her mind. "Things are going well."

"Apparently, since you're still here."

"It was a near thing," Lucy confided. "But we spoke last night, and I believe we came to an agreement."

"Good. I need a friend to help me fend off any suitors Aunt Beatrice might dig up."

"You do well enough. Besides, perhaps you will meet a gentleman who does not repel you."

Gin indicated a nearby mummy. "I'd rather marry him."

Lucy giggled. A footstep behind her had her glancing back, and the smile faded from her face.

"Good afternoon, ladies," Fox said. "Enjoying one last outing before you return home, Lady Devingham?"

"Mr. Foxworth." Lucy acknowledged him with a cool nod. "For your information, I am not returning to Devingham just yet."

"Really? I was under the impression that your stay in London was temporary."

"My plans have changed, which is really none of your affair."

"So how do you do that, anyway?" Gin asked Fox.

Fox cast her an ill-tempered glance. "Do what, Miss Matthews?"

"Walk so quietly when you use a cane. We didn't even hear you approach . . . probably not until you wanted us to," she mused.

Fox's face reddened, whether from outrage or anger or embarrassment, Lucy could not tell. "In polite circles, it is discourteous to comment on another's infirmity," he said tightly.

"It's also polite to acknowledge someone when you cross paths with them," Gin pointed out. "You didn't so much as look at me when you walked over here. And what are you doing out and about anyway? Aren't you something of a hermit?"

He sucked in a sharp breath, and Lucy thought for an instant the two might come to blows. Then he clenched his teeth in a clear effort to restrain himself. "I would not expect a woman of your background to understand."

"I doubt you know much about my background," Gin replied.

He gave her a menacing smile. "More than you might think."

Gin shook her head. "You don't scare me, Mr. Foxworth. I don't know what happened to you or why you're so bitter, but you should be glad that you can still walk, even if it's with the use of a cane."

"You know nothing about it," he snarled.

Lucy glanced about, realizing that the increasing volume of the heated barbs was beginning to turn the heads of those standing nearby. Across the room, Lady Wexford still engaged in animated conversation with her crony, but that would not last for long at the current volume.

She laid a hand on Gin's arm. "We are starting to attract attention."

Gin didn't shift her gaze from Fox, though she lowered her voice. "My uncle was in the war a few years back, Mr. Foxworth. He lost both legs and is confined to a wheeled chair. He nearly succeeded in committing suicide, but my father found him in time."

"As fascinating as that sounds—" Fox began in a bored tone.

"He was known for his dancing," Gin continued

softly, ignoring him. "The ladies all swooned for him because of it. And once his legs were gone, he didn't think anyone would want him anymore."

Fox stiffened.

"What happened to him?" Lucy asked.

Gin smiled at her. "He fell in love with the nurse we hired to care for him. They married and have five children." She looked back at Fox. "You can still walk, Mr. Foxworth, and you are a handsome man. Perhaps you would do better to think about what you have, rather than what you don't."

Fox stared at her for a long moment, his blue eyes sharp as daggers and rife with pain. Then, without a word, he gave a brief bow and walked out of the exhibit room.

Lucy let out a long breath. "Heavens, Gin, I thought the two of you were about to make a dawn appointment!"

Gin shrugged. "He's angry about what happened to him and taking it out on everyone. My uncle did the same thing."

Lady Wexford strolled over at just that moment. "Virginia, dear, was that Mr. Foxworth?"

"Yes, Aunt Beatrice."

"I did not realize you were acquainted with him." Lady Wexford's arched brows said more than her words conveyed.

"He's a friend of my husband's," Lucy said. "I introduced them at the Creston affair."

"Ah." Lady Wexford's face creased into a smile.

"Well, he is a handsome man, to be sure. He was quite popular with the ladies before the accident. Now it is rare to see him anywhere. Modest fortune, though that is completely at the benevolence of his father. And the two are known to be at odds more than they are amicable. I do not know that he would be a proper suitor for you, Virginia. He has become absolutely unpredictable these past three years."

"Was that when he had the accident?" Lucy asked.

"Indeed. There was a fire, and—" Lady Wexford glanced at their engrossed expressions and clamped her lips shut. "Dear me, how I do go on. Let us move along to the next room, shall we?"

"But what happened, Lady Wexford?" Lucy asked, hurrying to keep up with her.

"It is just old gossip, not fit for my goddaughter's ears." Lady Wexford gave Lucy a sharp look. "If you need to know more, Lady Devingham, I suggest you ask your husband. He was there."

Gentleman Jackson's provided just the sort of release he needed, Simon thought. It was a masculine environment, a place where he could forget about his problems with women.

But Stillwood was late again, curse him. He and the Earl of Stillwood had been boxing partners since their years at Eton, but even the responsibility of a wife and title had not cured Stillwood of his propensity for tardiness. Simon fancied buying the fellow a watch that ran an hour behind, just to see if the man would finally appear on time somewhere.

Even after years of dealing with such behavior, Simon still arrived at his appointments with Stillwood at the appointed hour, perpetually hoping this time would be the one where his friend did not arrive late. But here he stood at a quarter past three, watching a match and waiting—again—when Sir Adrian Hall walked up to him.

Sir Adrian was a tall fellow with a military bearing, a result of his early years in the cavalry. He was just a hint past his prime, at an age where silver just began to sprinkle the dark hair at his temples. His gray eyes always saw much and revealed nothing.

And he was Simon's superior in the organization.

"Afternoon, Devingham," Sir Adrian said, stopping beside him.

"Sir Adrian." Simon gave him a nod, wondering if this were a random meeting. Or had Sir Adrian sought him out on purpose?

"I had the pleasure of seeing your lovely wife at the Creston affair the other night. Quite a surprise, as I was under the impression she was at your estate in the country."

No random meeting, then.

"She arrived in Town unexpectedly," Simon said cautiously.

"Indeed. 'Tis a bit of an encumbrance to a man to have his wife hanging about while he tries to tend to his affairs."

"My wife is here for a specific purpose, Sir Adrian. A last request from a dying friend." He met and held the man's gaze. "As a military man, I'm certain you can understand why I am allowing her to remain a short time to complete her duty."

Sir Adrian's brows rose. "As long as her presence does not get in the way of your own responsibilities."

"You know better than that, Sir Adrian. Women have no place in men's business. My wife and I will keep separate social schedules while she is in Town."

"A good idea," Sir Adrian agreed. "I must admit, I find I am able to function more efficiently when my wife is home in Sussex."

"As do I. This is a temporary situation, which I expect to be rectified shortly."

"Good to know," Sir Adrian said. "Ah, there's Lord Stillwood. Good day to you, Devingham."

"Sir Adrian." He watched the other man walk away, hardly noticing when Stillwood reached him and began babbling his usual list of excuses.

He had just been warned. The situation with Lucy had just grown more precarious. Why didn't he just send her home?

He'd been raised to believe that business was

a man's province, something to be kept separate and private from women. A woman's role was to bear her husband's children and function as his hostess on social occasions. He could not slip and let Lucy know the truth about his dealings with Isabella. It was too dangerous. He really should send her back to Devingham, where she belonged.

But this assignment was temporary, and his marriage wasn't. He and Lucy had reached a level where a wrong move on his part could jeopardize what was growing between them. And he wanted that, more than he realized.

For the first time in his career, he hesitated about doing what he knew needed to be done.

It was impossible to tell Lucy the truth, and yet he wanted to spend more time with her. But the longer she remained in London, the more chance that she would hear about Isabella. And how would he explain that to her without either putting her in danger or ruining the fragile relationship they were starting to build?

"Devingham?" Stillwood was staring at him, and he realized the man must have been talking to him while he stood woolgathering. Managing a smile, he clapped his friend on the back and vowed to ponder the problem of Lucy and his assignment after clearing his mind with a rousing match of boxing.

Chapter 8

*It has been my experience that work is to a man
as hats or jewels or shoes are to a lady. We are
driven by our inner selves to overindulge no
matter what the cost.*

The journals of Simon, Lord Devingham,
on observations of the sexes

When Lucy arrived home from the museum,
she was told that her husband had gone
out for the afternoon and that her new gowns
from Madame Dauphine's had arrived.

As she instructed Molly to see to her new
wardrobe, she smothered her disappointment
at Simon's absence. After last night's encounter
in the greenhouse, she had every hope that they
were well on their way to establishing a firm and
loving commitment to each other, and she had
looked forward to seeing him.

It was foolish, of course, to expect that Simon would be lingering at home, waiting for her return. He was a busy man, with many important matters that required his attention. She preferred to believe he was dealing with issues of Parliament or one of his many investments—*not* continuing his pursuit of Isabella Montelucci.

It was late when Simon finally arrived home. Cook had been holding dinner while Lucy sat in the parlor, working on her embroidery and watching the fire burn lower and lower as the hours passed. She heard the front door close and the low rumble of Simon's voice as he addressed Dobbins, their butler, upon entering the house.

She set aside her embroidery hoop, but her distraction that afternoon had caused her to loop one of the stitches around her finger, and by the time she had untangled herself, Simon had already mounted the stairs to his chamber. She stood at the bottom of the staircase, biting her lip in indecision. She was his wife. She could enter his rooms while he attended to his toilette; after last night, she didn't believe her presence would be entirely unwelcome. But at the same time, she didn't want him to believe that she had been breathlessly awaiting his return, like an old hunting dog that hadn't seen its master for weeks.

Even though it was the truth.

She had some pride. He had clearly gone upstairs to change for dinner. She would simply return to her embroidery until he came back downstairs.

She returned to the parlor and picked up her hoop, but she didn't accomplish a single stitch. She merely sat there with it in her lap, watching the fire and listening for his descent down the staircase.

Finally, she heard his voice. She forced herself to remain calm. She even picked up her needle and stabbed it through the material.

Then she heard him talking to Dobbins, and the sound of the front door opening.

He was leaving!

Tossing aside her work, she hurried out of the parlor and into the foyer. Simon was dressed in evening clothes, and the door stood open. As she watched, his coach appeared and stopped at the curb outside the house.

"Simon."

He turned with one brow raised in inquiry. "Yes, Lucy?"

"Where are you going?" The words blurted from her lips in a plaintive whine that brought a hot flush to her cheeks. She sounded like that old hunting dog, whimpering at its master's departure!

Simon glanced at the servants, who were struggling to look as if they were not hanging upon every word. Abruptly, he took her arm. "A moment, if you please, dear wife."

She could tell he was displeased with her, but her flesh tingled at his touch anyway, her body warming with memories from the night before.

He led her into the parlor and closed the door firmly behind them. "Do not question me in front of the servants ever again."

His tone was quiet, but the warning in his eyes could not be misunderstood.

"I'm sorry," she said. "Cook has been holding dinner for you."

"I'm meeting Fox at my club."

"Oh." She twisted her fingers together, searching for the carefree lover of last night in the implacable features of the man before her. "Were you going to tell me?"

"I am unused to reporting my whereabouts. In the future, I will leave word of my plans with Dobbins. I would not want Cook to go through unnecessary trouble on my account." He turned to leave.

"Only Cook?" she whispered.

He glanced back at her, one hand poised to open the door. "Do you not recall our agreement, wife? Separate lives. Your suggestion, I believe."

"But . . ." Her heart sank at the inflexibility of his expression. She swallowed hard. "Last night . . ."

"Last night was most enjoyable, and I look forward to other such interludes," he said. "However, the agreement was that I allow you to remain in Town to complete your task upon Mrs. Nelson's return, but only on the condition that we each maintain our own separate schedules."

"Of course, you are right." Only pride prevented her from crumbling beneath the pain of bitter disappointment. "I apologize if I have overstepped."

He waved a hand in dismissal. "As long as we understand each other now."

"We do." She refused to cry, even though it felt as if a plum had lodged in her throat.

"Good evening then," he said. Then he gave her a half smile, and for an instant his eyes glowed with the passion he had shown her the night before as he reached out to touch her face. "Perhaps I will see you later this evening."

In your bed. The unspoken promise hovered between them.

Speech deserted her. She could only give a slight nod, then stood watching as he quit the room, leaving the door standing open.

The alliance she thought they were forging was a sham, the understanding between them a figment of her hopelessly infatuated imagination. Like many men of his station, Simon seemed to want a wife who would share his bed at night but leave him to his own devices during the day.

Which was not at all what she wanted.

She turned away, unable to ignore the sound of the house door closing, the distant jingle of harness, and the clop of horses' hooves as the carriage pulled away. She stared at the low burning fire, at her discarded embroidery hoop, and imagined sitting here alone, night after night, waiting for her husband to come claim her.

No. She had more pride than that.

She lifted her chin and glared at the quiet scene. Gin had asked her to accompany them to the Herrington affair. She had initially refused, expecting to spend the evening with Simon. But since he insisted that they maintain separate schedules, she would do just that. Why should she not enjoy herself with her friend if he was otherwise engaged?

She marched out of the room. She would send a note around to Gin that she would accompany them, and she would eat the dinner that Cook was desperately trying to keep warm.

As for what would happen later that night when Simon came to her, that would remain to be seen.

When Simon strolled into Boodle's, he found Fox waiting for him with a glass of brandy in his hand.

"Early, Fox? You're becoming absolutely sociable." Simon sat down across from his friend and signaled for a servant.

"I'm bloody well not. And I'm not early; you're late."

"I was detained, but only for a few minutes."

"I'd rather not be here any longer than necessary," Fox grumbled. "I've already chased off two busybodies who plagued me with their poking and prodding."

Simon shrugged and accepted his own brandy from the servant. "That's what happens when you become a hermit. People are curious about you,

Fox. And did it ever occur to you that they might genuinely care about your well-being?"

"Bollocks to that."

"As you say." With a grin, Simon sipped his brandy.

Fox sat back in his chair and placed his empty glass aside, one eyebrow raised and a sardonic twist to his mouth. "I saw your wife today."

Simon shot him a look. "Don't start on this."

"She indicates that she is staying in London indefinitely," Fox continued. His intense blue gaze never left Simon's face. "Would you care to explain?"

"My wife is none of your affair."

"Oh, but she is." Fox leaned forward. "Her presence may yet affect our business together."

"I have my own reasons for allowing her to stay. She will not make a nuisance of herself."

"How can you know that?" Fox lowered his voice. "You thought you had Georgina in hand, and look what happened there."

"Lucy is not Georgina."

"No, she's worse. You care for her, and that will affect the integrity of your decisions."

Simon stiffened. "I have the matter under control. All will be well."

"You are too quick to dismiss the danger." Fox's hands clenched on the arms of his chair. "The last time, I was the one to pay the price. Should history repeat itself, I am running out of currency."

Simon hissed with impatience. "I regret what happened more than I can tell you. However, has it occurred to you that the past is affecting your ability to estimate the risks of the present?"

"I think your infatuation with your wife has made you *underestimate* the risk," Fox snarled. "This is no game that we play, Simon. Lives are at stake."

"And one of those lives is my own." Simon stood and set his brandy snifter on the table. "I find I am not hungry after all, Fox."

"You're not in control," Fox shot out. "Your focus is skewed."

Simon leaned down and tapped the cane that rested against Fox's chair. "As is yours." He straightened and started to turn toward the door.

"Don't you dare walk out of here!"

Simon gave him a chilly smile. "I am going to do exactly that." He lowered his voice. "You live too much in the past, my friend. One day you will wake up an old man and realize you let your life slip away."

"Because of you," Fox said, his eyes glittering with rage and pain.

"I played a part in what happened to you," Simon agreed, the stab of guilt a familiar torture. "But you are the one who is ignoring the here and now. And that, John, is no one's fault but your own."

Simon walked away, leaving Fox in simmering silence.

* * *

"I am so glad you decided to attend with us," Lady Wexford said as she waited outside the Herrington's ballroom for the three of them to be announced. "A chaperone cannot be everywhere, and I will feel more comfortable knowing dear Virginia has you watching out for her as well."

Lucy exchanged amused glances with Gin. "I shall do my best, Lady Wexford."

"It is a great burden off my shoulders. I should not want some fortune-hunter to get his hands on my goddaughter's inheritance."

Gin gave an unladylike snort. "Mama and Father wouldn't care a fig who my husband is, as long as he takes the problem off their hands."

"Virginia!" Lady Wexford gasped. "Do not speak of your parents in such a way. Your mother is my dearest friend, as you know."

Gin shrugged. "I only speak the truth."

"Lady Devingham," Gin's godmother said, "perhaps you will be able to have some influence on this cheeky creature and convince her that marriage is not a prison!"

Lucy chuckled. "I can try, but I don't think anyone can convince Gin of anything."

Lady Wexford made a harrumph of disapproval. "I still miss my Harold every day. It wasn't a love match, but we came to care for each other."

"You were lucky," Gin said.

"Lady Devingham understands what I mean. She seems content in her marriage."

Lucy met Gin's glance. "I am still getting to know my husband," Lucy said.

"Everything comes in time," Lady Wexford said sagely. The group moved to the doors of the ballroom, the next to be announced.

"I am not certain I have yet forgiven you." Isabella pouted, the warmth in her dark eyes belying the scolding tone.

Simon handed her a glass of ratafia and gave her his best attempt at a rakish smile. "Come now. I must attend to duty before pleasure. Certainly you recognize that?"

"My head understands this, but my heart does not." She sipped her beverage, never looking away from him.

He lowered his tone, sensing that she was weakening. "Forgive me, Isabella."

"I have not given you leave to address me so familiarly," she sniffed in mock disapproval.

"Forgive me again." He sought for some piece of drivel to soften her further. "It is how I think of you in my dreams."

Her face lit with delight. "You are a clever man to say such things, my lord. *Bravo.*"

He touched her arm. "My name is Simon."

"Simon." She rolled the name around in her mouth like a cat savoring fresh cream.

"Say you have forgiven me. End my torment."

A smile tugged at her lips despite her efforts to remain stern. "You make it difficult to remain angry at you . . . Simon."

"I pray that is true." Good Lord, Fox had been right. Women really did succumb to pretty words, even if they were the most obvious kind of flattery. How would Lucy react to such talk?

Where Isabella left him more or less unmoved, just the thought of his wife woke his sleeping passion with a vengeance. Real ardor heated his glance as he looked at his companion—but it was Lucy's face he saw in his mind.

"I am inclined to excuse your neglect—this once," Isabella said, tapping his arm with her fan.

"My heart sings in gratitude."

She laughed, low and warm. "Just see that it does not happen again." She raised her perfectly arched brows and indicated the crowded ballroom. "Do you forget that there are other gentlemen who would enjoy my company?"

"Never. I promise I will not abandon you so shamefully ever again."

"We shall see." A secretive smile curved her lips.

"Why are you laughing at me?"

"I am not laughing." Isabella nodded her head in greeting to a passing gentleman.

"You are." Something about that mysterious smile unsettled him. As if she knew something he didn't.

Had she guessed his game? What if his name was on LaRue's list? He had wondered more than once why she seemed to favor him above men who were more handsome or wittier or more charming. Was this a trap?

"I do find you amusing," she admitted. "But I find all men amusing, Simon, with their passionate promises and words of devotion. However, actions speak louder than words."

"Then surely my actions tell you how much I want to be with you." He took her empty glass and placed it on the tray of a passing servant.

"If you can prove you are not so fascinated with your wife, *amore mio,* then I will believe you."

"She's a wife, just like a chair is a chair. She does not excite me nearly as much as you do." The lie nearly strangled him.

She gave him an approving smile. "*Bene,* Simon. You do well." She lowered her voice to a husky whisper. "Now remain by my side for the rest of the evening, and you may well find your way into my bed, *bello mio.*"

"Nothing could tear me away."

"Not even your wife?"

"Of course not."

"*Bene.* Because she is here."

"Quite the crush," Lady Wexford said, scanning the throng of bodies packed into Lady Herrington's ballroom.

"We can always go home." Gin nearly turned back toward the door, but a frown from her godmother stopped her cold. "I was just joking, Aunt Beatrice."

"How shall we ever find the eligible gentlemen?" With a sigh, Lady Wexford straightened her shoulders. "Come along then."

"Do you believe the number of people they've crammed into this room?" Gin hissed, casting her eyes over the crowd. "How does anyone talk privately when you're penned in like sheep?"

"Tête-à-têtes have no place at an event like this," Lucy commented, as they followed Lady Wexford. "Everyone can hear everything a person says."

"No wonder the conversations are so boring."

Lucy chuckled, looking around her at the richly dressed members of the Polite World. For once she felt like one of them in her new pink silk ball gown from Madame Dauphine's. Though the neckline of the dress bordered on scandalous with Lucy's generous bosom, she was comforted by the Devingham pearls adorning her neck and ears.

No longer the country bumpkin, but truly the Countess of Devingham.

Gin looked lovely in a deceptively simple white dress with delicate embroidery along the hem and sleeves that Lucy had helped her choose. Her vivid coloring and slender figure were emphasized by the very basic design, free of the unbecoming ruffles and lace. Even her spectacles—which she refused to tuck into her reticule—could not spoil her fresh, new look.

"Ah, Captain Standish, how is your dear mother?" Lady Wexford stopped by a handsome blond man.

Captain Standish gave a brief bow. "Good evening, Lady Wexford, thank you for asking. Mama is currently taking the waters in Bath and proclaims she feels ever so much better."

"Marvelous! May I introduce you to my goddaughter, Miss Virginia Matthews, and our friend, Lady Devingham?"

Captain Standish took Gin's hand and very properly bowed over it. "Charmed, Miss Matthews." Then he turned to Lucy, and his polite smile widened into one of charismatic flirtation as he took her hand as well. "Lady Devingham."

"Captain Standish." With a discreet tug, Lucy pulled her fingers free.

"The captain's mama is one of my dearest friends," Lady Wexford said. "We made our debut together."

"Will you lovely ladies allow me a dance? If they are not all spoken for already, that is!"

"We just arrived," Gin said.

"Then luck is with me today. Miss Matthews, may I request you reserve the country dance for me? And Lady Devingham—a minuet, perhaps?"

The interested gleam in the young man's blue eyes both unnerved and flattered. After a moment's hesitation, Lucy nodded, deciding to enjoy the masculine attention. After all, it was harmless.

Captain Standish gave her a slow smile. "Excellent. I shall return to collect each of you for the promised dance."

"Thank you, Captain," Lady Wexford said with an approving smile.

The young man bowed and with one last glance at Lucy, disappeared into the crowd.

"I think he likes you," Gin murmured.

Lucy frowned. "Nonsense. I am a married woman. He was just being polite."

"I don't think that matters much to him."

Lucy shrugged. "It's just a dance."

"Come, come!" Lady Wexford trilled. "I see Mrs. Fostham, and she has a very eligible son named Percy that I would so like you to meet, Virginia."

"I may just expire from enthusiasm," Gin said with a mock-English accent.

"Virginia, do keep a civil tongue in your head."

"If I must."

"Oh, look, Lady Devingham. Here is your husband!"

Lucy jerked her gaze around and saw that it was indeed Simon headed toward them, a scowl on his face.

"Lady Wexford," he said with a bow as he reached them.

"Good evening, Lord Devingham. Have you met my goddaughter, Miss Matthews?"

"I've not had the pleasure." He gave a brief nod to Gin. "Miss Matthews." Before Gin could respond, he turned a searing stare back on Lucy. "I've come to claim the first dance."

Lucy raised her chin at the challenge in his eyes. "You are in luck then, because it is not yet spoken for."

"Excellent." He took his wife's arm, his smile to the others little more than a brief flash of teeth. "If you ladies will excuse us."

"Of course, Lord Devingham," Lady Wexford said with a gay wave of her beringed hand.

Gin opened her mouth, but closed it again when Lucy sent her a quick look of warning. Lucy and Simon took their places for the dance.

"What are you doing here?" he asked softly.

"Accompanying a friend." The orchestra started playing, and she stepped into the dance. Their hands touched, and the jolt of attraction shook her.

The formation prevented any private conversation for a few moments, but then they came back together. Simon dipped his head low to her ear. "Why are you following me?"

"I'm not!" Anger came quickly on the heels of surprise. "How could I follow you if you did not tell me where you were going?" she hissed.

His frown told her he hadn't considered that.

They moved apart again, and she smiled by rote at her new partner. Then Simon was back to take her hand for the promenade. "Go home," he commanded in a voice only she could hear.

"I can't. The gossip."

He made a sound of impatience. "Within the hour then." They reached the end of the line of dancers.

"Fine," she whispered past the lump in her throat. Why did he want her gone so badly?

They parted, each to their separate positions. She glanced down the line of dancers and saw Isabella Montelucci staring at Simon, her eyes narrowed in displeasure. Her breath froze in her lungs. Was this why he wanted her to leave? So he could continue his flirtation with the Italian woman?

Tears stung her eyes, but she forced them back. She would not cry—not in front of him or all of the wagging tongues of Society. She finished the dance, the pain choking her, and yet still her flesh tingled when Simon took her arm at the completion of the dance. When they were within paces of Lady Wexford and Virginia, Simon leaned down to her.

"Within the hour," he reminded her.

She nodded without looking at him, barely aware of his tall form striding away. Gin came to stand beside her, laying a hand on her arm in silent support.

"The Viscount Weatherton seems taken with Virginia, don't you think so, Lady Devingham?" Lady Wexford asked, apparently unaware of Lucy's turmoil.

Lucy looked up as the youthful viscount made his way toward them through the throng, a glass of punch in each hand, and found herself unable to formulate an answer.

Gin squeezed her arm, then said, "Really, Aunt Beatrice, I wouldn't know whether to dance with him or hire him a wet nurse."

"Virginia, really!"

"Honestly, I can't consider a man that young as a husband. If I am forced to marry, I will at least have some say in the matter."

Lady Wexford sighed. "Very well. It's not as if you don't have a fortune to recommend you."

Lucy ignored the disagreement, grateful that Gin had successfully diverted her godmother's attention. Her heart felt frozen, her mind paralyzed with Simon's treatment of her. He had made it more than clear that he preferred the company of Isabella to that of his wife.

Even now she could glimpse him with Isabella. As she struggled to keep them in sight through the crowd, Captain Standish appeared before her. Sketching a bow, he offered his arm with a beguiling smile.

"I believe this is our dance."

Chapter 9

The flame of green burns hot and fast in rage;
To torch foul flesh where black hearts
*   are encaged.*

The journals of Simon, Lord Devingham,
on jealousy

Lucy took the captain's arm without think-ing and allowed him to lead her back to the dance floor. Gin watched with concern in her eyes, trapped beside her godmother and trying to discourage the young viscount's interest.

"How long have you been in Town, Lady Deving-ham?" Standish asked, as they took their places.

"Only a few days." Lucy glanced at the spot where she had last seen Simon with Isabella, but they were no longer there. The orchestra started, and they were swept into the dance.

"And how are you enjoying the delights of our fair city?" he asked.

"There is much to see. I never had a Season." Ah, there they were, tucked into a shadowed corner. Her heart wrenched as Simon bent his dark head toward the other woman.

"I have always believed that there are certain amusements that are better enjoyed by more mature adults. Things that unsophisticated debutantes simply cannot appreciate."

"Indeed." Lucy barely comprehended his chatter. Isabella had just stroked her fan down Simon's arm, and Lucy was astounded at the rage that exploded inside her. She wanted to take that fan and—

"I understand that your husband is a very busy man. Please allow me to offer my services should you need an escort."

Lucy glanced at his earnest face, struggling to hide her own emotional turmoil. "Thank you, Captain Standish. You are too kind."

"I enjoy the company of beautiful women. And I am preparing to leave for the Peninsula, so I must appreciate what pleasures I can before I go into battle."

Lucy colored. "You flatter me, Captain." She glanced back and found Simon watching her. Then Isabella claimed his attention again, and Lucy's heart wrenched at how eagerly he turned toward her.

"Lady Devingham, you look pale," the handsome captain said. "Is the dance too rigorous for you?"

"Not at all." She forced a smile. "Though I do not feel well, I admit."

"These affairs are usually dreadful crushes, and a body cannot breathe properly," he said. The orchestra finished with a flourish, and as he bowed he murmured, "Perhaps a breath of fresh air? There is a terrace just there."

The idea of escaping to the sweet coolness of the night gripped her and would not let go. Perhaps a few moments away from the ballroom would allow her to regain her equilibrium. "Yes, Captain Standish," she said with a genuine smile. "I do believe a moment on the terrace would be the very thing."

He gave her a slow grin that seemed just a shade too familiar. "My thoughts exactly."

Simon controlled his churning emotions with effort. Isabella's perfume surrounded him like a smothering cloud, filling his nostrils and lungs with the heavy scent. Her dress this evening was a daring affair made of nearly transparent gold-shot material and cut so low that he could sometimes see a hint of her dark nipples peeking above the edge of the bodice.

Everything about the woman was obvious and sexual, and he found he much preferred the sweet sincerity of his wife.

When he had first realized that Lucy was at the ball, his initial reaction had been fury. He'd known that he'd hurt her feelings earlier, but he hadn't expected her to follow him. Her sharp reminder that he hadn't shared his plans with her was what had brought reason back into play.

But he needed her to leave very soon. It was bad enough that the eyes of Society watched their every move. No doubt they found it highly amusing that he dallied with Isabella at an affair where his wife was present. But idle speculation didn't bother him. Isabella seemed to relish the salacious whispers, clearly pleased that he remained at her side while his wife kept other company in the same ballroom.

But his dance with Lucy had awakened his ever-lingering desire for her. Just the touch of her hand, the scent of her, had brought his hunger to life with full force. Memories of the greenhouse taunted him, reminding him of what awaited him in the marriage bed.

He thought back on the way he had laid her down on the table in the greenhouse, how he had held her legs up in the air and watched his cock slide inside her. The memory stirred his vitals, and when Isabella claimed his attention, he was more able to produce a seductive smile at her throaty flirting. He could see by her reaction that she noticed his aroused state, that she thought it was for her.

Good. Let her think that. If conjuring up memories of the woman he really wanted would help the cause, then that was exactly what he would do.

Then he saw Lucy step on the dance floor with another man.

His first instinct was to storm out there and rip her away from him. But Isabella whispered his name, and he forced himself to focus on his assignment.

They were just dancing, not making love. He kept repeating the calming words in his head, but the roaring jealousy refused to let him go. Taken aback by its ferocity, he struggled to retain his reason.

He couldn't stop himself from glancing over again, and this time he found Lucy watching him. The stricken expression on her face brought guilt rising to the fore to churn along with the jealousy that already ripped at his insides.

I don't want Isabella. She's just an assignment. In his imagination, he told her the truth.

Of course she couldn't know that this wasn't a real affair. He'd tried to send her home, hadn't he? He'd told her in no uncertain terms that the only way she could stay in London was to leave him to his own life, while she lived hers. Only in bed would they come together.

He'd hurt her, and the knowledge ate at him.

Now she thought he didn't care, and she was out there with that bounder Standish. The handsome

blond captain used his mother's failing health as
an excuse not to fight for his country and instead
spent his time seducing naïve women, each of
whom believed she was his last romance before
he went to war.

As long as the two remained on the dance floor,
he didn't need to worry. Now that he thought on
it, Lady Wexford was bosom bows with Standish's
mother, so no doubt that was how Lucy had come
to be introduced to him. It was all completely
proper. There was nothing to worry about.

The dance ended. He expected Standish to escort
her back to Lady Wexford and Miss Matthews.

Instead, they turned toward the terrace.

No! He took a step, but Isabella's clinging hands
on his arm stopped him. He looked at the other
woman, registering her annoyance, the pout of
the lips that many men had no doubt kissed. Her
eyes held a warning. If he left her side, he would
fall from her good graces. He hesitated.

Standish stood back to allow Lucy to precede
him through the terrace doors. Very well. If they
were gone for more than five minutes, he would
send someone to search for his wife. A servant
perhaps. Or Lady Wexford.

Then he caught sight of Standish's predatory smile
as the man swept a glance down Lucy's retreating
body, his gaze lingering on her lush bottom.

Control snapped. Simon jerked his arm from
Isabella's hold, his eyes on the other man stepping

out on to the terrace behind Lucy. Ignoring the temper that lit Isabella's face, he began shoving his way through the crowd.

Lucy inhaled the fresh night air, relishing the cool of the evening. She had needed a moment away, and gazing up at the stars gave her the perspective she needed.

How could he be so insensitive? She hadn't missed the whispers and the stares. Everyone was talking about the Earl of Devingham and how he dallied with his trollop in full view of his naïve country wife.

Shame flooded her, along with a hint of embarrassment at her own bitter jealousy. Isabella Montelucci was no common trollop. She was what one would call a mistress perhaps. Or maybe a lightskirt.

She gave a harsh little laugh, irritated at how easily Simon's public rejection had turned her into a foul-mouthed fishwife, even if it was just within her own mind. But she didn't know what to do.

She had feelings for her husband, though she hadn't yet figured out what they were, and his obvious preference for another woman struck her like a dagger through the heart.

She heard Captain Standish come up beside her.

"I thought you might need to escape all that," he said.

His compassion brought more shame, and she closed her eyes against the tears that threatened. Did he know? Did everyone pity her?

"Lady Devingham—"

"You were right," she rasped, fighting for composure. "Fresh air was just the thing."

He touched a hand to her shoulder, a tentative moment of comfort that was not really proper but meant as a kindness. "Is there anything I can do?"

She closed her eyes against the weakness that flooded her. "Just stay here with me for a minute while I collect myself," she whispered.

"Of course."

They stood in silence, listening to the muffled strains of the orchestra, the distant clop of a horse's hooves somewhere near the stables.

Then a shrill laugh came from the ballroom, slicing through the tentative serenity of the night. Lucy jumped.

"Calm yourself." Standish touched her shoulder again. "No one even knows we're out here."

She sucked in a deep breath. "Good."

He leaned closer to her. "He does not deserve you, you know."

She jerked her head around to look at him. "You saw?"

"Yes." He nodded, his blue eyes soft with sympathy.

She glanced down at her hands clinging to the stone balustrade. "I imagine everyone did."

"Your husband is a cad for abandoning a new bride this way. He clearly does not realize the treasure he has in you."

"You are very kind," she choked, not looking at him.

"You should be worshipped for your beauty. Appreciated by a man who values you." His hand stroked along her back. Startled, she looked up at his face. The warm desire she saw there alarmed her further.

"Captain Standish—"

"Michael."

"Captain Standish . . ." she began again.

"God, you smell sweet." He leaned down to press his lips to her shoulder.

"Captain!" She turned to face him, intent on delivering her setdown face-to-face, but he clearly misunderstood and scooped her into his arms.

"Sweet Lucy." He pressed his mouth to hers.

Lucy struggled to push him away, but he was strong, his greedy mouth insistent. She managed to rip her lips away. "No," she gasped. "Stop!"

"You're right. We're too close to the ballroom." He pressed his open mouth to her throat. "Come with me to the garden."

"No! I do not want this." She shoved against his chest, leaning back as far as she could go.

"This is just what your husband deserves," the captain said with a chuckle. "I am sure you agree."

"No, I do *not*! Let me go, Captain Standish, or I

will scream loud enough to bring the house down around us!"

"No, you won't." He trailed a finger along one breast. "The gossips are already talking. What a tasty tidbit this would be, eh?" He smothered her with another kiss. She beat at his shoulders with her fists, panicking with each moment of futility that passed. Would he take her by force right here on the terrace?

Suddenly he was torn away from her. She staggered backwards, sucking in deep breaths as she grabbed for the balustrade with a trembling hand. Her eyes widened at the murderous look on Simon's face as he gripped Captain Standish with his hands twisted in the man's coat. Where had he come from?

The captain gave him a cocky grin. "You have apparently neglected your wife too much, Devingham. She was begging for me to—"

Simon's knee shot up into Standish's stomach. The blond man's breath escaped with a whoosh, and he doubled over. A swift uppercut to the jaw sent the captain flying backwards to crash to the ground with a heavy thud.

Simon turned to Lucy. The swiftness and accuracy of his movements had shocked her. He'd laid the captain out with all the efficiency and coldness of a cobra. But where that altercation had elicited no emotion from him, now his eyes burned as he looked at her.

"Simon?"

Her uncertain whisper seemed to provoke him further. He took her by the arm, his grip like a manacle, and dragged her from the terrace and back into the ballroom.

Whispers followed them as he marched her through the crowd. She caught a quick glimpse of Lady Wexford's appalled expression, and Gin's worried one, before he led her out of the ballroom toward the front door.

"Where are we going?" she asked.

His pace did not falter. "Home."

Standish was lucky he'd left him breathing. Simon regarded his wife in the seat across from him as the footman closed the door to the carriage. The temptation to put an end to the bounder's existence still lingered, and all because he had put his hands on Lucy.

She watched him warily, her dark eyes enormous in her face, her hands gripping the edge of the seat. Good. She should be unsettled. Even country misses should understand the imprudence of wandering outside alone with a man.

A red haze swam before his eyes at the memory of Lucy in Standish's arms. He'd never felt a moment of jealousy until his naïve little bride had walked into his life. The only reason he'd managed any degree of control at all was because he had seen her struggling in the bastard's arms. She hadn't wanted the embrace, and that was a good thing, but her foolishness in going outside with him had created the whole sordid mess.

Didn't she realize how desirable she was? How no man would be able to resist a moment of privacy with her?

She looked as sweet and tasty as a frosted cake, with her pale pink evening dress and creamy skin. Her dark hair appeared soft and inviting, delicate, wispy curls brushing her ears and neck. Her eyes held an innocence that a man could not ignore, but he had seen those eyes burn with passion, too. The Devingham pearls rested against the tops of her generous breasts, the soft globes barely covered by the sophisticated cut of her new dress.

And only he knew what delights awaited beneath her skirts.

The memory of the greenhouse exploded in his mind, the unhindered passion that had created new bonds between them. He found his attention drawn back to her swelling bosom, watching the plump flesh tremble with each jostle of the carriage wheels as they set off for home. He remembered how she looked with her breasts exposed and her legs parted for him, and even now he could almost feel her soft skin beneath his hands.

The intimacy of the darkened coach throbbed like a heartbeat.

"You shouldn't have gone outside with Standish," he said.

She nodded. "I never meant . . ."

"You never intended a liaison with him, I know." He had been watching her lips as she spoke, and desire stirred, a sleeping dragon slowly awakening.

"You're not angry with me?"

"Not angry, no." He didn't dare elaborate. He was jealous as hell and still wrestled with that unfamiliar emotion. It had struck so suddenly, so completely, that he had acted without thinking, driven to violence for his woman.

Never before had any female made him exhibit such a lack of control.

"You seem angry."

"Angry at him for putting his hands on you." He let his gaze slide over her, possessive and hungry. "My wife."

She gave a quick, indrawn breath, then ferocity lit her face, making her look like an angry kitten. "I know exactly how you feel."

"I'm glad you didn't enjoy his attentions either. I won't have to call him out."

"That's not what I meant . . ." Then her eyes widened. "Call him out? Simon, no!"

"He touched my wife." Aggression edged his voice. "Perhaps a dawn appointment is just the thing."

"You'll be killed!"

He raised an eyebrow. "Madam, I will have you know I am a crack shot."

"Then *he* will die." She wrung her hands, looking for all the world like a Drury Lane heroine, panic sweeping across her features.

Jealousy nipped at him. "Are you so worried for him then?"

"I'm worried for *you*. The scandal—"

"I don't care about the bloody scandal." He held her gaze, hot desire pumping through his system with each breath. "No one touches my woman but me."

Her wide-eyed expression of shocked fascination made him want to lay her down and take her like a savage. She must have caught a hint of his feelings because her features softened.

"You needn't worry about that. I don't want anyone to touch me but you."

Her quiet words, so innocently uttered, snapped his control.

In one swift move, he shifted across to her seat, crowding her back against the side of the coach. "I want to wipe the memory of him from your mind."

He kissed her, unable to resist touching her for another moment, at last giving rein to the passions inside him that begged for release. The taste and scent of her spun in his head, stoking the fires that never fully died.

He would make certain no man lingered in her memories but him.

His kiss was like strong wine, stealing her breath and reason. Lucy closed her eyes as familiar desire surged through her. One moment Simon was a cold, deadly stranger. The next moment he kissed her as if his life depended on it. There was something she wanted to ask him, but his fingers stroking over her legs made the thoughts evaporate like morning mist.

His hands caressed her with a rough tenderness, and that small betrayal of his need filled her with her own, hot longings. Did he want her so much? She pulled her mouth from his, gasping for breath, and he dipped down to her throat, nipping and suckling the sensitive flesh. A soft moan escaped her lips.

He made a growling noise, then buried his face in her cleavage, shoving aside her pearls with an impatient hand. At the same time, his other hand tugged up her skirts.

With a squeak of surprise, she reached down to halt his progress. They were in a coach! Surely this sort of thing was better suited for the bedchamber? But though she rested her hand on his, she found she could not stop him. Didn't want to stop him.

She so wanted him to see her as a woman and not some naïve country miss who would faint at the mere notion of the marriage bed.

He pulled back, drawing her restraining hand up to his mouth for a kiss, then pressed it against his chest. The thundering of his heart pounded against her palm, and his breathing was ragged. She slid her hand to his shoulder, unable to give the most token protest as he turned his gaze to her lower body. Then his hands were beneath the delicate muslin, sliding up her thighs, pushing her skirts aside. He stopped when the material pooled around her waist, satisfaction in his eyes as he looked down at her.

"There she is," he murmured, and stroked a gentle finger over her exposed mound.

A soft groan escaped her.

"You are so beautiful." He turned his gaze on her face, but his fingers kept caressing her sensitive female flesh. "Standish wanted you, and it made me insane."

"I didn't want him. I never wanted him." She arched her back, lost in sensation. "I only want you."

His eyes darkened, and the skin pulled taut across his features as he continued to caress her intimately. "Sweet wife," he murmured.

"Simon." She panted his name, her hands gripping his shoulders as the craving grew. Her skin felt so sensitive that even the night air seemed painful. Her breasts tightened, the nipples hard little peaks that ached when they brushed the material of her dress. His fingers teased her female flesh, stroking, then dipping inside her and making her wild with need. She practically sang his name over and over in rhythmic tandem with his movements, throwing back her head as he pushed her toward the peak.

Then the pleasure hit, striking with devastating force that ripped a tiny scream from her throat.

With a hand behind her head, he swallowed the sound with a kiss, and she whimpered beneath his mouth, breathing quickly through her nose as her body rippled with satisfaction.

Moments passed. His fingers grew still, and he broke the kiss, stroking her hair with one hand and whispering soft words of praise. She remained there, shuddering in his arms, her world cast askew at the suddenness of her climax.

Then the coach lurched to a halt.

Simon's head jerked up, and he cast a narrow-eyed glance at the vehicle's door. "We are home."

Chapter 10

O respite that is found in sweet desire,
So cruelly quelled by honor's righteous fire.

The journals of Simon, Lord Devingham,
on the price of honor

They descended from the carriage with false dignity, hoping that the servants had not overheard any hint of their passionate interlude. Simon glanced at Lucy as they ascended the steps to his home. Her cheeks were flushed, and her eyes sparkled. And if her coiffure drooped a bit in the back, well, that could be attributed to rigorous dancing.

And the true dance had not yet begun.

He thanked God for his greatcoat; without it there would have been no way to hide his very visible hunger for his wife from the servants bustling about the coach. She walked ahead of him into the house, and he watched her round bottom swaying beneath her skirts, pondering the notion of taking her from behind tonight. How it would feel to grasp that smooth feminine flesh as he slid in and out of her body.

Dobbins appeared to take his outer garments, and if he noticed his master's aroused state, he gave no sign, bless him. He disappeared as quickly as he had appeared, leaving Simon and Lucy alone in the foyer.

She turned to face him, lush and beautiful, her face glowing with the aftereffects of his attentions. A playful smile teased her lips. "I believe I am tired from all the excitement, Simon. I am going to bed."

He raised a brow. "Indeed?"

She nodded solemnly, but mischief danced in her eyes. "Yes, I believe so."

"Perhaps I am tired as well." He appeared to think on the matter.

Her serious expression broke, and with a giggle, she threw herself into his arms. "You're a wicked man to tease me so."

He felt his lips curve, and he traced a finger along her jaw. "Of course I am wicked. You should know that by now."

Pink swept her cheeks. "I do, indeed." She hugged him tightly, burying her face in his chest. "I am so glad you chose me over that Isabella woman."

Though the words were muffled against the material of his coat, they struck like a sledgehammer.

Isabella. Bloody hell.

An image rose in his mind, a brief glimpse of Isabella's enraged features as he'd led Lucy out of the ballroom.

The very crowded ballroom.

The ballroom stuffed to the rafters with every gossip and gabster in London.

It was impossible to imagine that anyone had missed the spectacle of his jealous rampage from the ballroom, wife in tow. Perhaps fewer people knew how he'd floored Standish with a well-placed facer, but that story would spread quickly enough.

Right back to his superiors.

Oh, he'd made a fine mess of things!

Lucy snuggled closer to him, and he closed his eyes, seduced by the lavender scent of her hair, the sweet curves cuddled against him, and pained by the knowledge of what he must do. He put his hands on her shoulders and gently pushed her away.

"You are right," he said, nearly choking on the words. "It is late, and you should go to bed."

Her luminous brown eyes dimmed with confusion. "I thought you and I—"

"I have work to attend to." He stepped back from her, and the cool air smacked him where the warmth of her flesh had been. "Also, you will provide me with your schedule each morning so that unfortunate incidents like tonight will not happen again."

"My schedule?" She looked as though he'd slapped her. "But—"

"Good night, Lucy." He turned and walked down the hall to his study, barely resisting the urge to look back at her.

To beg her to forgive him.

Lucy's heart broke as she watched Simon walk away from her. What had happened? What had she said that had made him withdraw from her? This wasn't the first time he'd abruptly walked away in the middle of what she considered a moment of intimacy.

She went back over the conversation in her head. Isabella. That's what she'd said. And he'd stiffened and retreated from her.

His actions puzzled her. Even though he had spent time at the Italian woman's side at the Herrington affair, his behavior regarding Captain Standish had been that of a jealous husband—a husband who cared for his wife, not one enamored of another woman. His attentions in the carriage had underscored that assumption quite clearly.

Simon did have feelings for her, of that she was certain. His treatment of her in their intimate encounters was affectionate, like a man who was fond of his bed partner. He'd shown that tenderness and camaraderie at other times outside the bedchamber, only to abruptly switch to an impersonal man on certain occasions.

Tonight had been another of those abrupt shifts in attitude.

Why? Why did he seem to want her one moment, then despise her the next?

She began to climb the stairs to her room, the questions circling in her mind like vultures over a carcass. Was there something wrong with her? Or perhaps she did something wrong? Was she too lighthearted in her dealings with him? Too forward?

Remembering what had happened in the coach, she blushed and dismissed that last notion.

She just couldn't figure out what it was that made him step back from their increasing closeness. Sometimes she swore he was two different men—one kind and passionate, the other cool and impassive. Such disparities in nature did not make sense.

She reached her chamber and entered the room, grateful that Molly was nowhere to be seen. No doubt the maid hadn't expected her home so soon.

She set down her reticule and her fan and shrugged off her wrap, then sat down in front of her mirror. Her brow creased as she noticed her hair coming loose, and the neckline of her dress was not quite straight. She tugged the bodice into place. Which man had done this, Captain Standish or Simon?

She paused at the memory of tonight's incident, of her husband's swift, lethal defense of her honor on the Herringtons' terrace. Simon's calm, efficient actions had shown her the face of another man, someone whom she did not know. But she had glimpsed that man once before, on the evening she had arrived in London—for one fleeting instant when he'd stood on the stairs, surprised by her unexpected appearance.

The sting of Simon's rejection faded beneath the growing suspicion that there was something afoot.

If he was starting to care for her, if they were indeed beginning to build the sort of marriage she had always dreamed about, then why had the mention of that woman's name made him walk away from her? Guilt?

He hadn't looked guilty. In fact, she got the distinct impression that he had forgotten Isabella's existence until Lucy had mentioned her. Not at all the reaction of a man trying to juggle the affections of two women.

Something was not right. Simon seemed preoccupied with Isabella, and like everyone else, Lucy had assumed they were having an affair. But what if they weren't? What if Simon was involved in some other matter that involved Isabella?

What if Isabella was not what she seemed?

It made sense. Simon clearly didn't want his wife in London. Why? What was he hiding? Or was he trying to protect her from something?

From Isabella? No, that was foolishness. What danger could another female pose to her?

Perhaps he had some dealing with Isabella, something having nothing to do with an affair, that he wanted to keep secret. Something not quite legal, perhaps?

No. It didn't seem possible. Simon—a criminal?

She thought about the poem he'd written for her during their courtship. The hours he spent in the greenhouse, working with his roses. His somber, studious mien. Could she really be considering that a rose-breeding poet, an intellectual, a man who took his duties to his title so very seriously, might be involved in some havey-cavey business on the wrong side of the law?

Her own growing fondness for her husband made her want to deny the charge outright, but could she really afford to ignore the possibility?

What about his friend, Mr. Foxworth? The man was a curmudgeon, certainly, but why was he so determined to see her gone from Simon's life? Did she pose some danger to their scheme?

She put together the things she had seen that had never quite made sense. Simon's frequent changes in temperament. His insistence that she return home immediately. His fixation on Isabella. Mr. Foxworth's obvious desire to see her leave London as soon as possible. Isabella's secret meeting with the clerk at the bookshop.

She gasped, staring at her own wide-eyed shock in the mirror as the truth became apparent.

Simon wasn't having an affair—he was in trouble.

Simon closed the door to his study behind him, though a slam would have been more satisfying. And more betraying. He stalked to his desk and dropped into his chair, staring up at the ceiling.

Damn, what a coil. Every thought of his assignment had fled his head the instant he'd realized Standish's intentions toward Lucy. He'd just caused a huge scene at a very crowded ball and completely fallen from Isabella's good graces yet again. The project was in shambles, and he hadn't even realized it until just moments ago. His whole world had been filled with Lucy.

How had she so completely captivated him in so short a time? Was it her sweet and loving nature? Her beauty? The incredible passion that had them stripping each other naked on a regular basis? Her playfulness? Her honor and determination to do the right thing, even in the face of her husband's disapproval?

It was all those things and more. His carefully ordered lifestyle had turned upside down since Lucy had come to London, and while in the beginning his goal had been to send her home, now he found that idea distasteful. He wanted Lucy around, wanted her arms around him and her laughter echoing through his empty home. He wanted her to tease him into undignified food battles in the breakfast room, then seduce him into mindless passion in the bedroom.

He wanted Lucy in his life, always, every day.

Was he falling in love with her? Was that what this tightness in his chest meant as he had walked away from her?

What a blasted tangle. He'd been so enchanted by his wife that he'd nearly destroyed the whole plan to get close to Isabella. He needed to fix what he'd broken, and he needed to do it quickly.

And not just with the assignment.

Though his instincts clamored for him to go to Lucy immediately, to kiss away the distress he had seen on her face, he calmed himself with the knowledge that they were married. There would be time for him to sort out his feelings, a lifetime to mend things with his wife. He just couldn't do it this moment, not before he straightened out the mess he'd made with Isabella. Once his work was again on even keel, he could turn his attention to his marriage.

And he dared not go to her bed again until he had things under control.

Though the torture might kill him, staying away from the sensual delights found in his wife's arms was the only way to maintain his concentration. Fox had been right; he was losing his focus. But he'd found something so unexpected with Lucy that he'd been blinded by it.

He rubbed a hand over his chest, the center of his emotional turmoil. Did she feel the same way? He hadn't missed her ferocity in the coach when he'd talked about another man's hands on her. What had she said?

I know how you feel.

She'd been talking about Isabella, he realized. And she hadn't liked his spending time with another woman any more than he liked her going outside with Standish.

He found himself grinning like a fool and forced his attention back to the matter at hand. The first step was to somehow get back in Isabella's good graces.

A knock came at his door, and for one shining second, his heart swelled as he considered that it might be Lucy. Then he remembered that he must discourage any bonds between them, at least for a little while, and his shoulders sagged.

If it was Lucy, he would have to send her away, and he didn't know if he could stand seeing the hurt in her lovely eyes again.

The knock came a second time. Steeling himself in his resolution, he said, "Come in."

Anticipation fizzled as Dobbins entered the room. "This just came for you, my lord. Dreadfully urgent."

Simon took the note from the servant. "Thank you, Dobbins. Please close the door on your way out."

"Very good, my lord."

Simon was barely aware of the butler leaving the room. He recognized the writing on the outside of the missive, and he steeled himself for the well-deserved rebuke he expected to find within.

Devingham:

Present yourself at my home at eleven o'clock tomorrow morning. Do not be late.

Hall

Had Sir Adrian been at the Herrington ball? He didn't recall. But even if his superior hadn't attended that particular affair, clearly the gossip was already making the rounds. And Sir Adrian felt the need to discuss the matter in person.

Very well. He'd expected no less.

He set aside the note and reached for his own stationery. The sooner he wheedled his way back into Isabella's good graces, the sooner he could get the assignment back on course.

Lucy awoke the next morning and realized that Simon had never come to her. An inquiry of the servants revealed that her husband had already breakfasted and left the house.

The heaviness of her heart weighed on her as she dressed for the day and went about her daily tasks. She'd sent a note around to Gin and was expecting her friend to pay a call, so when Dobbins appeared in the parlor shortly before noon to announce that she had a caller, she anticipated hearing the American announced.

"Mr. Foxworth to see you, my lady."

Lucy set down her embroidery on the sofa and stood as John Foxworth limped into the room. He halted just inside the doorway, his blue eyes glittering, his mouth curving in a knowing smile.

Lucy flicked her gaze to the butler. "That will be all, Dobbins."

The servant withdrew without a flicker of emotion. Fox reached back and closed the door behind him.

Lucy raised her brows. "I do not think that is entirely appropriate, Mr. Foxworth."

"What I have to say is something I doubt you would want your servants to overhear." Without waiting for an invitation, he came over and sat down in a chair across from her. "Forgive my lack of courtesy, Lady Devingham, but my knee refuses to wait on ceremony."

"Lack of courtesy is something I expect from you." She sat and picked up her embroidery again. "If you are looking for my husband, he has gone out."

"I am looking for you."

Her fingers trembled at his smug tone, and she forced herself to concentrate on her stitches. She refused to let him intimidate her.

Or at least, she refused to let him see that he intimidated her.

"Why would you want to call on me?" Push the needle through the cloth, pull the thread through. Repeat.

"I have a matter to discuss with you, Lady Devingham."

"Oh?" Push the needle through the cloth. . .

"The matter of your leaving London."

She tugged on the thread so hard that the cloth crinkled. With a hiss of frustration, she turned the hoop over and used her fingernails to loosen the stitch. "I am not leaving for several more days, Mr. Foxworth. And I don't understand why it is your concern."

"I have my reasons."

"I am certain you do, and I am equally certain you will not share those reasons with me." She continued to pluck at the thread until she loosened the stitch enough to smooth the material. She tugged it gently, then went on to the next stitch.

"You are correct." He scowled at the embroidery hoop. "Must you do that while we are conversing? I like to think I have your full attention."

"You're a very demanding man, Mr. Foxworth, much like a spoiled child." She set aside her work and folded her hands in her lap, gazing at him with raised eyebrows. His jaw had tightened in obvious irritation, and she smothered a smile.

"This is no game, Lady Devingham. You must leave London immediately. Surely the trouble you caused at the Herrington affair last evening has convinced you of that?"

She winced. "The gossips have been working through the night, I see."

"The story of how you taunted your husband with another man until he resorted to violence in public? Yes, even the scandal sheets have picked up the tale."

"I did *not* taunt my husband with another man!" She clamped her lips shut. She did not owe this reprobate any explanation.

He chuckled. "Did that sting? So sorry."

"You are not sorry, Mr. Foxworth. You are a bitter man who takes delight in the suffering of others."

His expression hardened. "You know nothing about me or how I feel, Lady Devingham, so do not presume to speak of it."

"Yet you presume much, sir, by coming to my parlor and demanding I leave London. Why do you feel you have the right?"

"I'm trying to do what's best for your husband."

"Why do you think my company is not what is best for him? Do you know something I do not, Mr. Foxworth?" She held her breath, hoping his annoyance would goad him into answering.

Instead, he narrowed his eyes at her. "The question is, what do *you* know, Lady Devingham?"

The menace underscoring his words shook her. "I know he is having an affair," she lied. "And you are apparently trying to keep me from finding out."

He blinked, and she could practically feel the oppression of danger lift. "So you know. I tried so hard to shield you."

Despite the very convincing note of sympathy in his voice, she was not fooled. They were both playing a game here, but apparently Simon's friend underestimated her intelligence. "I appreciate your concern, Mr. Foxworth."

"Surely, now that you know, you can understand that the best thing for you to do is return to Devingham and pretend ignorance. It's a wife's lot, I'm afraid."

"Not this wife's. I am newly wed, Mr. Foxworth, and while these things are usually tolerated by Society, it is normally after an heir has been born that a man seeks out a mistress. Simon is somewhat premature in his dallying." Her face flushed at discussing such intimate topics with a virtual stranger, but there was no other way to learn the truth. She sent a silent apology to her departed mother in heaven.

"Simon is my friend, Lady Devingham, and friends protect each other."

"Even from a wife?"

"Especially from a wife." He sighed with a regret

that was not echoed in his eyes and pulled a packet of papers from inside his jacket. "I had hoped you would see reason, but now I have no choice."

"What have you there, Mr. Foxworth?" she scoffed. "Love letters from my husband to his mistress? I assure you, I already know more than I'd like about their liaison."

"Nothing so crude." He unfolded the papers and scanned them. "It is just some information I have gathered."

She laughed. "My entire life was spent in the country, Mr. Foxworth. If you had me investigated, I doubt you will have found anything of import."

"Yes, I'm afraid you're right." He lowered the papers to his lap and gave her that cocky smile again. "However, Miss Matthews proved quite entertaining."

She stiffened. "How dare you investigate my friends!"

His fingers tightened around the papers. "I dare much, Lady Devingham, for the safety of *my* friends."

"You're a despicable man."

"I do what's necessary." He glanced down at the papers. "I suppose you know your friend caused quite a bit of trouble for her parents. Lots of gossip, a few embarrassing scenes."

Lucy narrowed her eyes at him and did not deign to reply.

He shrugged, but she could tell he was enjoying

this. "She pushed the governor's son into the pond at his birthday barbecue. This did not endear her father to a very powerful political ally."

"The young man was forcing his attentions on her," she said with a disdainful sniff. "I would have done the same."

"Really." He raised his brows in that superior way that made her want to slap him. The unladylike urge shocked her into biting her tongue as he continued. "Do you also know that Miss Matthews staged various public protests for the right of women to vote, as well as other issues relating to the working conditions of the miners in her father's employ?"

She merely nodded, keeping her fingers locked together to retain her composure.

Fox perused his papers. "Do you also know, Lady Devingham, that during one of these protests, your friend Miss Matthews was incarcerated?"

"Are you making up tales now?" she snapped.

He gave her a slow smile, and she regretted her burst of temper. "It was in the newspapers. Her parents thought a few hours in prison would teach their daughter her proper place. It didn't work, however, and when she continued her unseemly behavior, they sent her here to England and charged poor Lady Wexford to find her a husband."

"I know that."

He leaned forward. "Did you also know that if she does not find a husband, she will be cut off from her family completely? No contact with them, no inheritance. She will be completely outcast, Lady Devingham." He raised a brow as he sat back. "*If* the information were to fall into the hands of the gossips, that is."

She leaped to her feet. "Please leave, Mr. Foxworth. I won't listen to your lies for another moment."

"No lies, Lady Devingham. It's all written right here." He folded up the papers, then stood and tossed the documents on the table. "Think long and hard about your options. If you do not leave London immediately, a copy of that report will find its way to every scandal rag in the city."

She held his gaze, never glancing at the papers. "Dobbins will see you out, Mr. Foxworth."

Smirking, he gave her a brief bow, then turned and limped out of the room.

Only when he was gone did she sink back onto the sofa, her legs trembling. The visit had only underscored her suspicions. Simon was involved in something more sinister than a vulgar affair. Why else would his best friend call on her and try to blackmail her into going home?

She didn't dare leave. Not until she discovered what Simon was involved in and with whom. How did Isabella Montelucci factor into it? What was Fox's role? Was Simon a criminal or just caught up in a situation he could not escape? She needed to find out the truth.

Her gaze lit on the sheaf of papers resting on the table. If she stayed, then she had no doubt that Mr. Foxworth would indeed send his reports to every gossip rag in London. The resulting scandal would ruin Gin and destroy any hope she had of marrying and retaining her fortune. She didn't want her friend to suffer, but at the same time, she needed to find out what was afoot so she could save her marriage.

But which to choose?

Dobbins presented himself in the doorway. "Miss Matthews is here, my lady."

Lucy jerked her gaze up as Gin entered the room. Today she wore a pale green morning dress that suited her unusual coloring. Lucy thought back to when they'd ordered it from Madame Dauphine and felt a moment of gladness that her suggestion had worked out so well. Then she glanced at the papers sitting on the table. How could she possibly do anything to hurt Gin?

"Your note sounded urgent," Gin said, sitting down in the chair Fox had vacated. "I came as soon as Aunt Beatrice left for her appointment with the dressmaker."

"It was urgent. Is, I mean." She looked down at her hands.

"Tell me what happened. Your husband looked so fierce last night, I was half-afraid he would beat you once he got you home!"

"Nothing happened. Well . . . that is not quite

true." She sighed and shook her head. "I just do not know where to begin, Gin. Things are in an awful mess!"

Gin frowned and leaned forward. "What's happened?"

"Mr. Foxworth was here."

"That overbearing oaf? What did he want?"

"He wants me to leave London."

Gin threw up her hands. "Why is everyone trying to send you home?"

"I do not know," Lucy whispered, staring at her twisting hands. "But I think Simon is involved in something. And I think Mrs. Montelucci is, too."

"What kind of something?"

"Something bad." She glanced again at the damaging papers, and this time Gin followed her gaze.

"What's this?" She picked up the reports.

Lucy watched the flicker of emotions over her friend's face. "Mr. Foxworth brought that."

"It's about me," Gin mused, rapidly flipping through the pages. "Every embarrassing situation I ever got myself into. What was he doing with this?"

Encouraged by the American's lack of concern, she said, "Mr. Foxworth threatened to take the reports to the newspapers if I don't go home to Devingham immediately."

"What? Why, that bully!"

"I don't know what to do, Gin. I want to learn

what Simon is doing with these people and yet at the same time, I dare not displease them. They will ruin any chance you have of finding a husband and retaining your fortune."

"I'm not worried about my fortune. I know what needs to be done. But these . . ." She set down the sheaf of papers. "He's holding this nonsense over your head if you don't leave for Devingham?"

"Yes, and if I do not do what he says, he will ruin you." The words came out more bitter than she expected. "I could not do that to you, Gin."

The American's features softened. "Don't worry about me, Lucy. I can take care of myself."

Lucy shook her head. "No. I cannot be the instrument of your social destruction."

"Then you won't be." Gin drummed her fingers on the reports. "All these people want you to leave London, right? They want you to leave this house."

Lucy nodded.

"What if you did? Leave the house." Gin leaned forward in her eagerness. "What if you *acted* as if you were going home, but you really came to stay with me?"

"That would not work. Simon could inquire about me and know that I had never reached Devingham."

"Would he do that? Or do you think he'd be grateful that you had gone?"

Lucy thought for a moment. "You are right. He

might not even inquire, and if he did, it would still take two or three days for him to receive an answer."

"And in that time, you and I could start looking into matters. It would be much easier to investigate your husband if he didn't realize we were around."

"I want to know that woman's connection as well. We can start with the clerk at the bookshop." A small smile crept across her face, then faded as another thought occurred. "Gin, what about Lady Wexford? Surely she will know what we are doing."

"She's not very pleased with your husband since he floored the son of her best friend. She'll probably help us keep you hidden."

"I will tell the servants that I am returning to the country," Lucy mused. "Then I will send the people who accompanied me to London back to Devingham. Except for Molly. I will need her to bring some of my things to Lady Wexford's."

"Won't she give away the game?"

"I will swear her to secrecy. Besides, perhaps she can help us. This plan could work." Lucy grinned. "Thank you, Gin."

The American shrugged. "What are friends for?"

Chapter 11

I've heard tell that righting a teetering ship is a necessary, but dangerous, undertaking. The captain must decide at which point the effort is too strenuous and abandon the endeavor. Luckily, I've never had much affinity for the ocean anyway.

The journals of Simon, Lord Devingham,
on making hard choices

Simon presented himself at Sir Adrian's home at precisely eleven o'clock the next day, steeling himself for the dressing-down he knew he deserved. He was admitted promptly and found himself standing before the man's desk before he could take another breath.

"Sit down, Devingham," Sir Adrian said, as his butler closed the door to the library.

Simon sat and waited.

Sir Adrian watched him for a long moment, then made a harrumphing noise and sat back, hands curling around the knobby ends of the chair arms. "You surprise me, Devingham. I rather expected you to begin our meeting with a plethora of excuses for your behavior last night at the Herrington ball."

"I know I made the wrong decision," Simon said.

"The wrong decision? Planting a facer on Standish in a jealous rage, then dragging your wife through the crowd and out to your carriage in an appallingly public display . . . Yes, I should say you made a wrong decision." Sir Adrian leaned forward. "You may well have ruined everything."

The stark truth of that statement only added to the regret that weighed on him. "I will make it right, Sir Adrian."

"I warned you, Devingham, and Foxworth warned you. Your wife is distracting you from your assignment. She is a liability."

Simon met Sir Adrian's steely gaze, his own will unyielding where Lucy was concerned. "She is my wife."

"I have a wife, too, but Eleanor is content to reside in Sussex with the children. I thought that was what you intended as well."

"It was. Originally."

"Originally? But not now?" Sir Adrian rose and

moved from behind his desk. "You'd best explain, Devingham, for I will allow nothing and no one to interfere with this project."

"You know why I married in the first place."

"Yes, yes." Sir Adrian slashed a hand through the air. "To discourage the matchmaking mamas from setting their sights on you. And your duty to your line, of course."

"I have responsibilities beyond what we do."

"You do, but many of those responsibilities are to the future, not to the present. In the present, Isabella Montelucci, former mistress to one of the deadliest assassins in France, is in possession of information that will cost men their lives. And *we* have to retrieve that information and save those lives."

"Antoine LaRue is dead. We are not dealing with him, we are dealing with a woman." Simon rose so that he and Sir Adrian stood eye to eye. "I have not given up. I will get that list from her."

"How? You walked away from her last night. I was watching her, and if looks could kill, there would be a dozen daggers in your back."

"I didn't say it would be easy," Simon muttered.

"Then again, clearly her passions are engaged." Sir Adrian narrowed his eyes in thought and turned away to pace to the mantel and back. "We have tried every other avenue. We have searched her home to no avail. Our informants know nothing about her. The woman we had placed in her home as a servant was discharged." He sighed. "Other men have failed to hold her attention."

"Other men? You have tried this before?"

"Of course we have tried this before." Sir Adrian sent him a look of patronizing disbelief. "We have tried sending women to befriend her and men to seduce her ever since she surfaced in Europe, and we discovered who she was. We would have charged Foxworth with the duty once she arrived in England, but since the accident . . ."

Guilt churned like bad porridge in his gut. "So that left me."

"That left you. With Foxworth's encouragement and your title and fortune as lures, we hoped you might be successful. And you have been—far more than any of your predecessors."

"But—"

"But your wife is in the way," Sir Adrian said with a sharp thrust of a finger. "Get rid of her. Send her back to the country where she cannot endanger our plans."

"Why?" Simon protested. "Other men have wives. Henderly has a wife."

"Henderly's wife does not meddle in her husband's business affairs."

"Yet Lucy is meddling in mine, however innocently."

"I am certain you recognize the problem."

He pondered the situation for a long moment,

the beliefs of a lifetime warring with his heart's desire. "What if I tell her?"

"You can't trust women with such delicate matters," Sir Adrian scoffed.

"I can trust Lucy." Even as he said the words, he knew they were true. He smiled. "I can trust her with my life."

"Well, that's what you would be doing." Sir Adrian marched back to his chair and sat down with a scowl. "I don't recommend this course of action, Devingham. You take everyone's life in your hands with such an ill-advised undertaking."

"I have to tell her," Simon said. "If I don't, it will ruin everything."

"If you *do* tell her, it will ruin everything," Sir Adrian shot back. "Everything we have fought for. We will be vulnerable. I forbid it!"

"Lucy will not betray me." Eager to tear down the wall between them, Simon turned away and headed toward the door.

"Devingham! Blast you, I said I forbid it!"

Simon paused with his hand on the doorknob. "Our work is important, but Bonaparte will someday be defeated. My marriage will last the rest of my life."

"You're a romantic fool," Sir Adrian snapped.

Unfazed, Simon nodded. "Yes, I do believe I am. Good day to you, Sir Adrian." With a curt nod, he left the room.

* * *

The ruse went off without a hitch. Lucy ordered her belongings packed up and loaded on the coach, then sent it on ahead to Devingham, along with the servants who had accompanied her. The entire process took very little time, as she had not accumulated much in her short time in London. She explained to her servants that Gin was coming with her to the country and that they would follow in the Wexford traveling coach as soon as Gin's things had been packed by her household.

Humbolt's bookstore was not yet crowded when Lucy and Gin arrived there. Only two other customers perused the shelves, both ladies of modest means as revealed by their manner of dress. Lucy and Gin stood near the counter, Gin's footman standing behind them wearing an impassive expression and lending considerable consequence to their presence. It was impossible for them to be recognized as anything else but Quality. A little bald man came hurrying forward himself, a surprised and somewhat panicked expression on his face.

"I am Mr. Humbolt, the proprietor. May I help you, ladies?"

"I am Lady Devingham," Lucy said. "And this is my friend, Miss Matthews."

He gave them a bow. "How may I be of assistance, my lady?"

"We're looking for someone," Gin said.

Lucy sent her a warning look. "There was a young man here a day or so ago who was most helpful to us."

"A tall fellow? Blond, handsome?" Gin said.

Mr. Humbolt nodded. "That would be Andrew."

"We'd like to speak with him," Lucy said. "Is he here?"

"No." The proprietor's face creased in sorrow. "I'm sorry."

"When will he be here again?" Lucy asked.

The man's mouth worked as if he'd swallowed something unpleasant. "I hate to mention such subjects to a lady, but Andrew doesn't work here anymore." He lowered his voice to the barest whisper. "He was found dead last night."

Lucy gasped and covered her mouth with her hand.

"What happened?" Gin asked, touching Lucy's arm in comfort.

"Thieves, looks like. He was found behind the Three Hounds, a tavern near the docks. All his money was gone, and the gold ring his father gave him." Mr. Humbolt shook his head. "He was a good lad."

"How was he killed? Was he shot?"

The proprietor gave Gin a narrow-eyed look, as if he didn't appreciate her directness. "Stabbed, miss."

"Thank you," Lucy whispered.

He glanced at Lucy with concern. "May I be of assistance at all?"

"No, thank you." Lucy gave him a look of apology. "We'll come back another time."

"I'm sorry to have distressed you." The proprietor bowed and turned away.

Gin led Lucy toward the exit. "That's an unexpected turn of events."

"Yes." Still reeling from the shock of the proprietor's bad tidings, Lucy gratefully sucked in a breath of air as they reached the street. "You do realize what this means, don't you?"

"What do *you* think it means?" Gin climbed into the carriage after Lucy.

Lucy sat back in the seat. "I do not believe this young man's death is coincidence."

"I was thinking the same thing."

Troubled, Lucy met her friend's gaze as the carriage lurched into motion. "I think the situation is worse than we thought. Simon is not only in trouble; he is in danger."

"But what do we do about it?"

"Go forward with the plan. As far as anyone at Severton House knows, I have returned to the country."

"And once your husband believes that, we'll be better able to investigate without his knowing."

"Yes. We can look into Isabella's background, perhaps find some link to what Simon's gotten involved with."

"And the handsome but utterly contemptible

John Foxworth can take his nasty reports and stuff them up his—"

"Gin!"

"Well, he can stuff them somewhere," Gin grumbled.

Simon knew exactly where to find Isabella. She preferred to go riding in the park in the late morning, as she hated crowds and, therefore, avoided the more popular afternoon forays. She had invited him to join her there for a picnic—before he had left her standing alone at the Herrington affair.

He doubted that she still expected him to appear after the way he had abandoned her yesterday, but there was a good possibility she had not skipped her habitual ride. This was an opportunity to speak to her and clean up the mess he had made of his assignment.

A public venue was his only option, as he was reasonably sure that the fiery Italian had given her butler orders to toss Simon into the Thames should he dare present himself at her door. So he guided Socrates in the direction of the park and prayed he would not make a complete muck of things.

And even if he did, he just wanted to get his business matters back under control so he could focus on his true concern—Lucy. The sooner he could tell her the truth, the sooner everything in his life would improve.

Especially his marriage.

He hated lying to Lucy, abhorred letting her think that there was any other woman in the world that interested him.

No other woman could compare.

He was reasonably certain that he was falling in love with his wife—falling in lust, certainly. The softer emotions that plagued him had not yet formed completely and so could not yet be named. But he trusted his wife with his life, and he would soon trust her with this precious secret. And he wanted her all the time, every hour of every day.

Was this love?

He was forced to abandon this train of thought when he reached the park. He slowed Socrates to an easy walk and sought Isabella. He knew her favorite places and found her after only a quarter of an hour.

She was not alone.

A picnic was spread out on a blanket, the sun sparking off wine in crystal goblets while her groom stood nearby holding the horses. One plate was piled high with cheese and fruit and another with sliced meat. Laughing together between sips of red wine was Isabella and that bounder, Standish.

He scowled, remembering Lucy in the other man's arms. How ironic that the coward had chosen Isabella as his next target! Then the dark-haired beauty slid a sly glance his way that let

Simon know she was aware of his presence.

Then again, perhaps she had been the one to approach Standish. What was her game now?

Isabella gave a throaty laugh as Simon approached their cozy setting. "Have a care, *il mio capitano*. We are no longer alone." The icy look she turned on Simon could not be mistaken. "What do you want here, my lord?"

Simon dismounted and made his way to the blanket, leading Socrates along. Standish stood, and satisfaction made Simon's lips twitch as he noticed the dark bruise marring the captain's chiseled jaw.

"What are you doing here, Devingham? Be off with you!"

"You may rest easy, Standish. I have not come here to call you out, as well I should." Ignoring the fury that lit the soldier's expression, he focused completely on Isabella. "I thought we had an engagement."

She raised her brows and took a sip of wine. "Surely you did not think I would want to see you again after last night."

"Last night was a duty, nothing more. This riffraff," he said with a nod toward Standish, "trod upon my honor. I could not ignore the slight."

"Yet you do not call him out." She tossed her head, sending her inky curls dancing in the midmorning sun. "I do not think your honor is quite that wounded."

"But now he has done it again." Simon glared at Standish. "Was one thrashing not enough for you, Captain?"

"The lady does not want you here." The blond man pointed to the path. "Do be on your way."

"You dig your grave with each word you utter." Simon dismissed the blowhard by turning back to Isabella. "Why do you waste your time with this weasel?"

She shrugged. "He amuses me."

"I will be happy to entertain you."

Standish took a step closer. "If you want a duel, you shall have one, damn you."

Simon halted him with a look. "I should have killed you."

"As if you could."

"Gentlemen," Isabella purred, "do you mean to duel over me now?"

Simon watched her as she sipped her wine again, knowing she relished being the focus of their quarrel. He chose to feed the fire of her ego. "You are worth dying for, my beauty."

"Say the word, and I shall dispatch him for you!" Standish declared.

Her dark eyes gleamed, but then she lowered her gaze to her wineglass. "I am but a woman and cannot decide such important matters."

"Then I will decide," Standish said. "Devingham, name your seconds."

Simon raised a brow. "I am not fooled by the

uniform you wear, Standish. Rest assured that I am a crack shot."

Standish gave a disbelieving laugh. "Everyone claims that."

"Ask," Simon said. "You will not walk from this duel alive."

Standish opened his mouth for yet another boastful comment, but Simon turned his attention to Isabella. "You know I do not lie, Isabella."

A small smile curved her lips as she regarded first one man, then the other.

"This is preposterous!" Standish protested. "I shall see this finished once and for all!"

"Hush," Isabella snapped, her lips thinning with annoyance. "He would kill you, Michael, just as he says. Have the good sense not to goad him."

She looked at Simon, her face smoothing to impassiveness. "And you, my lord, provoke me sorely. How can you expect to treat me in such a manner, then come to me as if nothing at all has passed? I've already given you a second chance, and you shunned me yet again."

"Because of this blackguard. I could not ignore such an insult."

"Perhaps." She set down her wine and stood with assistance from the captain, then brushed out her skirts. The downward motion of her hands tugged her bodice a shade lower, drawing the men's attention as she had obviously intended. "But I do not forget insults either. You have grievously wounded me, Lord Devingham, and you will find my memory is long and my heart unforgiving."

"Tell me what I can do."

She paused, considering him. "I do not know if there is anything you can do to win my forgiveness."

Standish smirked, but Simon ignored him. "There must be something. Is my sin so terrible that I may not see you smile on me again?"

"Yes," she said with a snap of her skirts as she turned toward the horses. "It is." She held out her hand to Standish, who proffered his arm. "Good day to you, Lord Devingham. I'll thank you not to trouble me again."

Simon stood with jaw clenched as Isabella mounted her horse and rode away with a smug-looking Standish, leaving her footman to collect the abandoned picnic.

He really should have called the bastard out.

As they disappeared down the path, he headed for his own mount. He had truly succeeded in destroying any trace of trust he had managed to cultivate with Isabella. He would have to start all over again, and the same methods that had first won her would not work a second time.

He would have to consult with Fox.

But first he needed to speak to his wife. The sooner he confessed the truth to Lucy, the sooner he could resume his plan to charm the list away from Isabella.

The lessons he'd learned from Fox rose in his mind, and it occurred to him that he'd never presented his bride with any sort of gift, not even a wedding present. He'd given her the Devingham pearls, but those belonged to the Countess of Devingham and were more a right than a gift. Since Fox maintained that tokens such as flowers and chocolate and jewelry tended to soften a woman's heart, he decided to divert to the shops before he returned home.

Home. He smiled, realizing that the cold halls of his town house truly felt like home for the first time. And it was all because of Lucy.

Chapter 12

I have never truly understood the pain Caesar felt when Brutus made his choice. I wonder, if Caesar had survived, would he have ever learned to trust Brutus again?

The journals of Simon, Lord Devingham,
on friendship

Simon arrived at Severton House with a smile on his face and a delicate gold-and-diamond locket in his pocket. As soon as he had seen the elegant necklace, he had known it would be perfect for Lucy.

He rehearsed in his mind what he intended to say, trying to figure out the best way to approach the subject. He was murmuring to himself as he walked through the front door and found Dobbins waiting for him.

"Good afternoon, Dobbins. Where may I find my wife?"

Dobbins's inscrutable expression did not flicker. "She is not at home, my lord."

"Oh." Deflated, he touched the pocket where the box lay. "Did she say when she will be returning?"

"She left this for you, Lord Devingham." Dobbins handed him a note.

Simon unfolded the delicate sheet of stationery and read the short lines written in his wife's hand. *Returned to Devingham. Lucy.* He jerked his gaze back to the butler's face. "There is nothing more?"

"No, my lord."

"Blast." He stared at the words again as if they would re-form before his eyes. "When did she leave?"

"Over an hour ago."

"Why did she leave?" he muttered, more to himself than Dobbins. "She was bound and determined to deliver that box. Perhaps Miss Matthews will know the why of it."

Dobbins cleared his throat. "I believe Miss Matthews has accompanied her ladyship."

"Indeed?" He frowned and refolded the paper. "Did any messengers come from Devingham, Dobbins? Any urgent summons that would send my wife racing home in such a fashion?"

"Nothing, my lord."

"I see." It must have been he. He thought about the abrupt way he had dismissed her last night and winced. Clearly she knew about Isabella; he had made no effort to hide the fact that he was flirting with the woman at the Herrington affair. And she had mentioned Isabella by name.

He closed his eyes, his chest tightening. He'd hurt her. She thought he was having an affair—all of London thought that. And at first he hadn't cared. Let the gossips prattle. He had deliberately courted Isabella to cultivate such rumors.

Had those rumors reached Devingham? Had Lucy known about Isabella before she'd even arrived in London? She must have.

He'd managed to botch his relationships with both women all in the same evening. And he was forced by obligation first to repair what he could with Isabella. He could not go chasing to Devingham to talk to Lucy, much as his instincts urged him to do just that. It would destroy the entire project. Isabella would sell the list of English spies to enemy powers, and innocent people would die. He could not put his own affairs before his duty.

No matter how much his heart demanded he do just that.

"She must have tired of London," he said to Dobbins. "There was no summons to return home, no crisis that needed her immediate attention."

"No, my lord. No one came from Devingham. Miss Matthews came to call."

"Of course." Simon folded the note and put it in his pocket next to the jewelry box.

"Oh, and Mr. Foxworth. He was Lady Devingham's first caller of the day."

Simon paused. "Fox was here? To see Lucy?"

"Yes, my lord."

Suspicion flickered in his mind. "Did she seem upset after his visit?"

"I can't say, my lord. Miss Matthews arrived not long after Mr. Foxworth left."

"And then my wife set out for Devingham with Miss Matthews."

"Yes, my lord."

"Thank you, Dobbins." As the butler walked away, Simon continued to stand in the hallway, absorbing the impact of this turn of events. He should be pleased that Lucy had finally left London. Even though he had intended to tell her the truth, she was safer away from the city, and his job became easier if he didn't have to take her presence into account.

But already the house felt barren, as if all the warmth had fled from it.

So no, he wasn't pleased that she was gone. Quite the opposite. After all the chaos she had caused during the time she had been in London, he had finally gotten used to her presence. Looked forward to her company.

Wanted her in his arms.

Damn and blast, but this was inconvenient!

And bloody unfair to boot. Why the devil had she gone running off just as he was about to open up to her completely? Just last night she had been bound and determined to stay firmly in London, no matter how hard he had tried to get her to leave.

Simmering disappointment gave way to a whisper of logic. The timing of her departure niggled at him.

Why now? What had happened between last night and this morning that she felt the need to leave immediately for Devingham?

He'd not gone to her bed last night.

He hissed out a breath through his teeth. Was that it? Had she come to believe that he'd wanted Isabella and not her? Well, why shouldn't she? He'd certainly encouraged such thinking, especially when he had left her to her lonely slumber. And last night, the gossip must have humiliated her.

She must have taken his actions to mean that he no longer wanted her, when nothing could be farther from the truth.

For a moment he simmered with frustration. Blast the woman, but if she hadn't run off in such a manner, she would have known the truth. Instead, she'd fled to Devingham, abandoning her duty to Mrs. Wolcott, giving up on the tentative relationship they'd begun to build. . .

His thoughts halted as if he'd hit a stone wall.

Lucy, renouncing the task she'd fought him to accomplish? Lucy, surrendering to gossip and fleeing because she believed he wanted another woman?

It didn't make sense. Suppose she had already known about Isabella before she ever arrived in London. Wouldn't it be more likely that she would attempt to distract him from the other woman? Fight for the relationship she seemed to want their marriage to be?

Yes. That was exactly what she would do, and exactly what she *had* been doing. Which meant that there was another reason she had left London.

Fox. And Miss Matthews.

The pieces fell into place. Fox. Why had he come? Had he been looking for Simon and simply paid his respects to Lucy? Not likely, given his current displeasure with her presence.

Had Fox said something to upset her?

The other option would be Miss Matthews, but Lucy had formed a fast friendship with the blunt American, and the two were forever in each other's company. He doubted it had been Miss Matthews who sent Lucy packing.

But Fox? Oh yes, John Foxworth was just ruthless enough, and certainly capable enough, to force Lucy to leave. Especially if he didn't think Simon was doing what needed to be done.

His hands clenched into fists. He'd intended to talk to Fox anyway about how best to handle Isabella. It appeared there were other subjects that also merited discussion.

He turned on his heel and headed for the front door, shouting to the servants to bring Socrates back around. He stormed out of the house, happy to leave it behind.

Without Lucy, his home already echoed with a silence that made his heart ache. And if John Foxworth was responsible, he would have a lot to answer for.

Fox had his head bent over a French communiqué when Simon burst into his study unannounced.

Fox jerked his head up. "Simon! What brings you here?"

"A number of things." Simon came to stand over Fox's desk even as the timid Peters stuck his head through the door.

"My apologies, sir, but his lordship did not wait for me to announce him properly."

"Back to your duties, Peters," Fox said with a dismissive wave of his hand. He sat back in his chair as the butler scurried away and regarded Simon with an expectant air. "I assume you wish to speak to me."

"I do. I need your advice on how best to handle a situation with Isabella. But before we speak about that, why don't you tell me about your visit with my wife this morning?"

Fox gave a surprised chuckle. "Why, Simon, do you think I am flirting with your wife?"

"If I thought that, you would be speaking with my second even now."

Hurt confusion flashed across Fox's face before he managed to regain his expression of ennui. "I've always been your second."

"And you will be again, depending on what you tell me."

"I suppose I should be flattered that you believe a woman would welcome my attentions."

"Fox, why did you go to see Lucy?"

Fox's expression flickered for a moment, then he was his smiling self again. "I wanted to warn her about Miss Matthews."

Simon blinked. "Miss Matthews? What about her?"

"The woman is not fit company for your wife, Simon." Fox yanked open a drawer and withdrew a sheaf of papers, which he tossed on the desk. "I had my contacts investigate her background. She's an heiress, all right, but only on the condition that she weds. Her parents have washed their hands of her with the scandals she has caused them. She was even arrested once and spent an evening in a common jail for protesting for miners' rights."

Simon picked up the reports and flicked through them. "And you told this to Lucy?"

"Of course. I wanted to protect her."

"Protect her, or force her to leave London?"

"What?" Fox tilted his head in puzzlement. "Why would you say such a thing?"

"Because she has left me, Fox. Gone home to Devingham." Simon threw down the papers. "But apparently your warning went unheeded, because Miss Matthews has gone with her." He leaned forward on the desk. "Why did you not come to me, Fox? It's my job to protect my wife."

"Because—"

"Because your real motive was to send Lucy away." Simon straightened. "What did you do, threaten to expose Miss Matthews's questionable past to the *ton*?"

"Something had to be done." Fox stood with a wince, bracing his hands on the desk. "You would not do the thing, so I did it."

"You had no right."

"I did it for the project." Fox lifted his chin, his eyes glittering with pride. "You were too besotted by your bride to put England first, Simon. And I remember what happened the last time a woman distracted you."

"Must we return to the past yet again, Fox?"

"The past is my present!" Fox exploded. He jerked a hand in the direction of his knee. "I have never been the same since Georgina followed you to the rendezvous and destroyed our carefully constructed trap. I saved your hide and became a monster."

"I had no idea Georgina would follow us."

"I know you were considering wedding the chit, but she was queer in the attic. Always thought you were lusting after other women. That night, she thought you were tumbling a wench in the stables." Fox gave a snort of disgust. "She came blundering into the meeting place, and the enemy realized it was a trap."

"I was there, Fox."

The silence of the stables as both parties looked at each other with distrustful eyes. Georgina bursting through the doorway, spewing some nonsense about Simon trysting with a housemaid. The panic in the eyes of the two men who had been moments away from revealing the location of Antoine LaRue.

The flash of a pistol in the lamplight. Simon leaping and pushing Georgina out of the path of gunfire. Fox charging forward to pummel one of the men. The other raising his pistol, aiming at Simon. . .

One man down and Fox throwing himself at the gunman. A shot gone wild. Simon shoving Georgina out of the stables, her screams for her father blending with the cries of horses startled by gunfire.

Fox wrestling with the gunman. A shattered lantern and fire racing like a demon up the walls and across hay bales. Horses shrieking in terror as flames devoured the dry wood and straw.

Grooms rushing in from their card game in the back room with a cacophony of shouting, yanking open stall doors and chasing expensive steeds out into the night.

Fox crashing through the door of a burning stall, still occupied by a panicked mare. . .

An equine shriek of terror. The thudding of hooves as the horse reared and crashed back down again, reared and crashed down. An inhuman howl of anguish. . .

Simon reaching into the stall and grabbing Fox, dragging his friend away from the crazed beast by his burning coat, Fox's leg mangled and bleeding from the animal's sharp hooves.

The horse charging from the stables, leaving behind the corpse of the enemy, his skull crushed from the animal's rampage.

Simon dragging Fox out into the night, rolling him painfully on the ground to extinguish the flames still greedily consuming his coat. His throat raw from smoke, tears stinging as he saw Fox's mutilated limb and his skin blistering from the fire. . .

It was all his fault.

"We got out." Simon refocused on his friend, pushing back the painful memories. "You're alive, Fox."

Fox gave him a bitter smile. "That depends on your definition of alive."

Simon ignored the sharp retort and centered on the present. "Do not think to interfere in my affairs again, Fox."

Fox gathered the papers regarding Virginia Matthews and shoved them back in the drawer. "I will do what is necessary for England."

"Leave my marriage alone. You got what you wanted. Lucy is gone."

Fox slowly closed the drawer. "She's safer, you know."

"Her safety is my responsibility. You over-stepped yourself. Don't do it again."

Silence stretched for a long moment as the two men regarded each other. Finally, Fox gave a nod.

Simon let out a quiet breath. He'd won. Fox would not interfere again unless he chose to risk their friendship.

"What have you there?" he asked, indicating the letter. "Another message intercepted from the French?"

"Yes." Fox smoothed the paper with his hand. "I have yet to decipher their cursed code. I was told it contains a message of some urgency, though. Men died to protect it."

"I'm certain you'll decrypt it eventually."

A look passed between them. Truce.

"So what is this matter with Isabella that has brought you to my door?" Fox asked, settling back in his chair with his hands folded across his stomach.

Simon winced. "I'm certain you heard about last night's incident."

"The one where you planted Michael Standish a facer, then dragged your wife home? Yes, I heard about it."

"Isabella now wants nothing to do with me. I

need to find out how to get back into her good graces."

Fox gave him a derisive smile. "You've put your foot in it for certain, my friend. You publicly chose your wife over Isabella, and she won't forget that."

"I must make her change her mind."

"That, my dear Simon, will take some doing."

Simon shrugged and for the first time, sat down. "That's why I've come to see you, Fox. If anyone knows how to woo the woman back, it's you."

This time Fox's smile was genuine and just the slightest bit crafty. "Let's get a piece of paper, Simon, and I'll give you some suggestions that no woman can resist."

Lady Wexford regarded the two young women sitting in her parlor with some gravity. "What do you mean, you will not be attending Lady Bargencroft's musicale this evening, Virginia? As pleased as I am to have Lady Devingham as our guest, we cannot interfere with your social schedule."

"Aunt Beatrice, I told you that Lucy wants her husband to think she has gone back to Devingham so she can find out the truth about his relationship with that Italian woman." Gin shrugged with feigned resignation. "We told her servants that I was going with her, so of course I can't appear anywhere socially if I'm supposed to be with her in the country."

"You should not even know of such things, much less embroil yourself in a plot to learn more." Lady Wexford shook her head. "Your parents entrusted me with your future, Virginia, and I cannot disappoint them."

"I can't pretend not to know about things I do know about," Virginia said.

Lady Wexford gave a deep sigh. "You are most definitely an Original, Virginia, though I don't know if I mean that as a compliment."

Lucy watched the byplay with some concern. When Gin had first suggested her plan, Lucy hadn't considered the ramifications for her friend. Her intentions in leaving her home had been to prevent Mr. Foxworth from ruining Gin's reputation while still remaining in the city to discover the truth about her husband's activities. "Lady Wexford," she said, "I don't wish to overset your household or do anything to ruin Gin's chances of making a good match. Perhaps we can put it about that Gin changed her mind about going to Devingham."

"Excellent notion," Lady Wexford said with an approving nod.

"No, it is not," Gin said. "Aunt Beatrice, surely you understand Lucy's predicament."

"I do." Lady Wexford cast Lucy a glance of sympathy. "Unfortunately, it is the lot of many married women to look the other way when their husbands dally. It is the nature of men to conquer, and oftimes that entails conquests of a romantic variety."

"But they've only been married a few months."

Gin's godmother sighed. "Yes, that is a bit scandalous, and I do understand your dismay, Lady Devingham. I've always thought of your husband as a levelheaded man with a strong sense of honor. I was disturbed to witness his behavior last night."

"He hit Captain Standish," Gin reminded her. "I would think you would be put out with him."

Lady Wexford gave Gin a maternal smile. "Virginia, I have known Michael Standish since he was born, and I have no doubts that if Lord Devingham engaged in fisticuffs with him, then the lad probably deserved it."

Lucy flushed as the older woman glanced at her, brows lifted in inquiry. "You are correct, Lady Wexford."

Her ladyship shook her head, her lips curving in fondness. "I suspected as much. That boy has always been too handsome for his own good and a bit spoiled by his doting mama. I'm sorry if he did anything to distress you, my dear."

"It wasn't your fault, Lady Wexford."

"I introduced him to you. But your husband seems to have handled the matter, despite the scandalous repercussions."

Gin looked from one to the other in astonishment. "Aunt Beatrice, I expected that you would be furious with Lucy's husband."

"Counted on it, perhaps?" Lady Wexford said with a knowing tone to her voice. "Virginia, you are so young, and yet you feel that you know how the world works. You don't, my girl, and that is what I have been trying to tell you."

"I do know how the world works. I've done what I can to try and change it."

"Which is how you ended up here," Lady Wexford reminded her. "Really, Virginia, there is only so much anyone, especially a woman, can do overtly. Our methods must be subtle, or else Society brands us outcasts."

"It's not fair that men can do anything they want and that women have to conform to such rigid constraints," Gin said, her volume rising with each word. "I don't want to marry. It's been my experience that men either want to control me and my fortune, or are so controllable themselves that I would become exasperated with them in a matter of days."

"You simply haven't met the right man, dear."

"Aunt Beatrice, I have no intention of marrying. I'm sorry."

Lady Wexford's face grew stern. "*I'm* sorry, Virginia, but that is not an option. I will not see you ruin your life with these crusades of yours. You must marry, and you will marry. I have sworn to your mama that I will arrange a proper match for you."

"No. I won't do it."

"You will, for it is your only choice lest you be sent to some remote corner of the world with no access to your fortune. Your father has threatened exactly that, Virginia, and you know he will do it. If you thought that letting people believe that you had left Town would allow you to avoid your future, I must tell you that your plan will not work. I will not stand for it."

Lucy rose, uncomfortable with the personal slant the conversation had taken. "Perhaps I had best not stay here. I would not want to ruin Gin's future."

"And where would you go?" Gin asked. "Back to Severton House? Or back to Devingham? I thought you wanted to know the truth."

"I do," Lucy said, "but not at your expense, Gin."

"Do sit down, Lady Devingham," Lady Wexford said. "Of course you may stay here, and we will instruct the servants to keep silent about your presence. But Virginia, you will attend Lady Bargencroft's affair tonight. We will say you grew ill and chose not to travel."

Gin made a face. "I'm never ill, Aunt Beatrice."

Lady Wexford shot her a quelling look. "Society will believe that, which is all that matters. The *ton* forever believes women are frail and delicate."

"Nonsense," Gin muttered.

"I agree," her godmother said, and Gin blinked in surprise. "If there is a battle to be fought here,

Virginia, we will fight it—have no doubt of that. But we will be more successful by using women's weapons. Subtlety. Gossip. Letting Society's perceptions of the fair sex work to our advantage."

"Don't ask me to simper," Gin warned. "I believe it is physically impossible for me to do so."

Lady Wexford laughed. "I would not suggest such a thing. But if you attend the musicale tonight, you will accomplish two objectives—you will meet eligible suitors, which is, of course, my goal for you. And we will also be able to both hear and start rumors about your cause."

Gin's jaw dropped. "Are you saying you intend to help us?"

"Why not? It's been ages since anything so interesting has diverted me."

"I was certain you would expect me to stand quietly in the corner or flutter my fan like a ninny," Gin said.

"I do expect you to act like a lady and not start a scandalbroth," Lady Wexford warned. "However, you have eyes, ears, and a brain that works way too well much of the time. You can see and hear much more if you listen rather than speak. Most men consider women to be of inferior intellect, and it might serve you to allow them to believe that for now."

"Drat. You do expect me to act like a ninny." Gin scowled.

Lady Wexford laughed. "The people without preconceived notions will not be fooled, my dear."

"And you really believe this will help Lucy?"

"My dear Virginia, a woman can glean more information at a musicale than a Bonapartist at a Carlton House dinner party. If she knows what to ask and with whom to speak."

Despite Gin's protests, Lady Wexford bundled her goddaughter off to the Bargencroft musicale. Alone in her room, Lucy looked out at the lights of London, feeling as if she were very far away from the hustle and bustle of society. Carriages swept along the street below her. Laughter echoed up to her window.

Where was Simon tonight? Did he miss her?

She wrapped her arms around herself and stared out at the night. What had he become involved in? And how did Isabella Montelucci and John Foxworth fit into the puzzle? Who had killed Andrew, the bookseller's clerk? Had his death been mere coincidence?

It couldn't be. Barely a day after they had witnessed Isabella paying the lad for some unknown errand, he was murdered. The timing was too neat and convenient to be mere chance.

Someone in this scheme was a killer.

Her mind shot back to the scene with Captain Standish. Simon had struck like a predator, swiftly and efficiently, and in seconds the other man had been on the floor, utterly defeated.

Such skills were unusual in a peer of the realm. Could Simon be the killer?

No. Her mind rejected the thought instantly. She would know if her husband were capable of such a thing, wouldn't she? How could he treat her so sweetly and yet be a cold-blooded murderer at the same time?

Then again, she hadn't realized until recently that he might be anything but the slightly eccentric intellectual he appeared to be.

Was Simon capable of taking a life? Was he the type of man who could end a person's days as easily as one might crush an insect?

Was she married to a murderer?

Was her life in danger?

Chilled, she turned away from the window. With Lady Wexford's assistance, Gin was going to attempt to ferret out information from the Bargencroft gathering. Their next move would depend on what she discovered.

She hoped Gin was successful. It was only a matter of time before Simon discovered she had not returned to Devingham, and it would not take much thought for him to figure out where she had been hiding.

She didn't know what he would do when they met again.

Her dreams for their marriage were slowly crumbling. Simon seemed genuinely fond of her, and he certainly seemed to desire her in his bed.

There had been laughter and companionship, and, if not for Isabella Montelucci, they might have possibly fallen in love.

She didn't want to love him. It would be so much easier if she could remain aloof. She didn't want to miss the sound of his voice or the touch of his hands. But she did. Curse him, she did.

Lust, she thought fiercely. That's all it was.

Their entire relationship had been a lie. He had married her for convenience and planned to leave her in the country. He had clearly never intended for her to come to London and discover his secrets. If Arminda had not died, Lucy would be still sitting at Devingham, a neglected bride, wondering when her husband was going to remember her existence.

And even if it turned out Simon was innocent of any sort of foul scheme, she needed to remember that he intended to send her right back to those lonely days as soon as the box was delivered to Mrs. Nelson.

She needed to discover the truth about her husband—what he was doing, with whom, and why. Then she would be able to act on those facts and determine how she was going to save their marriage.

If there had ever been anything to save to begin with.

Chapter 13

A tune has grace to lull a weary mind,
The player's ken, though, shapes the song
  in kind.

The journals of Simon, Lord Devingham,
on knowing the players in the game

No one was more surprised than Simon to
see Fox come through the doors of the Bargencroft musicale. He had been trying without
success to garner Isabella's attention, but the lady
had made a great show of ignoring his presence.
Even now, she entertained herself with the ubiq-
uitous Captain Standish and another admirer,
Viscount Farwell. Simon might as well be at the
other side of the world for all the notice she paid
him.

Gratefully, he met Fox halfway across the room.
They retreated to a quiet corner.

"What are you doing here?" Simon whispered. "I thought you abhorred musicales."

"I do, but I will submit to the torture of the Bargencroft chit's caterwauling in the name of duty."

"I'm glad to see you."

"How goes it?" Fox asked with a glance toward the corner where Isabella held court.

"She will not even acknowledge my presence."

Fox scowled. "That won't do at all. Which is why I'm here, by the way. To assure that you do not make a muck of things with the woman yet again."

Simon curled his lip. "Your confidence in me is staggering."

"Not at all, my friend. Just realistic."

"Well then, what would you have me do to gain the lady's favor?"

"Poetry."

"What did you say?"

"Poetry." Fox smirked. "Surely you, my bookish friend, can take a moment to compose a few lines in order to win back the fair Isabella's affection."

"You want me to write a poem for Isabella? Right here? Right now?"

"Exactly. Then have it delivered to her by a servant with something else ... but what? We haven't time to send for flowers." He thought for a moment, then snapped his fingers. "A glass of champagne. That should do nicely."

Simon regarded his friend with skepticism. "Are you certain?"

"All women succumb to pretty words, my good fellow. Even females as jaded as our Italian beauty."

"Very well. I will search for paper in Lord Bargencroft's study."

"Just don't get caught."

Simon cast him an irritated glance. "I never do." He made his way toward the hallway through the crowd waiting for the musicale to begin. And even as Fox watched him, one moment he lingered near the doorway, and the next he was gone. Fox never saw him move.

"Hmmph," Fox murmured to himself. "I've taught the boy well." He turned his attention back toward the assemblage and caught a glimpse of a familiar figure across the room. The woman turned her head at that precise moment, locking gazes with his.

A frisson of arousal vibrated through him, a sensation he had not felt in three years.

"Bloody hell," he muttered, even as the lady straightened and started toward him.

He didn't have time to escape, not with the dratted leg slowing him down. So he stood there and waited for her, ignoring the way his body tightened in anticipation.

"Mr. Foxworth," she said, coming to a stop in front of him. "How unusual to see you out and about."

"Miss Matthews." He cast a glance over her, hoping to find some item of sartorial faux pas on which to comment, but the lady had dressed this evening to perfection in a pale blue silk cut on elegant lines that made her look like a young queen.

Lady Devingham's doing, no doubt.

"I had heard that you had left Town for the country, Miss Matthews, so I must admit to my own surprise at seeing you here this evening."

Something flashed in those green eyes of hers. "I fell ill this afternoon. Bad fish."

Fox made a tsking noise with his tongue. "I cannot fathom that something so plebeian as bad fish kept you from the side of your dearest friend, Miss Matthews."

"It's the truth," she said through gritted teeth.

"Indeed?" He raised a skeptical brow.

She glared at him, then with a huff, she opened her reticule and pulled out her spectacles, which she perched on her nose. "There," she said with great satisfaction.

He snapped his fingers. "Ah. I knew there was something different about you this evening. I assumed it was because you were not head to toe in ruffles. How ever did you see me from across the room?"

"You have a very distinctive walk, Mr. Foxworth. While I do not see well across distances without my spectacles, I am hardly blind. Your presence was unmistakable."

Pleasure that she had noticed him clashed with

irritation that it was his damnable limp that had drawn her attention. He bared his teeth in a smile. "As is yours. You stand a tall, strong sunflower amongst these delicate English roses."

To his surprise, a blush crept across her cheeks. "Save your clever compliments for a more gullible girl."

"Come now, Miss Matthews," he purred. "You know you are quite the tallest young lady in the room."

"To Aunt Beatrice's everlasting dismay."

"Indeed, I see her point. You do tower over many of your potential suitors."

She scowled. "I don't care about them. Tiny English lapdogs always panting at my heels."

"Tiny?"

She glanced over his broad shoulders, then looked up to meet his gaze. "Present company excepted, Mr. Foxworth. I cannot fathom anyone considering you a lapdog. A rabid hunting hound perhaps."

"Yet still a dog." He chuckled. "It's a miracle you have not sent all your suitors fleeing with such unflattering comparisons."

"Not for lack of trying," she grumbled. "They seem unusually resilient."

"The lure of an heiress, no doubt."

"Probably so. Fortune-hunters." She nearly spat the words. "There are more important things in this world than money."

"From the lips of a woman who has never had to do without it."

She raised her brows. "I do not fear poverty, Mr. Foxworth."

"I doubt you know what it is, Miss Matthews."

She tilted her head to the side. "And you do? That coat is by Weston, isn't it?"

He pressed his lips together in annoyance. "For the last three years, I have depended on my father for my very existence, and his favor is often capricious."

Her face softened in compassion. "I'm certain you were quite successful before the accident. It can't be easy for you to depend on others for your living." She gave a little smile. "It's a woman's lot, however, so I do understand."

For some reason, her comprehension of his discomfort shamed him, then enraged him. Did she pity him? Damned if he would accept that from her!

"At least I do not make a habit of embarrassing my family as you do, Miss Matthews. Tell me, how do you enjoy your banishment?"

Hurt flickered across her face, and regret stabbed at him. In all his years, he'd done his best never to injure a woman's feelings. With Miss Matthews, it was becoming a habit.

She recovered quickly. "I forgot that you know all my secrets, Mr. Foxworth. By the by, let me tell you what you can do with those reports you have been showing around London—"

"Virginia." Lady Wexford appeared, glancing from one to the other with curiosity. "The musicale is about to begin. Good evening, Mr. Foxworth."

"Lady Wexford." He bowed, but he never took his gaze from Virginia's flushed face. Her green eyes shot sparks at him, and he fancied that had she the power, she'd have stabbed him on the spot with just the power of her gaze.

"Of course. We must take our seats." The American gave him a regal nod. "Good evening, Mr. Foxworth."

"Have a care to sit near the back of the room," he said. "Bargencroft's daughter screeches like an owl."

As the ladies made their way to take their seats, Simon materialized beside him.

"Egad, Fox, but isn't that Miss Matthews?"

"It was." Fox nodded, not taking his gaze from the slender redhead as she sat down beside her godmother—a goodly distance from the singer, he noted with a smile.

"I thought she was at Devingham with Lucy."

"The lady claims bad fish prevented her from undertaking the journey."

"Bad fish." Simon glanced at the American, then back at Fox. Their gazes held in silent communication.

"I suspect that we are being bamboozled by Miss Matthews," Fox said as the pianist coaxed the opening chords from the pianoforte. "And, perhaps, by your wife."

Simon winced as Lord Bargencroft's daughter wailed her first note. "I agree. Perhaps Lucy never reached Devingham."

"Or never left London." Fox shuddered as the young debutante's soprano nearly split his eardrums.

"We shall call on Miss Matthews tomorrow. Between the two of us, we can ferret out the truth."

"Indeed." Fox raised his voice slightly so Simon could hear him over the din. "And what of your other plan?"

"I sent the most revoltingly flowery piece of drivel imaginable to Isabella, along with a flute of champagne."

"Good. Let us see if it works."

The intermission was a blessing to the audience. The instant Lady Bargencroft announced the short break, the entire assemblage rose from their seats and mingled as servants walked about with trays of beverages. The roar of conversation rose like a waking beast.

Simon saw a footman bearing a tray with a single glass of champagne and a folded piece of paper approach Isabella. Surprised pleasure lit her features as she reached for the folded sheet and read it. A delighted smile curved her lips as she read his words.

She met his gaze, then lifted the champagne glass from the tray and raised it in his direction before sipping from it.

"It appears your poem has touched the lady," Fox observed. "Excellent work."

"Thanks to you." Simon frowned as Isabella placed the half-filled glass back on the footman's tray, then left the room, escorted by her two admirers. "It looks as though there are other obstacles, however."

"A military captain and a viscount. Poor competition for an earl."

"Perhaps." His attention was caught by a flash of auburn hair as Miss Matthews and Lady Wexford rose from their seats. The American glanced at him, then quickly looked away, and his instincts rose like a dog's hackles.

Something was afoot, something to do with Lucy, and Miss Matthews was right in the thick of it.

"Excuse me, Fox."

Fox followed his gaze and scowled. "Ah, I see what has caught your attention. Just do not lose sight of the objective."

"Have faith in me, Fox. You and I both know that something peculiar is going on with Miss Matthews—and it involves Lucy. Do you want to accompany me while I quiz her about it?"

Fox hesitated, his gaze following the tall American as she left the room. Then he shook his head.

"Go and talk to her. I intend to find a chair before my blasted leg gives out from under me."

"I shall return shortly." Eyes narrowed in determination, Simon followed the crowd out the door.

Gin knew the instant Lord Devingham stepped out into the hallway. She felt his gaze on her like a live thing as she stood chatting with Mrs. Standish and Lady Trudor, dear friends of Lady Wexford, while she waited for her godmother to return from the lavatory.

"Such a crush," Lady Trudor commented. "And yet Lavinia's daughter has yet to warble a note which is not flat or piercing. I do not understand why people have not moved on to other amusements."

"Dear Anne," Mrs. Standish trilled, "everyone comes to Lavinia's fetes not because of her daughter's musical talents, but because of her fabulous chef!"

"I thought your digestion was ailing you, Caro," Lady Trudor retorted. "Frankly, I am amazed to see you out and about, much less consuming the rich culinary treasures created by Lavinia's man, Perlain."

"Such delights aid in recovery," Mrs. Standish claimed. "Dr. Anthony has assured me this is so."

"Dr. Anthony fancies you," Lady Trudor grumbled.

"Fustian!"

As the two ladies erupted into a good-natured squabble, Gin was very much aware of Lord Devingham's approach. Would she be able to lie to him if he asked her about Lucy's location? Despite her fearless nature, there was something slightly dangerous about Lucy's husband that intimidated her. She got the feeling he was not a man she wanted to anger. Being a smart woman, she weighed her options and decided on the best possible solution to her problem.

She escaped.

The two ladies were still bickering over whether or not Dr. Anthony was after Mrs. Standish's fortune, and they didn't notice when Gin slipped away. A glance behind her revealed Lord Devingham's grim expression as he watched her slip down the hall, but he had been waylaid by the Dowager Marchioness of Strye and would not be escaping that lady soon.

But to be safe, Gin hurried down the hall until the tall earl was out of sight, then slipped into what looked like a small library. For a moment she stood there, calming her nerves and gathering her thoughts in the semidarkness of the small room.

Muffled voices came through the door, and she froze. But the voices passed on, two servants grumbling about the number of people flooding the house. She backed away from the door, then hurried over to the windows. In her mind she could envision Lord Devingham striding down the halls in search of her. She shoved open the window. They were on the first floor. The ground was only a short drop away. Gathering her skirts, she thrust her leg over the sill and slipped out into the night.

Immediately, she felt foolish. Did she really consider that Lord Devingham would pursue her like a villain, through empty rooms and open windows?

Recalling his fierce expression, she decided that perhaps caution was the better option after all.

Still, Aunt Beatrice would be frantic if she were gone too long, and that lady had worked very hard to make certain that Gin was accepted into Society. She would not disappoint her by falling into scandalbroth now. The sooner she returned to the music room, the more quickly she and her godmother could make their exit before Lucy's husband caught up with them.

She stayed along the back wall of the house, following the dull roar of conversation and the light streaming out into the night. There had to be another room with an open window somewhere. . .

"Everything is set." The male voice, hushed and secretive, made her jump. She glanced around but saw no one around her. So where had the voice come from?

"You are certain?" A woman this time, her words slightly accented. . .

Isabella Montelucci.

Cautiously, Gin stepped away from the wall of the house.

"They are gone to visit his ailing father," the man continued. "This is the perfect time."

The voices were coming from above her, she realized. A careful glance up revealed two shadowy figures on a small, darkened balcony. A bedroom, perhaps.

"Agreed," Isabella said. "You will meet me at the abbey tomorrow, Michael, and bring the others. You *have* found others, have you not?"

Even Gin shivered at the menace in the woman's voice. And Michael—was that Michael Standish?

"Of course," the man said, a hint of submission in his voice. "I told them all to meet us at Ravenforth Abbey, eleven o'clock."

"They'd best not be late," she hissed. "I am to attend Lady Blayney's luncheon at one o'clock."

"All will be well," he replied. "I think you will be most pleased with what I have found."

There was a tense silence, then Isabella said, "You had better not disappoint me."

A scrape of shoes against stone reached her ears, and she realized the two had moved off.

Ravenforth Abbey. Where was that? Who were these "others"?

Lucy would know.

She found an open window in a darkened morning room and climbed back into the house, then followed the voices until she found the music room. The intermission was almost over, and she slipped into her chair beside her godmother. That lady gave her a stern look, but Gin shook her head, indicating she would explain later.

A glance about the room found Lord Devingham standing near a wall, John Foxworth seated nearby. His lordship's dark gaze never left her, and Gin knew that while she had escaped him for the moment, she might not be so lucky a second time.

Chapter 14

Truth is not unlike a seat at the opera. Its value is directly proportionate to the perspective it affords one. Additionally, that perspective can add value to an otherwise lackluster evening!

The journals of Simon, Lord Devingham,
on perceived value

At ten o'clock the next morning, Miss Virginia Matthews and a mysterious, cloaked lady climbed into Lady Wexford's traveling coach.

"Ravenforth Abbey is an abandoned monastery owned by the Earl of Rothstone," Lucy said, settling into a seat and pulling back the hood of her cloak. "I believe the Standishes are a family connection."

"So that explains why they might be meeting there. Michael Standish probably got permission from the earl."

"Possibly. It only proves my suspicion that Simon's interest in that woman is something more than an affair."

"Maybe this meeting will tell us something." Gin arranged herself on her seat as a servant closed the door.

"I hope so. What did you tell Lady Wexford about our outing?"

Gin shrugged. "That we're going to view the ruins. I explained that you are going mad cooped up inside the house, and since you are supposed to be at Devingham, we need to find amusements outside of London."

Lucy grinned. "At least you did not lie to her."

"No need. With you as my chaperone, it gives her more time to spend gossiping with her friends. She even sent a footman with luncheon for us."

"How lovely." The coach pulled away from the curb.

Across the road, a hired hack lurched into motion and began to follow a short distance behind them.

Ravenforth Abbey was an ancient monastery just outside London that had been in the family of the Earl of Rothstone for generations. No one lived there, though occasionally Lady Rothstone would hold parties on the sprawling grounds. On Tuesdays and Fridays one could pay to go on a tour of the place, but today, Thursday, it was quiet indeed.

Lucy and Gin walked along the pathways, ostensibly enjoying the delightful gardens. Donald, the footman, followed behind them, a picnic blanket in his arms should the ladies need to stop and rest.

"What are we looking for?" Lucy whispered, conscious of the servant's presence.

"Isabella," Gin murmured back. "But we can't allow Donald to follow us to the meeting place. Wherever it is."

Lucy thought for a moment. Donald did pose a problem, as not only might he try and prevent them from witnessing this meeting of Isabella's, but he was bound to report their activities to Lady Wexford. "We can select a spot, then tell Donald we are hungry and send him back for the luncheon hamper. While he's gone, we shall continue on to the monastery. That seems the most likely place for a meeting."

"Good idea."

At an area near a small pond surrounded by flowering shrubs and graced by a statue of Saint Augustine, Lucy said, "How about this place, Gin? It is nearly eleven o'clock already, and this rigorous exercise has me quite ravenous."

"Me, too. Donald, do go fetch the luncheon hamper for us, won't you?"

"Of course, miss." Donald spread his blanket out on the grass.

"Oh, and tell Hume he may take the coach

down to that inn we passed along the way—the Swann Inn? I don't like to think of him sitting in the hot sun with the horses while we take our time touring this place."

Donald nodded. "When shall he return, miss?"

Gin glanced at Lucy.

"Two hours should be sufficient, I would think."

Gin gave a nod and turned back to the servant. "Two hours, Donald. That will give us plenty of time to enjoy our meal and tour the ruins."

Donald gave a brief bow. "Very good, miss."

As the footman started back down the pathway they had come, Lucy murmured, "Good idea about the coachman."

Gin shrugged. "I hate to see the servants waiting on my convenience. Besides, the sight of the other coach might scare Isabella away, and we'd miss an opportunity to learn what she is really doing."

"Well, you certainly did not lie about the hot sun." Lucy discarded the suffocating cloak and dropped it on the blanket. "There, much better."

Gin had been craning her neck to watch Donald, and now turned back to Lucy. "All right, he's gone. Let's head up to the monastery. Do you know how to get there?"

"Just follow the path. All paths lead to the monastery."

"Convenient."

They hurried along the well-kept walkway, and after a moment, Gin asked, "How are we going to find them in this huge place?"

Intent on reaching the concealment of the trees surrounding the ancient building, Lucy could only shrug. "I have no clear plan on how we shall accomplish that. I am assuming that if this meeting is for more than two people—those 'others' you spoke of—then, she will need a place that is easy to find. And the monastery is easy to find."

"I suppose you're right. How do you expect to get inside the monastery if it's locked? There are no tours today."

"I expect Isabella to do that for us."

"Oh. All right then."

It took them about a quarter of an hour of searching the building before they came upon an unlocked door. Lucy eased it open a crack. Instantly voices reached them—a woman's tones, slightly accented and imperious. The mumble of multiple male voices.

"Can you see anything?" Gin asked, trying to peer over Lucy's head into the dark interior.

"I think this is a chapel," Lucy whispered back. "They must have arrived while we were on the other side of the building."

"Shall we go in?"

"I don't know." Lucy eased the door open a little more. "There's a small hallway here, but we might easily be trapped if they come out."

"Can you hear what they're saying?"

"Some of it."

"If it's a chapel, there must be windows. You listen here, and I'll go around the corner to see if I can find one. I'll watch, and you listen, and we'll put the pieces together."

"Good idea. Be careful."

"You, too." Gin slipped along the side of the building and disappeared around the corner.

She was alone. Suppressing a shiver of trepidation, Lucy continued to hold the door open and pressed her ear back against the narrow crack.

"This can . . . rich . . . night in question . . . servants' livery."

Lucy strained her ears to better hear what Isabella was saying, but sporadic words kept getting lost in the echoing chamber of the chapel. She heard a man speak, but the deep, growling timbre of his voice made it impossible to discern what he said. She could tell from his inflection that he was asking a question.

Isabella's voice reached Lucy in response to the question. " . . . date is not yet . . . will let you know . . . ready."

Someone else asked a question, another male with a voice too low on the scale for her to distinguish individual words.

Isabella again. "The captain . . . ready to take . . . to safety."

The captain? Captain Standish perhaps?

She leaned a little closer, hoping to hear something that would prove it was Michael Standish of whom she spoke. Suddenly a strong male arm wrapped around her waist from behind, and a man's hand covered her mouth before she could scream. He lifted her feet off the ground, yanking her against his body and away from the door. She kicked her heels backwards against his knees, clawing at the hand over her mouth with both of hers as the abbey door closed with a muffled thud. She couldn't see her assailant. He held her head immobile against his broad chest and dragged her backwards into the trees.

She tried to open her mouth to bite his hand, but he held her too firmly for even that. Her mind began registering details. He was tall. Strong. Was it one of Isabella's men? Smelled like sandalwood and earth. The cloth of his sleeve felt smooth and expensive. A well-tailored coat. Probably not a common man then. Michael Standish?

The door to the abbey opened. Her captor muttered a curse and dragged her down deeper into the shrubbery as three rough-looking men exited the building. She felt the tension in his body and realized he didn't want the others to see him. Not Isabella's man then.

Then who? Someone who worked for Lord Rothstone to keep trespassers off his property?

The three fellows started off down one of the paths, laughing and talking about the things they would buy with their fortunes. The door opened again, and another man walked out, this one with the rolling gait of a seaman. He looked neither right nor left, just picked a different path from the other three and disappeared from sight.

Her captor seemed distracted. The hand over her lips loosened a bit. She started to bare her teeth, but his fingers clamped hard over her mouth again.

"No, you will not, my girl," he growled, and relief flooded her system at the familiar voice.

Simon.

She didn't have even a moment to consider what he was doing there because the door opened a third time, and Isabella Montelucci strolled out on the arm of Captain Standish. A satisfied smile curved the other woman's lips, and something about it made Lucy's stomach curl with dread. The captain paused to lock the door, then slipped the key in his pocket. Then he offered his arm to Isabella again, and the two wandered down yet another pathway, their pace casual and unhurried.

It seemed like it took an eternity for them to disappear from sight.

Finally, they were gone. Simon released his hold on her and rose, dragging her up with him. She brushed at the leaves that clung to her dress, then sucked up her courage and looked at him.

His eyes blazed with emotion, his mouth a grim line. She bit her lower lip, knowing he had every right to be vexed with her after the way she had deceived him. He reached out to pluck yet another leaf from her hair. His hand continued down along her cheek, a sweet, unexpected caress.

"Lucy." Then he swept her into his arms, claiming her mouth in a hard, hot kiss.

The taste of her exploded inside him, and he fed greedily on her mouth, a starving man finally given a meal. Her scent surrounded him, that heady hint of lavender that drove him more wild than any perfume. Her body fit against his as if they'd been made for each other, two pieces of one whole, and he filled his hands with her curves as he slaked the hunger that roared through his veins.

Lucy was back where she belonged.

He finally managed to break the kiss. "Lucy," he rasped, cupping her face in his hands, "what the devil did you think you were doing?"

Lucy met his gaze squarely. "Now, or when I let you think I had returned to Devingham?"

"Now." He narrowed his eyes. "Though I will insist on an explanation for the other as well. Later."

She bit her lip, wariness flickering across her face. "I was following Mrs. Montelucci."

"What? Why?"

"Because I was trying to find out what hold she has on you." Straightening her spine, she lifted her chin. "I am no fool, Simon. Rumors of your supposed affair with Mrs. Montelucci reached me long before I ever came to London."

"I suspected as much." Guilt rose that she had thought him unfaithful so soon after their marriage.

"I've been trying to see the truth for myself," she continued.

He braced himself for accusations, for tears. "Lucy, there is more here than meets the eye."

To his surprise, she just nodded calmly. "There is no affair, is there?"

Shocked, he could only gape at her. "No, there is not."

"It is something else that draws you to that woman. What is it—blackmail? What hold does she have on you?" She laid her hand on his chest. "Whatever it is, Simon, we can fight it together."

Her tender declaration of loyalty squeezed his heart. He placed his hand over hers to ease the sweet ache. "No, my dear, not blackmail."

"Are you involved in something illegal then? I need to know."

His lips curved despite the seriousness of the conversation. "No."

She let out a huge sigh, her shoulders sagging with relief. "Thank goodness."

"Are you pleased that you are not wed to a criminal?"

"I am indeed. But you must tell me what is going on, Simon. My imagination has conjured all manner of things."

He chuckled and hugged her to him, gaining

intense satisfaction from the way she returned the embrace, her arms strong and fierce. "I will tell you everything."

"Lucy!" Gin called softly, coming around the corner of the monastery.

Simon released her as reality returned with a crash. They were in danger as long as Isabella was in the vicinity. Giving Lucy a warning look that forestalled further questions, he stepped out of the trees, pulling his wife along with him.

"Miss Matthews," he said, "come this way. I have a carriage waiting."

Gin froze where she stood. "Lord Devingham, what are you doing here?"

"Following the two of you." He looked from one to the other, then let the exasperation play into his voice. "Did you really think I would believe that Lucy had left me once I saw that you were still in Town? Really, Miss Matthews."

Gin glanced at Lucy, then shrugged.

Simon shook his head. "Come with me, both of you. The sooner we leave this place, the better."

Fox met them at the carriage, where the frantic Donald had been quite relieved to see the ladies recovered and unharmed. They dropped him at the Swann Inn that he might join up with Lady Wexford's traveling coach and her coachman. Simon, Lucy, Gin, and Fox all rode home in the hired hack (obtained only because the ladies would have recognized the Devingham rig following them) and congregated at Severton House.

After sending a note around to Lady Wexford to notify the lady of Gin's whereabouts, the four of them sat in the Devingham drawing room, tension thrumming among them.

Lucy watched her husband with some uncertainty. He leaned against his desk, arms folded, and she and Gin sat in the chairs right in front of him. Fox had settled into a seat by the fire, idly rubbing the place where his thigh met his knee.

Simon regarded the two women with a stern expression. "There are several issues to be addressed here. First of all, why Lucy only pretended to go to Devingham and in fact relocated to Lady Wexford's house. Secondly, why were you two following Mrs. Montelucci to such a secluded place? Surely you know such an action is rash if not utterly dangerous."

"Thirdly," Gin interjected, "how you two happened to come along."

"No mystery there," Fox said. "I knew when we saw you last night, Miss Matthews, that something was amiss. We decided to follow you to discover the whereabouts of Lady Devingham."

"Luckily for us, you came out of the house and saved us the effort of paying a formal call. All we had to do was keep your coach in sight," Simon said. "But still, this hardly seemed like a simple outing to view some old ruins."

Lucy sighed. "I told you already that we were following Mrs. Montelucci, Simon."

"What?" Fox exclaimed. "Why?"

Gin turned her head to look at him. "Because we know that Lord Devingham is not having an affair with her, despite the rumors to the contrary."

Fox looked as if someone had smacked him across the face with a fish. "The devil you say."

"Oh, enough of this dancing about!" Lucy stood, her fists clenched at her sides. "I'm tired of being treated like a child who has misbehaved. Mr. Foxworth, you know good and well why I had to pretend to leave London." She turned to Simon. "I knew there was something afoot with Mrs. Montelucci, something besides a common affair. Nothing made sense. And then Mr. Foxworth came to me and *strongly encouraged* me to go home to Devingham, lest he accidentally reveal some gossip about Gin to the scandal sheets."

"Blackmail," Gin grumbled, glaring at Fox.

Lucy never took her eyes from her husband, hoping he could read the sincerity behind her words. "I thought you were in trouble, Simon, yet Mr. Foxworth had just threatened Gin. I could not stay, yet I could not go. So I pretended to leave Town and hid at Lady Wexford's."

"Just what sort of trouble are you both in?" Gin asked, glancing from one man to the other. "I know it's not just Lord Devingham, Mr. Foxworth. You're both involved in this mess."

Fox's face hardened, and he stared into the grate, mute.

"We are not in trouble," Simon said. He went to his wife and caressed her shoulder, easing her back down into her chair. "Tell me this: How did you know Isabella was going to be at Ravenforth Abbey?"

"I overheard her talking at the musicale last night," Gin confessed. "I think she was talking to Captain Standish, but it was dark, and I couldn't really see them."

"It *was* Captain Standish," Lucy confirmed. "We saw her leave the abbey with him. And we were right, Gin. He had a key."

"He must have gotten it from Lord Rothstone. What was the connection again?" Gin asked.

"Their mothers are second cousins, I believe."

"Stop." Simon held up a hand. "So what you are saying is that Miss Matthews overheard a conversation involving a meeting at Ravenforth Abbey, and the two of you concluded that her partner in this was indeed Standish because he has a family connection to Lord Rothstone?"

"Yes," Lucy said.

"And because she called him Michael," Gin added. "But Michael is a common name, so I wasn't certain until now that it was Captain Standish."

"Amazing," Simon murmured, shaking his head. "You have no idea of the danger you narrowly avoided today."

"I overheard some of their conversation," Lucy said. "But most of it was not very clear. I'm afraid my eavesdropping did not prove useful in this case."

Simon met Fox's gaze over the women's heads. "There were three thugs and a fellow who had the look of the sea about him. And Standish."

"A ship?" Fox asked.

Simon nodded. "Perhaps."

"No more cryptic comments," Lucy said. "We will tell you nothing more until you explain your connection to Isabella Montelucci. I deserve that much, Simon."

He hesitated for a long moment, then nodded. "You are correct. You do deserve to know the truth."

"Oh, blast it, Simon!" Fox growled.

"Isabella Montelucci is suspected of being a French spy," Simon said, locking gazes with his wife. "And Fox and I work to protect England against people like her."

"That's it? That's why you were with her . . . why you wanted me to go home . . . ?"

Simon nodded. "I'm sorry, my sweet. I didn't want you hurt."

She could only stare at her husband, stunned.

"Does this mean we're all spies, too?" Gin glanced at Fox.

Fox covered his face with his hand and groaned.

Chapter 15

How ironic that deception brought so much joy, yet honesty brings naught but strife. One would think the reverse would be true.

The journals of Simon, Lord Devingham, on expected outcomes

Her husband was a spy.

As Gin and Fox engaged in a quarrel about why the ladies could not be spies, too, Lucy studied Simon's face, looking for some clue as to whom she had actually married. Of all the possible scenarios she had envisioned . . . victim of a swindler . . . blackmail . . . driven by poverty into some illegal activity. . .

In none of them had she imagined that her husband, the quiet intellectual, the poetry-scribbling gentleman who preferred roses to people, could possibly be engaging in secret missions for the Crown.

She met his gaze as the squabbling continued and saw the same familiar hazel eyes she always had seen. He looked no different, and yet she found herself wondering about this unfamiliar man she saw before her, confident and in charge of the situation, the efficient weapon who had felled Michael Standish in a matter of seconds.

She should be happy to hear that he worked for the good of England. She should be relieved that he was not a criminal, nor was he pursuing an affair with Isabella Montelucci. But after this business was done, they would continue with their lives, and how would they go on?

She had married a stranger. Anger began to simmer as she remembered the sweetness of their courtship. The intimacies they had shared. Her slowly growing feelings for a man who did not appear to exist.

Had he used her? Had he assumed a mild-mannered persona when in reality he was a man with dark secrets? What sort of life would they live now? Need she worry about his enemies interfering in their lives, attempting to kill him or anyone close to him?

Who *was* this man she had married?

Lucy seemed somewhat withdrawn. She watched him as if he were someone she barely knew, and the disquiet in her eyes disturbed him.

He longed to get her alone so they could talk. So he could tell her everything.

But there was Fox and Miss Matthews to worry about, the two of whom might come to blows at any second.

"Enough!" Simon roared, and all three of them stared at him. "Fox, stop plaguing Miss Matthews. And you, Miss Matthews, kindly cease antagonizing my associate so we can all sort out this muddle."

"There's no muddle," Gin said. "We followed Isabella; we learned some things that you don't know. In my book, that makes us spies."

Fox opened his mouth to protest, but Simon glared him into silence. "Miss Matthews, what else do you remember about the meeting today?"

"Nothing," she replied with disappointing cheerfulness.

Simon sighed and turned his attention to his wife. "Lucy?"

"You saw what we did," she replied, her voice hushed. "Though there was one other thing— somewhat odd, actually. Gin and I stumbled across it quite by accident."

"Oh, the clerk at the bookseller," Gin said, nodding.

"What clerk?" Simon asked.

Lucy kept her hands folded in her lap as she replied. There was something about her demeanor, something sad or disheartened, that made him want to hold her close and protect her from the world. "Gin and I were at Humbolt's bookstore when we witnessed Isabella meeting a young clerk outside the back of the store. She was paying him to do something."

"Which clerk?" Simon demanded. "When?"

"Last week. Perhaps Friday."

"His name was Andrew," Gin put in. "We tried to go back and talk to him, but he'd been murdered."

"Murdered?" Fox stood up and limped over to Gin's chair. "What makes you say that?"

"Mr. Humbolt told us," Gin said, her gaze direct on his. Fox was the first to break eye contact.

"It's terrible," Lucy whispered. "He told us poor Andrew was killed behind a tavern—I don't remember which one."

"He was stabbed," Gin added.

"Indeed." Simon glanced at Fox, his mind racing. "It might be worth investigating young Andrew's death. Date, time, style."

"I agree." Rubbing his thigh, Fox began to limp back and forth across the room. "When did you want to do this? Leg's stiffening up."

"Tonight." Simon glanced at Lucy. The shadows still lingered in her eyes. He hesitated, knowing they needed to talk privately, yet hungry to have her in his arms again. "I mean, tomorrow is soon enough."

"Very well then. I'll await word from you. In the meantime, I am going to go deal with this cursed knee."

"Fine. If there is nothing else you ladies can tell us?" Simon looked from one to the other, but both women shook their heads. Simon turned to his friend. "Fox, do escort Miss Matthews home, won't you?"

"I can get home by myself," Gin protested.

"Do have some regard for your own safety," Fox scolded. "Not to mention your reputation."

"As if my reputation could withstand being seen with you!"

"Take my carriage," Simon suggested.

"As long as the chit minds her manners," Fox said.

Gin's eyes widened. "This from the rudest man in London?"

Fox merely laughed, and said, "Come along, Miss Matthews. I shall protect the footpads of the city from your sharp tongue by escorting you home."

Gin made a face at Fox, then looked at Lucy. "I'll send Molly along with your things."

"Thank you." Lucy looked down at her hands, suddenly uncertain, now that she would be left alone with Simon.

Fox escorted Gin from the room, the murmur of their bickering echoing back long after they had stepped through the door.

Lucy continued to twist her fingers around, conscious of the growing silence between her and Simon. They heard Fox talking to Dobbins and, a few minutes later, the front door closing. They were alone in the house.

Simon went to the door of the drawing room and closed it, his footsteps padded by the thick rug as he made his way back to her. His boots creaked ever so slightly as he crouched down to her level. "Why did you leave me?"

A touch of lament, of confusion, flavored the words, and the ache in her heart grew. "I told you, I had no choice."

"You could have come to me."

Tears stung her eyes, and she said nothing.

He tilted her head up with a finger beneath her chin, compelling her to look at him. "You could have come to me," he repeated.

"No," she whispered. "I did not know the husband I saw before me. I still do not."

Bewilderment creased his brow. "I am the same man I have always been."

"And who is that? I cannot say." A tear escaped, sliding down her cheek, and she swiped at it with impatience.

"Lucy, why are you so distraught? I thought you would be pleased to discover the truth about my actions."

She nodded, moisture still welling in her eyes

despite her will. "I am glad you are not in trouble. But Simon, you are still in danger."

"I know what I am doing."

"Well, I do not! How can we live as we were now that this is between us?"

"What are you talking about?"

"You lied to me, husband. *Lied*. Every day we were together, you told me untruths with an innocent face." She swiped both hands across her cheeks, dispelling the tears that revealed her weakness. "How can I believe anything you say to me now?"

His stricken expression made her feel even worse, but she couldn't allow herself to feel guilty. She needed to know what would happen next. How they would go on.

"I never meant to hurt you," he said.

"I believe you. But you *have* hurt me." She sniffled, and he handed her his handkerchief. She dabbed at her face, but the scrap of linen smelled like him, rousing memories of the intimacies they had shared. Sucking in air against the lump in her throat, she crushed the handkerchief between her fingers.

"I no longer have to deceive you," he murmured, stroking a hand down her arm. "You know the truth now."

"And such a truth! I thought you were in some kind of trouble. Gambling debts. Blackmail. Something dire that would lead you to abandon your newly wedded wife the day after the wedding."

He flinched. "I was summoned away by my work. I had no choice."

"Do I have a choice? I am wedded to you, Simon. Bound as long as we both shall live. Yet you never confided in me, never trusted me enough to keep your secret."

"I was forbidden to tell you," he explained.

"By whom, your superiors? You constantly put yourself in harm's way with your activities, husband. Did it never occur to you that I might be in danger as well? That some enemy of England might think to approach you through your wife? Through our children?"

He paled. "That is why I thought it best you remain in the country. Out of sight."

"My life was in danger, and I would never have known. What else have you not told me?"

"Ask me anything," he vowed, "and I will answer."

"Then tell me this, Simon—why did you marry me?"

His eyes widened in surprise. "You know why. I needed a wife."

"Why?"

"The usual reasons."

"Which are?"

He frowned. "I need heirs, Lucy. Surely you understand that."

"I do. But why me? Certainly there were any number of debutantes here in London who would suit an earl. Why a squire's daughter?"

"You were raised near Devingham. You loved the area as much as I do."

"So you wanted a country wife, is that what you are saying?"

"Devingham is where my children will be raised. My wife needed to be comfortable there as well."

She heard it then, the stiffness beneath the very correct words. "You are lying to me again, aren't you?"

His expression betrayed his surprise before he could hide it. "Not really."

"Tell me the truth, Simon. Did you expect that by marrying a squire's daughter, you would gain a wife who preferred to stay in the country rather than join you in London?"

His jaw clenched. "Yes," he replied, reluctance in his very posture.

"I thought as much." She sat back in the chair, putting distance between them. "You wanted a wife who would happily live at Devingham and leave you to your life of intrigue here in London."

"It was safer. Better."

"For a marriage of convenience." Her lips curved in a sad smile. "I want children with you, Simon. And I am happy to be your hostess and manage your estate while you tend to your business. But I want more than that."

"I thought we had more." He glanced away, his throat working.

"Bed sport is not all things in marriage," Lucy said. "Though to find the passion that we have is truly unique."

"How would you know?" Simon demanded. "You, a proper lady who should not know of such things?"

"I am a married woman now, so if I choose to speak on such topics in my own home, I shall do just that." She raised her brows, challenging him to disagree. "My parents cared for each other very much, so I have seen how marriage can be. Loving. Trusting. A partnership."

"My parents barely saw each other," he said, leaning on the edge of his desk. "After my younger brother was born, they went their separate ways."

"Lived separate lives."

"Yes. They each died alone."

Her resolve softened. "I do not want that to happen to us. I want to laugh with you, Simon, and cry with you in times of sadness. Play with you, fight with you. Make love with you."

"I like the sound of that. I suppose I just do not know how to share myself." He stood again, seeming to have collected himself. "I work for England, Lucy, and sometimes that means I must do things I dislike."

"Like lying to your wife?"

"Yes." He slashed a hand through the air. "Or

trying to pretend passion for a woman for whom I care nothing."

She gasped, paling at the implication.

He shook his head. "Not you, Lucy. Never you. I mean Isabella. That was my assignment. To become one of her admirers."

She let out a long breath. "Oh."

"If I tell you the whole of it, will that make things better between us?" He came to her, knelt before her again. "I want things to be the way they were."

"They can never be the way they were."

His expression fell.

"But the truth can certainly help." She gave in to the urge to touch his face. "Things have happened, feelings have been hurt. We must make amends and move on. This is how a marriage grows stronger over the years."

"I want to make amends." He put his arms around her and laid his head against her bosom. "I missed you."

Stunned, she hesitated before tentatively caressing his soft, thick hair. "I missed you as well."

"Do not try to go away again." He looked up, his dark eyes fierce. "I shall find you more quickly next time."

His determination took her breath away, and she forced herself to think about things other than how much she wanted to be back in his arms. "Tell me about Isabella."

He let out a long sigh and sat back on his heels. "I told you that she is suspected of being a French spy. What I neglected to mention was that she is rumored to have been the lover of a very dangerous French assassin named Antoine LaRue."

"If you know this, how is it she is here in England, welcomed with open arms by the *ton*?"

"It is all rumors and hearsay. We have no proof, so she moves about Society as she wishes." He paused. "The rumors also say she is in possession of a list of English sympathizers in France. If that list gets into the wrong hands, many people would die."

"She intends to do something with the list? Sell it or some such thing?"

Simon nodded, his approving expression warming her like sunshine. "That is what we have heard. But how and to whom, we do not know."

"So you are to befriend her in hopes of discovering her plans?"

"Yes, or stealing the list."

Her eyes widened. "Can you do that?"

He chuckled. "My sweet, you are unaware of many of my talents."

"Yes." She gave him another sad little smile. "This is our problem, husband. Despite our time together these past few days, we are yet strangers."

"In some ways." He gave her a wicked grin that immediately melted her insides. "In other ways, my dear, we are intimately acquainted."

Her cheeks warmed. "I told you, there is more to marriage than bed sport."

"Yes, but if the marriage bed is cold, then so is the marriage." He stood and held out a hand to her. "But if it is warm, then both parties find satisfaction no matter how little they know one another."

She allowed him to help her from her seat. "It would seem to me that the marriage bed would be an excellent place to get to know one's spouse."

His hazel eyes glittered. "I agree completely. Shall we prove our theory?"

She hesitated. "Passion cannot solve all problems, Simon."

"No." He caressed her jaw with his thumb. "But it is a good way to find our way back to each other."

Her stomach did a little flip-flop. "I would like that," she whispered, and allowed him to lead her from the room.

Fox chose to take Simon's barouche to escort Miss Matthews to her door, assuming that the openness of the carriage, along with the presence of a coachman, would satisfy propriety. The Devingham coat of arms emblazoned on the side of the vehicle would help to squelch most rumors.

He sat with his back to the coachman and carefully stretched out his leg. The knee was throbbing again, curse it. Probably more blasted rain headed their way.

Miss Matthews, perched in the forward-facing seat, said nothing, but as she watched the bustle of the pedestrians on the street, she wore a considering expression that kept him on his guard. The carriage pulled into traffic, and they enjoyed a comfortable silence.

As they turned a corner, the sunlight hit the curls peeking from beneath her bonnet, making her hair glow like flame. She really wasn't unattractive, he decided. In fact, the pale blue dress made her skin look like fresh cream, despite the freckles. Her straw bonnet had no garish fruit or birds as adornment, simply a wide blue ribbon that tied on the side of her face.

All in all, she looked rather fetching.

She turned to face him just then, her green eyes alight with intelligence and curiosity behind the lenses of her spectacles. "I would like to be a spy," she said.

His fanciful notions evaporated like water thrown on hot coals. "Do not be ridiculous."

"Ridiculous? Why? Doesn't England have female spies?"

"Of course it does. But they are a different sort of female altogether."

"Different how? Prettier?"

He gritted his teeth. "No. Just different."

"That doesn't answer my question."

"*A different sort of female*, Miss Matthews." At

her perplexed stare, he ground out, "*Not* innocent debutantes."

"Oh." She pursed her lips and frowned. "I shall be the first then."

"Rubbish."

She scowled. "Mr. Foxworth, am I correct in understanding that you have some objection to women doing their part to protect the country?"

"Miss Matthews, you are not even English."

"Not now. I might be, if I end up married to an Englishman."

He shook his head, strangely disturbed by her warped logic. "Impossible."

"Why? I'm smart and willing. I want to help."

"Out of the question."

"Mr. Foxworth . . ."

"No. You do not understand that dark world, and I shall not be responsible for showing it to you. For all your colorful past, Miss Matthews, you are a young woman of good family and an innocent. There is no place for you."

The carriage turned another corner and approached Lady Wexford's town house. Miss Matthews never took her gaze from him.

"Mr. Foxworth," she said, "you have seen the full gamut of my exploits, it is true. But as you pointed out, I am not some frail English flower. I am an American woman with a mind of my own."

"Do not think to interfere, my girl."

Her lips curved in a way that made him believe she knew the secrets of Eve. "I would not do such a thing," she replied, "for to blunder in where one is uncertain would only cost valuable lives. But do think about the notion, Mr. Foxworth. Who would suspect an American of helping the English defend their country?"

Her unexpected wisdom stunned him, and as the carriage came to a stop and a footman stepped forward to help her from the carriage, he still had no reply.

It seemed a scandalous thing, to be naked in the middle of the day.

Lucy watched Simon from beneath lowered lashes as he slipped the last of her garments from her body. His eyes gleamed as he looked over her nude form, one hand around her waist and the other caressing her hip.

"You're so beautiful," he murmured.

Despite what had happened, despite deception, she believed him. The glow of his gaze warmed her like sunlight.

"And what about you, my lord?" she teased, tugging at the sleeve of his coat. "How very odd that you are clothed while I am not."

"I have no complaints." He bent to nuzzle her neck, cupping one of her plump breasts with a quiet rumble of pleasure.

"I know what you are about." She gasped, her eyes sliding closed as he nipped the sensitive flesh beneath her ear. "You seek to take advantage of me, sir."

"I thought it was rather obvious." He pulled her against him, his hands greedy as they swept over her hips and buttocks. "Dear God, I have missed you, Lucy. One day seemed an eternity."

A thrill jolted through her before common sense asserted itself. She should not weigh his words too carefully. He was skilled at falsehoods.

But oh, how much she wanted to believe him!

She tugged at his coat sleeve, unable to resist the pull of desire even as her mind swam with doubt. She wanted him in her bed, wanted that insane pleasure jangling every nerve. No matter what happened between them now, they were still husband and wife. And this might be all she ever had of him. Just hot passion and fleeting bliss.

A knot formed in her throat. Could he ever be the man she needed him to be? A man who could love and trust and be a friend as well as a lover? Or would he always be the stranger she had married, the man who kept all his secrets locked away from her?

He stepped back to tug at his coat, shrugging off the garment with ill-concealed impatience. His hazel eyes burned with hunger, and her doubts drifted to the back of her mind as he methodically stripped off his clothing. Expensive tailored garments hit the floor with alarming speed, and she gloried in his eagerness.

"Hurry," she urged, trailing her fingers along her own body. "It's been too long."

He let out a growl, his features growing taut with lust as his gaze followed the path of her hands along her flesh. "Wicked woman." With difficulty, he jerked off his boots and tossed them aside.

She laughed, delighted to be female. "I'm waiting."

"And I am finished waiting." He stripped off his tight pantaloons, his erection an obvious testament to his need. "Come here, wife."

She giggled and eluded his hands, but in two steps he had caught her, pulling her wiggling form against his. In that instant, with her breasts crushed against his chest and his hardness jabbing her thigh, all humor vanished. She stared up at him, at his beloved face, and the rest of the world fell away.

He traced a hand along her temple, gently tucking a stray lock of hair behind her ear. "Lucy."

"Simon." She moved first, raising on tiptoe and pressing her mouth to his.

Like a spark to tinder, his passion erupted. With a growl that thrilled her, he wrapped both arms around her and lifted her off her feet. One step . . . two . . . and they were on the bed.

Her back hit the coverlet as he came down on

top of her, the heat of his body delicious as his weight trapped her beneath him. With both hands, he cupped her face and kissed her, his mouth demanding, his fingers greedy as they thrust through her hair to hold her head still. He fed on her mouth as if it were nectar, and every bone in her body melted. Every defense dissolved, every ounce of resistance faded away.

Dear Lord, how she wanted him.

She gripped his shoulders, cradling him between her thighs, dying against all reason to feel him inside her.

Liar.

Deceiver.

Lover.

He joined their bodies fast and hard, never breaking their kiss. And as she felt that hot flesh penetrate her body, the floodgates opened. Tears stung her eyes, and she clung to him, emotion surging through her veins as she matched the primal rhythm of his thrusts.

She wanted him. She had just started to love the man she'd thought him to be. And the pain of his deception pricked her soft heart and left a bleeding wound.

Desire and dismay tangled like unruly vines, choking her with the force of their demands. He slowed his movements, breaking the kiss to look into her eyes. It was as if she were looking at his soul, a mix of vulnerability and confidence, tenderness and ruthlessness. Were there shadows there as well? He moved slowly now, tugging one of her knees up to cradle his hip, and bent to brush away one of her tears with his lips.

Like a whirlpool, everything spun wildly, drenching her with sensation. Love, confusion, distrust, desire. He made love to her slowly, pacing himself as the tension slowly built. And when it finally snapped, the release shattered her. She cried out his name, shuddering with reaction, gasping sobs shaking her from head to toe.

He held her close, shushing her with nonsense words, trembling from his own climax. She continued to weep, moisture streaming down her cheeks even as her body vibrated with satisfaction. They clung to each other, bathed in her tears, and drifted to sleep.

A long time later, Lucy opened her eyes. She lay in her husband's arms, his steady breathing telling her that he slept. She curled against him, her head on his shoulder and her hand over his steady heartbeat.

Her body hummed with satisfaction, but her mind spun with uncertainty.

Passion alone did not make a marriage.

She threaded her fingers through the crisp hair sprinkled across Simon's chest, the memories of their heated, frantic lovemaking playing through her mind. Did he show her his real self during those moments? Or was the role of lover just another part for him to play?

Perhaps she should not have given in to desire. Perhaps she should have insisted they work out their differences without the fog of physical craving overshadowing the very real complications of their marriage. But he had wanted her so badly, and, weak woman that she was, she hadn't been able to resist his need. How could any female turn away a husband who so clearly hungered for her?

She would never be able to deny Simon her bed. No matter how they might argue, no matter what obstacles lay in the path of their marriage, she could not refuse him.

Was this weakness? Or the bond that would hold them together in times of trouble?

Did he love her? She didn't know. But he wanted her, and apparently he also wanted something more than a marriage of convenience.

That would have to be enough for now. She didn't know if she could ever give her whole heart to him unless he decided to trust her completely. Until then, the pleasure found in the marriage bed would have to bind them together.

Chapter 16

While constant chatter is not a necessary ingredient to a successful marriage, the words that go unsaid can be the most critical, much like eggs to a bread pudding.

The journals of Simon, Lord Devingham, on awkward silences

Simon felt as if he were a theater player, treading the boards of a production for which he had no script. He was uncertain of his lines and attempted to take his prompts from the other members of the cast.

But there was only one other member, and she was a bit too stingy with her cues for comfort.

For three days they had lived in the same house, eaten at the same table, slept in the same bed. They went their separate ways after breakfast—he to continue his campaign to woo the ever-stubborn

Isabella, or to meet with Fox and Sir Adrian, or to vent his frustrations at Gentleman Jackson's. She engaged in shopping expeditions with Miss Matthews and heaven knew what other sorts of female pursuits. But he noticed that they never again met up at the same social event. He attended whatever balls and routs where he might find Isabella. She appeared at Almack's with Miss Matthews, as well as other dinner parties and soirees favored by those in the marriage mart.

They lived separate lives during the day, and at night they came together in scorching passion that felt almost desperate in its intensity.

This was exactly what he had wanted, exactly the way he had intended his life to be when he had first offered for Lucy. And he hated it.

Now that she knew the truth about him, she took great care to leave him free to do his work. Sir Adrian had gotten past his initial resistance to Lucy knowing the truth and had voiced his approval of the current arrangement. Fox no longer stung him with verbal jabs about sending Lucy home and instead directed all his energy toward finding the key to the coded French missive, a prize that continued to elude him. Simon focused on the incremental softening of Isabella's pique, slowly wooing his way back into the lady's good graces. Things were moving along exactly as they should.

And he was miserable.

He walked into the breakfast room, not really

hungry at all, and slowed his pace as he noticed Lucy already at the table. She was slicing a piece of sausage as he approached, and he could not help but remember that morning after she had first arrived, and she had tossed the sausage at him. Plath had turned puce at the sight of the greasy stain on his pristine coat, but Simon had regarded the mark with fondness, recalling the playful exchange with his wife.

Lucy never laughed anymore. She smiled, but it was always a very polite smile. She never teased him anymore, never tried to engage him in silly antics that were beneath the dignity of an earl. The only time he ever caught a glimpse of her natural tendency toward mischief was in bed, when the darkness hid their faces and they could lose themselves in each other's arms.

But even that was different. Something was missing, as if she were holding a piece of herself back from him. And it disturbed him greatly.

She glanced at him as he helped himself to eggs and meat at the sideboard. "Good morning, Simon."

"Good morning, Lucy." So civil. So very polite. They were the very picture of correctness. Of a marriage of convenience. He slapped his plate down on the table, rattling the silverware and earning a questioning look from his wife. "Sorry," he muttered.

She turned back to her meal, cutting that

damned sausage into smaller pieces and placing each bite between her lips with a daintiness that charmed and irritated him at the same time.

Was this what she wanted? This sterile civility? He could not believe that the Lucy he had married would settle for such a state of affairs. Where was the passionate woman who had embraced the idea of marriage so fervently? Perhaps she did not know how to handle the change in their relationship any more than he did.

The thought cheered him, though only marginally. If she was just as confused as he was, then they were on common ground.

"Mrs. Nelson is expected back in Town tomorrow, so I anticipate that I shall be able to return to Devingham on Wednesday," she said.

He laid down his fork with a clank. "I thought you were staying for two weeks."

"You told me I could stay until I delivered Mrs. Nelson's inheritance to her. When I spoke to her butler, I was told that she was in Scotland for a fortnight and would return a week from Tuesday. Tomorrow is Tuesday."

"You do not have to leave." He wanted to reach over and touch her hand, but the stillness of her expression discouraged any such contact.

"I think it best." She glanced down and took another bite of sausage.

He signaled for the servants to leave the room.

Once they were alone, he said, "I thought you enjoyed Town."

A sad smile curved her lips. "It has been an education for me," she admitted, "and I shall miss Gin. But I believe that it is better that I return home after I have discharged my duty."

He refused to beg. Giving a reluctant nod, he turned his attention to his own breakfast. "As you wish. However, I want you to understand that there is no longer any reason for you to cloister yourself at Devingham. You are certainly free to stay here with me and enjoy the Season."

She sighed. "That sounds lovely, Simon, but you and I both know that I would not be enjoying the Season *with* you."

His hands fisted around his utensils. "You understand how important my work is."

She nodded. "I do. And I shall leave you to it. But please do not ask me to follow you about London like a lost puppy while the world whispers about your pursuit of Mrs. Montelucci."

Shame flooded him immediately. Why hadn't he realized? "My apologies. I did not consider that the gossip would hurt you, since you know the truth about our relationship."

She shrugged. "There is no way to avoid the chatterbroth of Town. The slightest incident will set the tongues to wagging, and a newly wed husband dallying with an exotic foreign widow is certainly fuel for the fire."

"If I had a choice . . ."

"I know." She rose. "If you will excuse me, Simon, I must get ready to accompany Gin and Lady Wexford to Mrs. Eversham's poetry reading."

"A poetry reading? I should like to accompany you to that."

She paused, her hands clenching on the back of her chair. "I do not believe it would serve your cause to be seen escorting your wife to such mundane amusements, Simon."

"Bother that," he snapped. "I miss your company, Lucy."

Her guarded expression softened. "We both have duties, Simon. Mine is to deliver the box to Mrs. Nelson, then return home to Devingham where I belong. Yours is to win the affection of this woman to save our country."

"And after that? What happens next? This assignment with Isabella is a temporary thing. Afterward, you and I still have a life to lead as husband and wife."

"I cannot even imagine that far into the future," she said with a dismissive wave of her hand. "After we have both discharged our responsibilities, then we may look at how we intend to go on."

"I want more than that." He thumped a fist on the table, making the china rattle. "More time with you."

"Time is something we do not have. I shall see

you at dinner, Simon." She left the room, her posture stiff and defensive.

He stared at the uneaten sausage on her plate. In his mind he recalled how she had cut the meat with graceful precision and placed each bite in her mouth with a deft flick of her wrist. Just the memory stirred him, as everything about her stirred him.

With one swift move, he grabbed her dish and flung it against the far wall.

The china shattered. Servants scurried in, shouting in alarm. He stared at the grease stain on the wallpaper as the footmen exclaimed over the shards of the destroyed plate. How could she remain so calm? Did she no longer feel the attraction between them? Was he losing her?

He had told her the truth, but in so doing, appeared to have pushed her farther away than when she had leaped to her own conclusions. Blissful ignorance had brought him a passionate and playful wife, one who had been determined to fight for his attentions when threatened with another woman. But full disclosure had introduced this woman, a woman who doubted him, a woman who was content to spend hours away from him. Only in bed did he glimpse the Lucy he had come to know these past few days.

Did she think he couldn't see it? That he didn't notice the wariness in her eyes every time he spoke to her? She didn't know what to believe, and he didn't know how to convince her of his sincerity. Her caution cut him to the quick.

He ignored the servants fussing over the broken plate and left the breakfast room.

What he wouldn't give to turn back the clock to the naïve bride who had arrived on his doorstep nearly two weeks ago. He had been a fool not to realize the precious gift he had been given. He had pushed her away over and over again, but she had always come back, willing to fight for them.

Now it seemed as if she had given up.

Very well then. If she wouldn't fight for what they could have together, then he would take up the challenge. Though at the moment he had no idea how he would possibly convince her to trust him again, and he didn't dare ask Fox about this one.

This was a problem he had to untangle for himself. He had handled many a dangerous mission for the Crown, but never one so complex and delicate as how to convince his wife to fall in love with him.

Lucy stood near her bedroom window and looked out onto the street as Simon exited the house and mounted his horse. He glanced up at her window, and she jerked behind the curtain, a tear trickling down her cheek.

When would this torment end?

Every day he left the house alone. She didn't

know where he went, and she didn't ask. She had vivid imaginings of his bedding Mrs. Montelucci in order to win that list away from her, and despite the fact that she knew he was playing this game to protect England, the idea of it set a choke-hold on her heart.

Where once two weeks in London had seemed too short a time to spend with her husband, now that same time appeared to stretch on into the eternity of a private hell. She longed for the peace of Devingham, where every aspect of her life proceeded with the same comforting predictabil-ity. How much longer could she stay in London, watching her husband woo another woman?

She knew he did not choose this other woman over her, that he had good, honorable reasons for his actions. But she was selfish enough, female enough, to resent England and Bonaparte and any other po-litical excuse that had created the current situation.

She wanted her husband for herself.

Did that make her a horrible person? Was she shallow and greedy because she wished the entire association of spies to the bottom of the ocean?

At least if he loved her, they might have been able to weather this difficulty with less pain. They would have had the comfort of each other and their love to hold fast through the storm.

All they had instead were hours of awkward silences and separation.

The nights were the only thing that gave her

even a little hope that their marriage would survive this challenge. At night, he came to her, or sometimes she went to him. They never spoke, except to encourage. They looked into each other's eyes, but never too deeply . . . for to view the true person inside might shatter the delicate balance of accord that their physical relationship brought to them. They touched and kissed and engaged in innumerable intimacies—some of which she had never even imagined could exist.

But always there was a door closed firmly between them, and only in the midst of this uncontrollable passion they had for each other did it open the slightest crack.

Then to close again when the sun rose.

She had married this man with certain expectations—expectations of being a wife and companion and, eventually, a mother. Expectations of developing a bond with her husband that might grow into love or, at the very least, friendship and respect. She had never imagined that he was a spy, that he lived a whole other life outside what she had already seen.

She had learned rather harshly that the husband she thought she had married was not truly the man who now shared her life, and it was difficult to maintain her idealistic dreams for their future. Their torrid nights in each other's arms were all that sustained her now. If nothing else, in the end, they would have that.

But hot passion with a stranger was a poor substitute for the higher union of souls for which she longed. She was forced to get to know her husband all over again, and while she supposed the fact that he had unbent enough to tell her the truth could be viewed as a victory, in a way it had set her back to before their courtship. Did the man she had begun to care for even exist?

She had certainly never imagined that she would be supporting him in his efforts to secure another woman's attentions.

Her stomach lurched, and she clasped a hand over her middle, turning away from the window. At least at Devingham she would not have to watch his pursuit of Isabella. She would not be the butt of ridicule and pity. She would hear an occasional rumor, but far away in the green hills of the country, she would be able to ignore it with only a pang of bitterness.

Tomorrow Mrs. Nelson returned. The sooner Lucy presented the box to Arminda's daughter, the sooner she could escape London and the heartbreak it held for her.

Simon arrived at Fox's home, still disturbed by the awkwardness between him and Lucy. She wanted to leave him, go back to Devingham. Once he would have celebrated such an event.

Not now.

He was shown into Fox's study only to find his

friend standing at the sideboard, pouring a glass of brandy. Fox looked up as Peters slammed the door behind Simon. As they listened to the scurry of the butler's footsteps as he fled, Fox grinned, a wide, toothy expression Simon had not seen on his friend's face in years.

"Mad as a hatter he is," Fox said. "But an excellent butler nonetheless. Brandy?"

"That sounds just the thing." Simon walked over to stand beside his friend. "You seem to be in excellent spirits today."

"I am indeed." Fox handed Simon the second glass of liquor. "I have found the key to that encoded message that has been plaguing me these past two days."

"Excellent news, Fox! What does the letter say?"

"I haven't finished the translation. Once I decoded the first sentence, I felt the need to celebrate." He clapped a hand on Simon's shoulder. "Come, let us read what the French have to say, shall we?"

"Lead on."

Fox sat behind his desk and set down his glass near the papers that littered the surface. Simon remained standing nearby, sipping his brandy as Fox pulled the top document toward him. "Let me see . . . Dear friends, I bring you good news. Our numbers are strong once again. Rumors have been proven false, and our enemies will once more feel the sting of the emperor's . . . what? Oh, arrow. The sting of the emperor's arrow. Let his enemies beware. Antoine LaRue—" He stopped.

"What about Antoine LaRue?" Simon came closer, peering over Fox's shoulder at the gibberish on the page.

"That cannot be correct." Fox rummaged through his papers, muttering to himself, comparing this page with that one.

"What is it?" Alarmed, Simon set his glass beside Fox's. "What does it say?"

Fox ignored him, reading one of the pages, murmuring the words aloud but in a voice so low that Simon could not understand him. Fox threw down that page and picked up another, scanning that one just as quickly. "Bloody hell."

"Fox . . ."

"That has to be it. Bloody hell."

"You said that already. Now tell me what the blasted letter says."

Fox sent him a black glare, then picked up the page again. "Dear friends, I bring you good news. Our numbers are strong once again. Rumors have been proven false, and our enemies will once more feel the sting of the emperor's arrow. Let his enemies beware." He looked up at Simon with foreboding in his eyes. "Antoine LaRue lives."

"What?" Simon reached for the paper, then realized he couldn't read the message anyway. "You must be wrong."

"Did you not see me check my references just

now?" Fox shoved the papers away and fell back in his chair, frustration twisting his features. "There is no mistake. Antoine LaRue lives."

"What does that mean for us?" Simon paced to the sideboard and back. "Where is he? Does he know about Isabella and the list?"

"Do I look like a mystic? We can only speculate. Wait!" Fox shuffled through the papers. "Where is that report on the young clerk's death?"

"The bookseller's clerk?"

"Yes. Andrew something ... ah, here it is. Andrew Chandler, found murdered behind the Three Hounds tavern near the docks." Fox's mouth tightened as he handed the report to Simon. "His throat was slit. Precision slice to the jugular from the ear to the base of the throat."

"A cut throat is nothing new in that area," Simon murmured, glancing over the paper, "but what is the likelihood that this young man, who had a connection to LaRue's mistress, should mysteriously die in a manner consistent with LaRue's favorite method of killing just when we receive word that Antoine LaRue might be alive?"

"I don't believe in coincidence." Fox took back the report and slipped it back into the pile. "I think there is every chance that LaRue may be right here in England."

"Tracking Isabella." Simon stroked his chin. "He might have heard that she was going to sell the list."

"Or he might have been part of the plot all along."

"She could sell the list—"

"And they both reap the profit and disappear."

"Damn it all." Simon began to pace again. "Either he is her partner, or he is coming here to stop the auction. In which case, we may never get that list."

"We need to know who is on it. Anyone's name could be there, including yours and mine."

"I know." And if his name was listed there, would that put Lucy in danger as well? Simon shoved that concern to the back of his mind. He needed to focus on the problem. If he worried too much about Lucy, he would not have the concentration necessary to do his job and keep her safe.

"LaRue is a bloody ghost, and was even before rumors of his death," Fox said. "No one could ever find him. Isabella is our best option. Do whatever you must to regain her favor. Time is of the essence now."

"What about the dead bookseller's clerk?" Simon asked. "Where does he fit in?"

"A messenger would be my guess. I have a man working on that angle, as well as one tracking Michael Standish."

"But it all comes back to Isabella," Simon mused. "If LaRue is not involved in the plot, he may well intend to kill her. Perhaps she betrayed him and stole the list."

"All the more reason for you to get close to her. He may be planning to act at the auction."

"That auction is the crux of the whole thing. I wish there were another way besides pursuing a romantic attachment to accomplish this."

"We have tried everything else," Fox reminded him. "And the game is already started. Your best choice now is to step up the chase. Go to her home. Ignore her refusals and push your way past the butler if necessary. Force her to see you." Fox grinned like the scoundrel he had once been. "A woman like Isabella cannot resist a man who will fight for her."

Remembering Isabella's delight at the prospect of a duel between himself and Standish, Simon had to agree. "I believe you have the right of it, my friend. I will go there right now."

"Bring flowers," Fox reminded him as Simon turned to leave. "They will soften her heart even if you plant the butler a facer."

"I was thinking diamonds, actually."

"Even better. I see you have been listening to my teachings."

"I have always been a quick study."

Chapter 17

My passion burns for Love's reluctant heart,
And scorches deep when Love is set apart.

The journals of Simon, Lord Devingham,
on love

Though Simon had been prepared to battle his way into Isabella's home, there was no need. The butler stepped back to allow him in, and he found himself escorted to Isabella's morning room without incident.

"Ah, *bello mio,*" the lady cooed after the butler announced him. "I have missed your company."

He arched his brows as he came forward to kiss her hand. Garbed in a simple white dress, with her lustrous hair pulled back with a satiny ribbon, she might have been any debutante accepting calls from her suitors—except that the generous bosom revealed by the plunging neckline of her dress gave an impression that was anything but virginal. "I am gratified you have granted me forgiveness at last."

She smiled and patted the place next to her on the sofa. "Naughty Simon. Do come and talk to me a while."

"I've brought you something." He sat beside her, the musky scent of her perfume nearly stifling him. How he longed for the sweet, fresh scent of Lucy.

"A gift? For me?" Her eyes gleamed. "Where is it?"

"Here." He removed the jeweler's case from his pocket. "I saw this and thought of you."

She reached for it, but he held it beyond her grasp.

"Tell me you forgive me," he coaxed.

She gave him a slow smile, slanting him a glance from beneath her lashes. "You are a true romantic, *bello mio*. How can a woman's heart resist?"

"I don't want you to resist." He brought the box closer to her and opened the lid. "I want you to surrender."

"Che la bella collana!" Reverently, she lifted the glittering strand of diamonds from the velvet-lined box. "Such a beautiful necklace!"

"For you." He set the box aside and took the string of diamonds from her. "Allow me."

She turned, and he slipped the necklace around her neck, then fastened it. As soon as the clasp snapped, she turned around to face him, caressing the jewels with her fingertips. The sparkling stones tumbled along the tops of her breasts, emphasizing her bountiful attributes. "How does it look?"

"Stunning."

"I must see." She rose from the sofa and hurried to a small mirror hanging on the wall. She stared at the necklace, stroking it. "*Che bella*," she murmured.

He smiled, pleased that his plan appeared to be working. "I'm glad you like it."

"Like it?" She whirled to face him. "I am enchanted with it!"

"Excellent."

Her dark eyes smoldered, and she regarded him with a teasing curve to her lips. "I fear you are trying to seduce me, Simon."

"Is it working?"

"Perhaps." She approached the sofa, her hips swaying with invitation. "These diamonds—they are a temptation."

"And how do you feel about temptation?"

"Sinful." She stopped in front of him and bent forward, her breasts nearly spilling out completely. The plump flesh dangled before him in invitation, but he felt no desire to accept. "You make me think wicked thoughts, *bello mio*."

"You do the same to me." He raised his gaze from her breasts to her face. "And I can be very wicked."

"Good." She traced a finger along his jaw, then walked back to preen before the mirror.

"So," Simon asked, "does this mean I am forgiven?"

She glanced at him, her brows arched. "It is certainly a good start."

"A start? That necklace cost a fortune."

She gave a dismissive wave. "You are a man. Women do not measure love in English pounds."

"Oh? What must I do then?"

She pursed her lips in thought. "A favor perhaps."

He shifted in his seat, stretching one arm along the back of the sofa. "What sort of favor?"

She tapped her lower lip with her finger and began to walk toward him. "I would like to have a small dinner party."

"A dinner party."

"Yes." She approached the sofa and turned away just as she reached him, letting her skirts brush his legs. "At one of your houses."

He straightened in surprise. "At my house?"

"One of them." She glanced back over her shoulder. "Something near the sea perhaps."

He frowned, surprised at the odd request. "I have a small manor in Essex."

"It would be lovely if you allowed me to use it for my party." She turned toward him again and placed a finger over his lips when he would have spoken. "And asked no questions."

He hesitated, his instincts vibrating with urgency. Was this all she wanted? He'd expected more, gowns and carriages and expensive jewelry perhaps. But all she wanted was to use his house for a dinner party. . .

Or an auction.

She tilted her head so her dark curls swept across her shoulder. "Is this small thing too much to ask, *bello mio*? Can you not trust me?"

He gave her what he hoped was a besotted smile. "Nothing is too much, my precious. Consider it yours—as long as I am invited."

"Of course you are invited . . . but only you."

"No, my dear." He took her hand and pressed his lips to her fingers. "Only *you*."

Simon came home well after the dinner hour had passed. Lucy put down her book as she heard his footstep in the hall. She'd thought to lull herself to sleep with a novel, but the love story only reminded her of the tangle of her own love life.

Simon appeared in the doorway to the library. "Lucy, I expected you would have retired by now."

"I could not sleep." She closed the book and set it aside. Questions were poised on her tongue, but she dared not ask them. Wasn't certain she wanted to ask them. Instead, she simply folded her hands in her lap and waited.

He came into the room. "Have you eaten?"

"Some time ago."

"I had dinner with Fox." He went to the fire and stared into it.

Silence stretched between them, awkward and uncomfortable.

"Thank you for telling me," she said finally.

He glanced at her. "You have not asked me if I saw Isabella today."

"No, I have not." She rose from the chair and reached for her book. "If you will excuse me, Simon, I am very tired."

"Lucy." He stepped in front of her when she would have left the room. "Please, do not go."

She went to step around him, but he matched her movement.

"Lucy," he murmured, "we cannot go on like this."

She jerked her gaze to his, nearly undone by the tenderness in his eyes. "I do not know any other way."

"I hate this discomfort between us. I hate that we never talk or laugh anymore. I want things back the way they were before."

"Before, I thought I knew you. I thought we were building a marriage together. But Simon, you are a different man than I thought you were."

"I am still the same man." He smoothed his hands down her arms from her shoulders to her to her elbows. "Our first night together lingered with me long after I returned to London. You have captured my attention in a way that no woman ever has."

"But not strongly enough for you to come back to me." She jerked away from him. "You wed me, bedded me, and left me all in the span of hours. When I came here to be with you, you lied to me and let me believe you were engaging in an affair with another woman." She sniffed the air. "And I can still smell her perfume on you."

He closed his eyes and let out a long sigh. "I went to see her today, yes. But I came home to you. Every night, you are the only woman in my bed."

"Men are easily led by the physical. And I am so very afraid that our nights of passion may be all we ever have to recommend this marriage."

"Would that be so horrible? I am rather amazed by it myself."

She clasped the book to her breast in an instinctive gesture. "I want more than that. I want to learn who my husband really is, and I need to know if this marriage has a future outside of the bedchamber."

"This is who I am," he said quietly. "But I think I begin to understand. You have always been open with me, always allowed me to see your true self."

She shrugged. "I know no other way."

"Whereas I hid part of myself from you, so now you fear that I am someone other than the man you married." At her nod, he appeared to give the matter serious thought. "I am still Simon," he said finally. "Still the man who writes poetry and breeds roses. That has not changed; I just have not shown you the rest. Very well, then."

"Very well, what?"

"You are afraid that sex is all we have. I believe there is more, but we may never find it as long as the physical distracts us. I propose—" He paused, then sucked in a breath and continued. "I propose that we not share a bed for a while. That we begin our courtship all over again."

Her eyes widened. "My heavens!"

"I have always regarded marriage as a business contract," he hastened on. "Since meeting you, I realize it can be more. And I want to see how much more. I do not want to lose what we have, Lucy. Or what we might have in the future."

She knew enough about men to know that this was a huge concession on his part. Her heart warmed. "Simon, are you certain?"

He nodded, though she could tell he was not looking forward to abstinence.

"Then I accept your proposal." She chuckled. "Again."

He grinned. "I do not intend to propose marriage a second time. In fact, I rather look forward to skipping right to the honeymoon."

She blushed even as her heart tripped at the sincere desire in his eyes. "That is no way to court a lady, you scoundrel."

"Then how about this?" He pulled a jeweler's case out of his pocket and opened the lid to reveal a set of earrings with a matching necklace. The diamonds and rubies glittered like cold fire against the dark velvet.

"They're beautiful." Stunned, she hesitantly touched a stone.

"They looked like jeweled flames," he said, watching her. "They reminded me of you."

"Of me?"

"Fire. And elegance."

"Oh." She placed a hand on her bosom. "Thank you, Simon. They are stunning."

He closed the case and pressed it into her hand. "You deserve much more."

She placed the case on top of her book and clutched both items to her. "Are you certain about this?"

"Yes. Take the time you need," he said, "but not too much time. I won't be able to wait very long to hold you in my arms again."

The hunger in his tone, in his stance, warmed her throughout her body. "Good night, Simon."

"Good night, Lucy. Pleasant dreams."

He watched her go, his gaze drawn to the sway of her hips beneath the modest nightgown. Sweet heaven, he hoped this period of self-restraint would not last long.

He turned away from temptation and went directly to the small portrait of his great-uncle Bartley. He pressed a concealed spring, and a small door opened in the wall, taking Great-uncle's portrait with it. Inside the hidden cubbyhole were stacks of well-worn leather-backed journals. He took out the most recent one and shut the cupboard door, making his way to his desk.

Already the urge to write consumed him. There was so much to say, so many thoughts crowding his mind to be expressed in the private pages. . .

He paused in the act of putting ink to paper. He had been keeping these journals ever since he could write. In a family that never spoke of emotion, never admitted any true feelings for fear of offending the rules of civility, he had needed a place to express himself. All that he had ever thought, all that he was, could be found in the pages of these journals.

This was what Lucy wanted. She wanted to learn about him, wanted to sort the deception from the real man.

Why hadn't he thought of this before?

Lucy sat in bed, the novel open on her lap, but she wasn't looking at the words. Instead, she stared at the door to Simon's room, listening despite her better judgment for sounds of someone moving about.

For the first time since she had learned the truth, hope glowed within her that they might yet salvage this marriage.

The knock at the door to the hall startled her so much that she jerked, and the novel slid to the floor with a thump. Slowly she peeled back the coverlet, her mind sorting through the various possibilities but steering away from one. . .

"Lucy?" Simon called in a low voice.

She froze with one foot on the floor. He couldn't be . . . he had said. . .

He tapped again. "Lucy, let me in."

Had he changed his mind? If he looked at her and smiled at her, or, Lord help her, if he touched her. . .

She would not be able to refuse him. She never could. And then they would have accomplished nothing.

"I can see the light under the door," he said, patience heavy in his voice.

She slid completely from the bed and slowly made her way to the door, her nightrail billowing like the gossamer wings of a butterfly. She grasped the door latch with white-knuckled fingers and laid her head against the portal. "Simon, it is late."

"Open the door, Lucy. I have something for you." His voice was so close, it was as if he were speaking directly in her ear. He had to be standing as close to the door as she was, no farther away than a kiss.

She closed her eyes, trying to banish the tempting image in her mind. "Give it to me at breakfast."

"I would rather give this to you tonight."

"Simon." His name came out on a sigh. "We made an agreement. We said good night."

He was silent so long that she would have thought he had left, if not for the rustling of his clothing. "Open the door, Lucy. Trust me to keep my word."

She took a deep breath, intellect battling with longing, then swung open the door.

He stood waiting on the other side, his cravat undone, his hair askew as if he had run his hands through it. His sober gaze pinned her, and she knew that if he asked it of her, she would welcome him into her bed without a second's hesitation.

Then he reached for her, and it took her a moment to realize that he wasn't making an advance. She glanced down at his hand and saw that he held out a ragged leather journal.

"What is this?"

"My journal from the year I first got recruited into the organization." He gestured again. "You wanted to know who Simon Severton really is. Take it."

Surprise slowed her movements as she took the

book from his hand. "You want me to read this?"

"Of course I want you to read it. Just . . . have a care not to leave it lying about. These pages contain my every thought and feeling during those years. I'd prefer to keep those things between us."

She clutched the book to her bosom as she realized what he was saying. "No one but me will read your words."

He gave a jerky bob of his head. "Good. My thanks."

She nodded in acknowledgment, and they stood there, just looking at each other as long moments ticked by. She was tempted to invite him in, but before the words could leave her lips, he took a step backward into the hallway.

"Very well then. Good night, Lucy."

Her fingers tightened around the precious piece of himself that he had given her, scribbled on paper and wrapped in leather. "Good night, Simon."

He gave a small bow, then started down the hall to his own chamber. Lucy closed the door and leaned back against it, looking down at the book in her hands as if it were made of diamonds.

Unlike the romantic novel she had taken from the library, this volume was bound to keep her awake until the cock crowed at dawn.

Chapter 18

I cannot live my life as a useless aristocrat when others around me are suffering. I was given the gift of intellect, and I would rather use it to help my fellow man, rather than compose witticisms for the jaded and corruptible.

The journals of Simon, Lord Devingham,
on living a life of purpose

The jaded and corruptible.

The words stayed with Lucy as she yawned through her morning toilette, then made her way downstairs. As predicted, she had stayed up until the wee hours, devouring the pages of Simon's diary until she could no longer keep her eyes open. Though she had yet to finish the book, she had already learned with vivid clarity the sort of man he was. The diary covered the first few months after he had begun his service to the

Crown and had given her a glimpse into the idealist who lurked in the body of the sober earl.

Who would have thought that bookish Simon, a man who had been handed everything by virtue of his birth, should feel such a compelling need for purpose?

Dobbins met her as she reached the bottom of the staircase. "Good afternoon, my lady."

"Afternoon? What time is it?"

"Nearly three o'clock."

"Oh, dear! I did sleep later than I'd expected."

"Miss Matthews has just arrived," Dobbins said. "She is waiting for you in the gold room. I have ordered refreshments."

"Thank you, Dobbins." Stifling a yawn, Lucy went to meet Gin.

Her friend was seated on the sofa, leafing through the latest issue of *La Belle Assemblée*. She looked up as Lucy came into the room. "Good Lord, I don't understand how Aunt Beatrice spends so many hours studying these things. I'm bored silly."

"I would say it is definitely not your sort of publication." Lucy sat down across from Gin and admired the blue spotted muslin her friend wore. "Is that a new dress?"

"The last one we bought at Madame Dauphine's."

"It suits you." She stifled another yawn.

Gin closed the magazine and regarded her with raised eyebrows. "Didn't you sleep well?"

"Actually, not much. I was up until nearly sunrise, reading."

"I can't imagine any book being that fascinating."

Lucy smiled, keeping the secret of Simon's journal to herself. "It was the most riveting piece I had ever read."

"Well, I hope you can keep yourself awake for our outing today."

Lucy fought through the drowsiness of her mind, trying to recall. "Outing?"

"It's Tuesday, Lucy. Today is the day you can deliver that box."

The box. Memory came crashing back to her. Today was the day Mrs. Nelson was due to return to London. The day Lucy was supposed to deliver Arminda's legacy.

Up until last night, she had wanted this day to come, had looked forward to returning to the peace and serenity of Devingham and leaving the confusing mess of her marriage behind. But now that Simon had stepped forward and handed her a key to himself, she had hope that it wasn't too late.

She might not be returning to Devingham after all.

"Are you all right?"

Gin's concerned question brought her out of her thoughts. "Yes. Yes, I am fine. I just had not realized what day it is."

Her friend's face creased in worry. "Is your

husband still going to force you to go home afterward, Lucy? Even now that you know the truth?"

"I do not know. Perhaps not."

"I wouldn't go," Gin declared. "I would stay right here and fight for what I wanted."

Lucy couldn't help but smile. "I know you would."

Dobbins came in just then, and Lucy looked up, expecting him to be accompanied by a servant with a tray. Instead, the butler announced, "Mrs. John Nelson to see you, my lady."

Gin and Lucy exchanged startled glances. "Send her in, Dobbins."

The butler bowed, then showed the lady into the room.

Daphne Nelson was not a small woman. Tall of stature and of queenly proportions, she made up for her very ordinary looks with a pair of stunning blue eyes.

Her mother's eyes.

Mrs. Nelson hesitated, looking from one to the other. Lucy smiled in greeting. "I am Lady Devingham," she said. "And this is my friend, Miss Matthews."

"I am Mrs. Daphne Nelson. I understand you called on me while I was away."

"That is true." Lucy looked up as the footman entered with the tea tray. "Will you sit down and have some tea?"

"Thank you." Mrs. Nelson sat down in an armchair.

"Shall I pour?" Without waiting for an answer, Lucy took up the teapot and filled a cup for her unexpected guest. The next few moments were taken up with each of the ladies preparing her tea to her taste and selecting a biscuit to go with the steaming beverage.

Once they were all settled, Lucy said, "How was your trip, Mrs. Nelson?"

Her visitor gave her a considering look, and Lucy was jolted once again at the sight of Arminda's eyes in a stranger's face. "Lady Devingham, I thank you for your courtesy, but I must admit to being at a loss. You and I do not know each other, yet you paid a call at my home. Curiosity is what brings me here, and I apologize, but I am too impatient to engage in pleasantries until that question is answered."

Lucy smiled. "No, forgive *me*. Of course you must be puzzled as to why a complete stranger would call on you with no warning."

"Much less a countess." Mrs. Nelson glanced around at the tasteful, yet expensive, décor. "No offense to you, Lady Devingham, but we do not move in the same circles."

"I understand completely, Mrs. Nelson." Lucy paused, trying to find the right words. "Unfortunately, I am sorry to tell you that I came seeking you to relay some bad news."

Mrs. Nelson's fingers tightened around her teacup. "What sort of bad news?"

Lucy sighed and set down her own cup. Meeting the other woman's gaze, she said, "Mrs. Nelson, I regret to be the one to tell you, but your mother passed away two weeks ago."

Mrs. Nelson fumbled the teacup, then set it and the saucer down on the table with a clatter. "I do not know what you mean, Lady Devingham. My mother died some years ago."

Lucy frowned. She knew there had been some bad blood between the two, but would that history cause the woman not to acknowledge her own mother? "How odd," she said, watching the other woman carefully. "For Arminda Wolcott died just two weeks ago at Devingham. And you have her eyes."

Mrs. Nelson's face froze, her expression a combination of fear and defiance. "Blue eyes are quite common."

"Actually, Arminda's eyes were quite distinctive. As are yours." Lucy leaned forward, touching the woman's hand. "I knew Arminda quite well, Mrs. Nelson, and I am confident that you are indeed her daughter. The resemblance is unmistakable."

The woman jerked to her feet. "I have told you that this woman is not my mother. I do not understand your game, Lady Devingham, but I shall not tolerate it for another moment. Good day to you." She started toward the door at a brisk pace.

Lucy stood as well. "I lost my mother when I was twelve years old, Mrs. Nelson, and no matter how angry I was at her, I would never have denied her to be anyone but who she was."

Mrs. Nelson paused, her trembling hand on the door latch. "I am sorry for your tragedy, but that has nothing to do with me."

Lucy came toward her, sensing progress. "In the end, she was still my mother, and I lost her. The pain of that does not change, no matter how harsh the words between you."

Gin stood as well. "We know you haven't spoken to her in years, but she's dead now. Whatever happened between you, it's finally over."

"Over?" Mrs. Nelson whipped around, her eyes wild and tearful. "What do you know of it? My mother's scandals humiliated me to the point where I had to change my name to escape the gossip."

"So Arminda Wolcott is your mother then," Lucy said.

"Wolcott? Is that what she was calling herself?" Mrs. Nelson dug out a handkerchief and dabbed at her moist eyes. "My mother's name was Arminda, yes. But as far as I am concerned, she has been dead to me for years."

Lucy flinched. "Surely—"

"It is true, Lady Devingham," Mrs. Nelson continued, tucking away the handkerchief again. "I'm sorry I have shocked you with such a vulgar word, but it is the truth. After my father died, my mother courted scandal with all the abandon of a debutante discarding evening dresses. Her exploits generated such gossip that I left her house when I was fifteen years old. I changed my name and made my own way in the world. As far as I am concerned, that is the day my mother died."

"She left something for you," Lucy said quietly.

"I do not want anything from that woman," Mrs. Nelson declared. "Toss it into the fire and burn it. That's what I would do anyway." She jerked open the door and marched out of the room, leaving Lucy staring after her.

"Well," Gin said, as they listened to the staccato of the woman's angry footsteps toward the front door. "I suppose you'll be staying a while longer in London."

The letter was delivered by a servant rather than by post. Simon retired to his study to read the missive in private.

He knew who had sent it as soon as he tore open the seal. Isabella's distinctive perfume wafted from the paper and surrounded him.

As discussed, I would like to hold a small dinner party at your estate in Essex this Thursday. Naturally you will escort me.

Keep your promise and ask no questions.

At last. It had to be the auction—why else would Isabella want to hold an affair in one of his homes instead of her own town house? And now she had set the date.

He folded the missive, a grim smile curving his lips. LaRue was bound to hear about the auction if he wasn't already involved in it. Everything would be resolved soon, and Simon could turn his attention toward his wife.

He tucked away Isabella's note in his secret cabinet, realizing that he would have to tell Lucy about his promise to Isabella. On the one hand, he didn't want to reveal his plans because he didn't want to hurt her. She understood his reasons for courting Isabella, but the situation apparently still wounded her.

On the other hand, he did not want to cause more of a rift between them with deliberate deception.

He wondered if she'd read the journal, if it had helped his cause at all. If the writings of his heart and mind did not move her, then this marriage would eventually degrade into a cold association where each of them lived separate lives with separate lovers.

Just the thought of another man sampling Lucy's intoxicating passion made him want to break something. Preferably the nose of her hypothetical lover.

A knock came at his study door. "My lord," Dobbins called. "Mr. Masseri is here."

"Excellent," he muttered, shutting the door firmly on the hidden cabinet. He raised his voice to answer the butler. "Thank you, Dobbins. Do show him to the ballroom."

"Very well, my lord."

Simon made his way swiftly out of the room. Perfect. He was in the mood for a fight, and Giovanni Masseri would provide it.

Mrs. Nelson's words lingered with Lucy even after Gin had left. The woman had been so vehement, so unforgiving. Her mother was dead, yet she wanted nothing to do with even her memory.

Is that what would happen to her and Simon if she could not find some way to accept the truth about him?

She didn't want that, didn't want to be a wife who saw her husband a handful of times a year and otherwise lived a life of solitude. Neither did she want a marriage where each of them sought solace in the arms of a lover. She wanted a true union based on trust and affection, but if she could not reconcile herself to the facts, then that would never come to pass.

Simon had taken the first step by revealing part of himself through the words in his diaries. Now it was her turn to take a step toward him.

Upon inquiring as to the whereabouts of her husband, the servants directed her to the ballroom.

The hiss of blades reached her before she had even walked through the door. Curious, she peered inside the cavernous room. Two men in fencing masks danced around each other in a spirited bout, foils flashing in the fading sunlight.

She slipped into the room and watched the match, marveling at the grace and speed of the opponents. One of them noticed her and stopped in his tracks, and the other fencer jabbed him in the heart.

"Ha! You are dead, my lord."

"Too true, Giovanni." Simon pulled off the protective headgear and looked at her, surprise lingering in his eyes. "Lucy, what are you doing here?"

"Looking for you." She glanced at his companion.

"Lucy, this is Signor Giovanni Masseri. Giovanni, my wife, Lady Devingham."

"Piacere," the fencing master said with a bow.

"Mr. Masseri," she acknowledged with a nod.

"I believe we are finished for today, Giovanni," Simon said, extending a hand. "Same time next week?"

"Va bene," the Italian replied, shaking it. "I will be here."

"And I look forward to evening the score between us." Simon handed the mask to the fencing master and came forward to offer Lucy his arm. "Come, my dear, let us take a stroll on the terrace while Signor Masseri collects the equipment."

Lucy took Simon's arm, craning her neck to observe as the Italian fencing master collected the equipment. Only when she and Simon reached the doorway leading from the ballroom to the back terrace did she focus on her husband.

Simon watched her, amusement tugging at his lips. "Have you never seen a fencing match before?"

"Now that I think on the matter, I should have expected that, as a gentleman, fencing would be among your abilities," she said, "but I had no idea that you had developed such expertise. I imagine that a man in your position would find such a skill to be useful."

"It can be."

"I was quite impressed."

"Thank you, but you really only saw a few minutes of the bout. And I got killed."

"Does that mean I am a wealthy widow?" She sent him a mischievous grin.

He chuckled. "Are you so eager to see me dispatched to the netherworld?"

"Of course not." Her humor faded. "I would never wish you ill, Simon."

"I know." He stroked a knuckle down her cheek. "I was simply funning with you."

"So much has happened." She stepped away from him, unable to concentrate when he touched her. "Mrs. Nelson came to call."

"And who is that?"

She gave him an exasperated look. "Arminda's daughter."

He stiffened. "Oh. Of course. I imagine you left your card when you called on her last."

"Indeed, and so she came to visit this morning, having just returned from Scotland."

He moved to the balustrade and looked down at the gardens below. "Does this mean you are going home to Devingham then?"

His impassive tone made it impossible to discern his mood. "Do you want me to?"

"It might be safer for you there."

Her heart sank. "Then you do want me gone."

He turned to face her, and her breath caught at the emotion blazing in his eyes. "Had I my way, Lucy, you would never leave my side as long as we both still breathed."

Her heart pounded in her breast, hope like an elixir singing through her veins. "I do not want to go."

"Then don't." He pulled her into his arms. "I have been trying to exercise patience, but I miss you, Lucy. I miss the way things used to be, the way you feel in my arms, the way you make me laugh at breakfast."

"Only at breakfast?"

He chuckled and rested his forehead against hers. "I do believe I am falling in love with you, Lucy Severton."

"Oh, Simon." She stared up into his eyes, amazed that he had confessed such a thing yet wishing she could return the sentiment. She had come to care for the Simon she had married, and she didn't doubt that once she had absorbed all that had happened, those feelings would grow to the point where she could make her own declaration.

"I can see the emotions chasing across your face. You need not return my feelings, my sweet. At least not yet." He kissed her, and all rational thought evaporated from her mind as she lost herself in the power of his touch.

The sound of one carriage driver shouting at another reached them from the street and broke the spell. Lucy pulled back, her heartbeat skipping around like a child's ball.

"What is it?" His arms remained around her, the warmth and scent of his body a nearly irresistible temptation.

She bit her lower lip, hating that she must shatter their brief euphoria. "I have not yet been able to completely accept what has happened recently."

"Did you read the journal?"

"Most of it."

"It seemed to be what you wanted."

"It is helping me to get to understand you better." She cupped his cheek. "But only time can truly do that. Now that I know the truth, it will take a while for me to get used to it, to learn my husband all over again without the shadow of deception between us."

"I never intended to hurt you, Lucy."

"I know." She gave him a sad smile. "But you never intended me to find out either."

"That was true in the beginning. However, I had recently decided to tell you the truth. I could not bear lying to you anymore."

Her mouth fell open. "When did this happen?"

He gave her a rueful grin. "The day you left for Lady Wexford's house. I had come home to tell you, but you were gone."

"It comforts me to know that." She pressed her lips to his, then pulled back as the kiss again showed signs of exploding into mind-numbing passion. She blew out a hard breath, struggling to think clearly. "Well. I did come looking for you to talk about a different matter entirely."

"Very well." He sent a heated glance over her as she stepped out of his arms. "I will do my best to concentrate."

A thrill shot through her at the desire in his tone, and it was an effort to keep her own voice steady. "I told you Mrs. Nelson came to call. What I did not mention was that she wants nothing to do with the box. She is very bitter about her relationship with her mother."

"Really. Quite an unexpected turn."

"She tried to deny that Arminda even was her mother and went so far as to tell me her mother had died years ago." She sighed. "It was very unsettling. How can a daughter hate her mother so?"

"Ah, my sweet, innocent bride. You would be amazed how many close family relatives despise each other."

"They say hate is the other side of the coin of love," Lucy mused. "I suppose it is true."

"More often than not." He stroked a hand over her hair, and she took comfort in his touch. "Did she give any reason for her feelings?"

"She did not give specifics, but apparently Arminda lived an adventurous life, and her daughter was very hurt by the gossip. Mrs. Nelson left home when she was merely fifteen, changed her name, and built a life away from her mother. They never spoke again." Lucy shook her head. "I cannot equate the Arminda I knew with a woman who lived so scandalous a life that her own daughter disowned her. And now Mrs. Nelson refuses to accept the box, so my duty to Arminda is still unfinished."

"There is more to the story that you do not know." Simon paused, as if searching for words. "Arminda Wolcott was one of us."

"One of who?"

He gave her an exasperated look. "Arminda was part of our organization. She was a spy, Lucy."

Lucy could only gape at him. "A spy? A female spy?"

"There are several such women," he said, watching her with careful deliberation. "Arminda was quite effective in her youth. Her exploits, as you put it, were directly related to her assignments to uncover information for the good of England. When she grew older and her health began to deteriorate, she retired to the cottage on my estate to live out the rest of her life under my protection."

"Gracious me! I would never have imagined such a thing!"

"I have to wonder in this case if Mrs. Nelson was aware of her mother's true reasons for her actions."

"She did not give any indication one way or the other." Lucy pursed her lips in thought. "Do you suppose that knowing the truth would help her accept her mother's legacy?"

"I do not know." He shrugged. "I thought telling you the truth would make things better, but it is apparently not quite that simple."

She glanced away. "Perhaps not. But at least we are both trying to rectify the problem."

"I suggest you approach Mrs. Nelson and tell her the whole of it. Tell her that Arminda confided it to you before she died. The lady has passed on now, and there can be no harm in comforting her daughter."

"I will try doing just that." Lucy stood on tiptoe and pressed a kiss to his cheek. "Thank you, Simon. Perhaps knowing will make her at least accept the box. She can wait to open it until she is ready."

"And when will you be ready, my sweet?" He took her hand, unfolding it slowly to press a kiss to her palm.

Heat exploded between her thighs at his low, passionate words. She longed to lean into him, to let him strip the clothes from both of them and take her on a mind-spinning journey of skin-scorching desire right there on the terrace. Instead, she closed her hand as if to preserve his kiss. "Soon, husband."

"Wife." His eyes burned with hunger. "It had best be *soon*, lest I forget I am a gentleman."

"You are always a gentleman."

"I have my limits." The warning in his voice sent a delicious quiver through her.

"Then we had best not test them." Her voice sounded husky to her own ears, and she cleared her throat. "Will I see you at dinner?"

He bared his teeth in a predator's smile, and she knew then that she was looking at the side of Simon that he had always hidden from her, the part that made him a dangerous man to those who threatened England. "Yes, I will be dining at home this evening."

"I will see you at dinner then." She hurried back into the house, prickling with awareness that he held himself on a very tight leash—a leash that might snap under the right circumstances.

She had a vision in her mind of Simon pursuing her into the house, of him catching up to her and yanking the clothes from her body right there in the middle of the ballroom. Of his laying her down on the polished wood floor, his hungry kisses setting fire to her own simmering passion, his greedy hands sweeping over her bare flesh, spreading her thighs wide ... of his taking her hard and fast in the middle of a room where propriety was worshipped like a deity while scandal was whispered behind open fans.

Of her joyfully exploding with release, begging him to do it again.

She quickened her pace out of the ballroom, lest she give in to her own lurid imagination and beg him to make the fantasy come true.

Chapter 19

*I have heard that the Oriental people have roses
with repeating blooms. A clever people, they
found that nature was not as effective as they
desired. So, rather than change their desire,
they changed nature to suit their necessity. I would
that such a thing were as easy with a woman!*

The journals of Simon, Lord Devingham,
on resourcefulness

Three days had passed—three days where
Lucy and Gin had tried in vain to call on
Mrs. Nelson again, only to be turned from her
door by her manservant. Three days where they
had waited outside the Nelson residence to catch
a glimpse of the lady, to successfully follow her
to Pall Mall to try and have a word, but she had
caught sight of them and left abruptly in her
carriage.

And three days since Simon had told her he was falling in love with her.

Lucy sat before her vanity table, garbed in one of Madame Dauphine's fashionable creations, and watched Molly in the mirror while the maid arranged her hair.

The connecting door between their rooms opened, and Simon entered, dressed in traveling clothes. Their eyes met for one, hot second in the mirror, then his gaze dropped to the daring décolletage of her new gown, frankly admiring the swells of her breasts. Her breath caught at the look on his face—voracious, barely leashed need.

"Leave us, Molly," she said, her voice trembling with answering desire.

"But, my lady, your hair—"

"Molly," Simon said. "Go."

The maid cast him an anxious look, then fled the room.

Lucy chuckled, the sound husky in the sudden silence. "You frightened her, Simon."

"Do I frighten you?" He came up behind her and laid his hands on her shoulders, watching her in the mirror.

"Frighten is not the word I would use."

"What is the proper word then?" He splayed his fingers across the bared skin of her collarbone. "Excite?"

"Definitely excite." Her eyes closed to nearly slits as he trailed his fingers lower along the plunging neckline of her dress. "I have never denied what your touch does to me."

His hands flexed on her delicate flesh. "Have a care, my sweet. It would not take much to make me forget myself."

"You tempt me to forget as well."

He made a low, growling noise and leaned forward to nip her ear. "I am but a man, Lucy, and can only take so much." He nuzzled his mouth against her neck, and she jolted as pure, sweet desire shot right to her loins.

"Oh, Simon," she breathed.

He slid his hands beneath her dress and cupped her breasts, pulling them free of their fragile covering without effort. Her hardened nipples were a testimony to his effect on her. "Now there's a lovely sight." He rubbed his thumbs over the pouting tips, and fire pooled between her thighs. "I have missed looking at you, my beautiful wife."

She parted her lips, sucking in air as she watched his hands caress her in the reflection. "We cannot," she panted. "I have an engagement this afternoon, and from your dress, I would say you do, too."

"Indeed, you are correct." He straightened, taking his hands from her breasts. She reached down to tug her bodice back into place, but he said, "No, leave it."

She dropped her hands to her lap. He reached over, flipped open her jewel box, and withdrew the ruby necklace he had given her. "Allow me to play the lady's maid, my dear." He draped it around her neck and fastened it. She reached up to touch it, aroused by the pagan appearance of her bared breasts combined with the glittering crimson jewels.

He bent down again, his eyes level with hers in the mirror. "You look magnificent, Lucy. Like Hippolyte leading her Amazons into battle." Then he tenderly tugged her dress back into place and stepped away.

"You are a wicked man, Simon." She turned in her chair to face him. "How am I to concentrate on my task with a memory such as that haunting me all evening?"

"Welcome to my private hell." He bowed.

She shook her head and turned back to her mirror, stirred up just by looking at him. Her fingers trembled as she unfastened the necklace which, stunning as it was, did not go with her less-extravagant afternoon garb.

His gaze followed her movements as she put back the rubies and withdrew the simple yet striking Devingham pearls. Silently, he took the strand from her and fastened it around her neck.

She watched him in the mirror, still shaken by his attentions. "Tonight I intend to have a word with Mrs. Nelson. She has been avoiding me for the past few days, but this time I believe I will be able to catch a moment with her."

"And how will you accomplish that?" Finished with his task, he met her gaze in the looking glass as she reached for one of the matching pearl earrings.

"Gin prevailed on Lady Wexford to have her friend Lady Trudor invite Mrs. Nelson to the theater tonight," she replied, fastening the jewel to her lobe. "Apparently Lord Trudor is acquainted with Mr. Nelson through their military careers."

Simon picked up her other earring and handed it to her. "I assume that you have also endeavored to be present at the theater?"

"Yes. Lady Wexford has obtained a box for the seven o'clock performance."

"And dinner?"

"We plan to have a light meal before the performance and a proper dinner afterward. I am to be at Lady Wexford's by half past four."

"I wish you luck then."

Something in his voice struck her as odd. She tilted her head to fasten her earring and fixed him with an inquisitive look. "Dare I ask about your plans tonight, Simon? Or would I prefer not to know?"

He rubbed the back of his neck. "I meant to tell you before now, but you have been out much of the time, chasing after Mrs. Nelson. And of course, our evenings have been spent . . . apart from each other."

The earring in place, she pushed aside her own

pang of longing for marital relations and focused on the fact that he was finally confiding in her. "Tell me what is going on, Simon."

"I leave for Bridgemoor today."

"Bridgemoor?"

"A small manor house we have in Essex." He paused. "Isabella is coming with me."

She should have expected the pain that statement brought, but the ache in her heart still shocked with its intensity. "I see." She turned back to her mirror and reached for her face powder.

"Isabella has asked to use the house for a dinner party. I believe this will be the setting of the auction for the list. It is the opportunity we have been waiting for."

"So you hope to obtain that list tonight."

"Yes." He came and laid his hands on her shoulders as she dusted powder on her face. "This is business, Lucy. You know I do not want Isabella."

"It is still hard for me to watch you go, knowing you will be charming another woman." She tilted her head to rub her cheek against his hand. "I am greedy, Simon. I do not want to share you."

"I like that you are greedy." He dropped a kiss on her temple. "After tonight, Isabella Montelucci will no longer be part of our lives."

"I like the sound of that. Is Mr. Foxworth going with you?"

"No, Fox does not participate in these types of assignments anymore."

"I do not like the idea of your going alone. You have no idea what this woman might do."

"I will not be alone. We have arranged for some men to masquerade as servants. They are already in place."

"All well and good, but I would feel better if Mr. Foxworth was with you."

He sighed. "Fox has been limited to decoding French communiqués since his accident. His leg cannot handle the stress of a fight."

Lucy turned in her chair. "What happened to him, Simon? I have heard rumors, but Lady Wexford says you were there that night."

"I was." He pulled out his pocket watch. "It is nearly two o'clock. I had best leave now if I hope to arrive in Essex on time."

"Simon." She put her hand on his arm to stop him when he would have walked away. "Please tell me what happened to Mr. Foxworth. I would really like to know."

His mouth tightened. "It was my fault. I do not like to talk about it."

"I understand that, and after today, I will never ask you again."

He tucked his pocketwatch away. "Very well. I will make this quick, since I must leave within the next quarter hour. On the night he was injured, Fox and I were to meet some people who had information on Antoine LaRue."

"That French assassin you mentioned."

He looked impressed. "Yes. Your memory is excellent. At any rate, a woman I was courting at the time—her name was Georgina—followed me to the meeting. She burst in with some wild notion in her mind that I was tumbling a housemaid."

"Which you were not because that is not the sort of man you are."

Surprise flickered across his face and then he smiled. "Thank you for realizing that."

"I am learning about you," she said softly.

"Indeed you are. Needless to say, her arrival spooked the other men, and they tried to run away. In the melee that followed, Fox was hurt when he saved my life."

"I see now why you were so determined to send me back to Devingham. No doubt you expected something similar to happen with me."

"I did." He shook his head, no doubt reliving the events in his mind. "It scarred Fox, too, and not just on the outside."

"I understand." She rose and went to fetch her reticule where Molly had laid it on the bed. "What happened to Georgina?"

"My superiors made an agreement with her father, and she was married off to a wealthy peer who spends most of his time in Scotland."

"Convenient." A thought occurred as she checked the contents of her bag. "This is why you wanted a wife who would stay in the country."

"It was. I could not take the chance that a woman

would endanger herself—and my assignment—by being in the wrong place at the wrong time."

"So much of what has happened makes sense now. Your strange mood changes when I first arrived, for instance."

"I wanted you to stay with me, but I knew you had to go, for safety. It was killing me."

"And now I must step back and watch you go into danger." She closed the little bag and slipped the string over her wrist. "You are much more than the sweet, bookish poet I thought I had wed."

"I am bookish. And a poet."

"And many other things." She came to him and kissed his lips. "Come home to me, Simon. Whatever the outcome tonight, just come home to me."

"There is no place else I would rather be. And Lucy?"

"Yes, husband?"

"I shall send Molly in to finish arranging your hair."

Lucy glanced in the mirror and gave a cry of alarm as she saw that her hair was, indeed, only half-done. "Wicked man! You might have told me sooner!" She plopped down in front of her vanity table again.

He left the room chuckling. Lucy hugged the sound close to her heart, more than aware that there was always a chance that things could go wrong, and she might never hear his laughter again.

* * *

When the Nelsons first entered Lady Wexford's theater box, Lucy thought Mrs. Nelson would turn and flee once she realized who was waiting for her. The woman maintained her poise, probably for the sake of her husband, who clearly wanted to impress Lord Trudor, but she took care never to look in Lucy's direction.

At the intermission, they all filed out of the box to seek refreshment. Lucy tried to catch Mrs. Nelson, but the lady and her husband slipped out and rapidly disappeared into the crowd. Lady Wexford and Lady Trudor hailed an acquaintance and hurried to speak to her.

Lord Trudor stopped on his way out of the box. "May I fetch you a lemonade, Lady Devingham?"

Lucy smiled at the elderly man. "Thank you, Lord Trudor. That would be lovely."

As he made his way to the refreshment area, Gin came up behind Lucy. "I've got to find the privy," she whispered. "You wait here for Mrs. Nelson."

Lucy nodded and went back to her seat, hoping she would be able to get Mrs. Nelson alone. She was contemplating her exact words when two women entered the box, giggling and whispering to each other. They both looked to be a bit older than Lucy, one with dark hair and one with auburn. They stumbled into the back of one of the seats, and that was when the dark-haired one noticed Lucy.

"Who are you?" she demanded. "Why are you in our box?"

Lucy raised her brows at the shrewish tone. "I am Lady Devingham, and I believe it is you who is in the wrong box."

The auburn-haired woman tugged at her friend's sleeve. "She has the right of it, Maude. There is your Percy, over there in the next box."

The one called Maude squinted across the way. "Oh! So sorry," she stammered, her words slurring. "Wrong box."

Lucy wrinkled her nose at the unmistakable scent of spirits emanating from the woman. "Good evening to you."

The dark-haired woman started to leave, then stopped and looked back. "Did you say you are Lady Devingham?"

"I am."

Maude snickered. "Then that would be your husband sniffing after that Italian woman."

Lucy stiffened, and the auburn-haired lady shushed her friend. "Maude, be civil."

"Sally, this is the Countess of Devingham. Newly wed, are you not? Terrible thing to happen so soon after the vows are spoken."

Sally sent an apologetic look toward Lucy. "That is nothing more than common gossip, Maude. Let us leave Lady Devingham to enjoy the play."

"You are right. Poor thing needs some amusement. After all, her husband is entertaining himself, eh?"

"I am sorry," Sally whispered. She guided her intoxicated friend out of the box and past Mrs. Nelson, who stood frozen near the doorway.

Lucy glanced around, noting the whispers and pitiful glances from the patrons around her. She clenched her hands in her lap, stung by the malicious tongue-wagging even though she knew it was based on deception. Society tended to believe the obvious, and with Simon's concerted pursuit of Isabella, the clear conclusion was a sordid affair.

And she was the naïve bride who was the target of rumor and laughter.

Mrs. Nelson sat down in the seat beside her. "I remember what it felt like," she said quietly. "I am sorry you must endure such hurtful words."

Lucy looked at the woman. "Thank you. You are very kind."

Mrs. Nelson nodded and began to rise to move back to her seat.

"Mrs. Nelson," Lucy said, laying a hand on her arm. "May I ask you a question?"

The lady hesitated, wariness evident on her face. Then she lowered herself back into the chair, her expression wary. "Ask your question."

The thrill of victory was enough to soothe the sting of the drunken woman's words. "I grew to know Arminda very well," she murmured, conscious of the people around them. "Are you aware that her actions were designed to distract people from realizing that she was doing something else? Something to help keep England safe from its enemies?"

Mrs. Nelson stiffened. "She told you that?"

"Yes. Did you know?"

The lady gave a stiff nod. "I did. But by the time she confided in me, the damage was done. I could no longer stand the constant scandal."

"So you could never forgive your mother, even knowing the truth."

"No." Blue eyes blazing, Mrs. Nelson rose. "And do not attempt to make me change my mind. I have a good life, Lady Devingham. Let me be." She stormed over to her chair just as Mr. Nelson reappeared with a lemonade for his lady. He sat down beside his wife, and the opportunity for more private conversation was gone.

So Mrs. Nelson had known the truth, but she had still chosen not to forgive her mother. Instead, she had left home and created a new life for herself and never contacted Arminda again.

Because Arminda had waited too long to confide in her daughter, their relationship had been destroyed forever.

Is that what would happen to her and Simon? Was their marriage doomed?

No. She refused to accept such a thing.

She glanced over at the Nelsons. Until she managed to resolve her own problem with her marriage, she would not be able to encourage Mrs. Nelson to forgive her mother and accept the box. She refused to be the hypocrite.

Suddenly, it all seemed too much to bear. Too many people in the theater, too much drama outside of it. She came to a decision and stood.

"I have a headache," she told the startled couple. "Would you convey my regrets to Lady Wexford? I am going home."

"Of course," Mr. Nelson said. "It will be my pleasure."

"Thank you." She glanced at Mrs. Nelson. "Good evening to both of you."

She left the box and headed for the exit, working her way against all the people who were headed back to the theater after intermission. She called for her carriage. As soon as the equipage was brought around, she climbed inside the well-sprung vehicle and settled back against the squabs with a sigh. She was glad she had brought her own carriage instead of riding with Lady Wexford and Gin. She had not been certain if she would need to leave in a hurry, but it was best to be prepared.

A servant had just closed the door behind her, when the one on the other side opened. A slender man leaped into the carriage, his brow sweaty and his eyes desperate. In his shaking hands, he held a pistol pointed straight at her heart.

"Good evening, Lady Devingham," he panted, wiping his face and forehead with his sleeve. "I suggest you be very quiet and do exactly what I tell you."

"Who are you?" she asked, staring at the weapon.

"I do not want to hurt you," he told her. "I simply want to talk to you about something. Or rather, someone."

"Who?"

The man's thin face hardened. "Antoine LaRue."

Chapter 20

I can remember the first time I ever had to rush to the aid of a comrade in danger. I was not quite fast enough, and poor Buckley paid the price. At least Fox is alive and as irascible as ever, though I still regret that his injuries came at the cost of saving my life.

The journals of Simon, Lord Devingham,
on accepting the past

"I do not know anyone named Antoine LaRue."

"Ah, but I believe your husband does." The coach lurched into motion, and the man scrabbled to keep his balance though the pistol did not waver.

He seemed somewhat sickly, and she wondered if she would be able to wrest the weapon away from him. "We are newly married," she said. "I do not know many of my husband's acquaintances."

"I do not think even your husband knows how dangerous LaRue can be." His breathing had become more labored. "I must warn him." His hand began to shake. "Take me to . . . take me to your husband."

"He is out of town."

"The devil take it! Do you know where he is? Can we get word to him?"

"Yes, I know where he is."

"There isn't much time." His hand fell down into his lap, as if he could no longer hold his arm extended. He sucked in air like a man who had run for miles. "Devingham is in danger."

"Who are you?" she demanded.

"My name . . . is Avery Felix." He dabbed at his sweating brow with his sleeve. "Until a few days ago, I was in France."

She drew back. "You are French?"

"No." He gave her a wan smile. "I am English."

"What were you doing in France then?"

"My duty." He closed his eyes. "My duty . . . for England."

She slowly reached out a hand for the pistol, but just as her fingers grazed it, he opened his eyes. She jerked her hand back.

"Take it." He opened his hand, and she gingerly claimed the weapon. "I did not mean . . . to frighten you."

With the gun safely in her possession, she focused on the stranger, who clearly was ill. "Shall I summon a physician for you, Mr. Felix?"

"No. I must find your husband." His eyes drifted halfway closed. "Must warn him."

"He may already know," she said, struggling to decide if she should believe that the man worked with Simon. What if this were a trap, and he was the enemy?

Mr. Felix shook his head. "No, he does not know. No one does." He coughed, great heaving spasms that shook his thin body.

Lucy frowned at him. If he was the enemy, he was the saddest example of one she had ever seen. "I still believe I should send for a physician, Mr. Felix. You do not look well."

He managed a pained grin. "If you had cheated death, my lady, you would not look well either."

"You had best explain yourself, sir, as I am still unclear if I should summon a physician or the watch."

"LaRue tried to kill me. Left me for dead." He sucked in a breath, clearly an effort. "Never made that mistake before."

"Good heavens, are you saying that Antoine LaRue thought he had killed you, but you survived?"

He nodded. "No one ever has."

"So you saw his face. You know what he looks like."

"She," Mr. Felix corrected. "Antoine LaRue . . . is a woman."

"A woman! Are you certain?"

He opened his eyes and stared right at her, his own blazing with indignation. "When someone tries to . . . to kill you, you remember what she looks like."

The famous assassin was a woman? Could it be . . . ? "Isabella," she murmured.

He jerked, his eyes blazing as he struggled to sit up straighter. "Isabella," he repeated. "Yes. Isabella . . . Montelucci. She is LaRue."

"And Simon is with her."

"Get help."

"Yes," she agreed. "We must get help." She thumped on the ceiling of the carriage and shouted a new destination to the coachman.

"Devingham . . . in danger."

Lucy regarded her fading companion grimly. "Not if I have anything to say about it."

John Foxworth was astonished when Peters announced not only Lady Devingham on his doorstep at nearly half past eight o'clock, but also Miss Matthews and a sickly fellow of unknown identity.

"What are you doing here? Have you no care for your reputation?" Fox abandoned his latest encoded missives and came forward as the three entered his study.

"Fiddlesticks. Reputations are the least of our worries," Lucy said, helping Mr. Felix to a chair.

"Perhaps for you. Dev would thrash anyone who spoke ill of you. But *you*, Miss Matthews . . . what madness brings you to the home of a gentleman, especially at this hour?"

"I followed Lucy," Gin said. "I saw this fellow jump into her carriage, and I was afraid she was in danger."

"So you chased after her, alone? Of all the feather-witted schemes—"

"Mr. Foxworth," Lucy snapped, "this is not the time. Mr. Felix did leap into my coach. He says that Simon is in danger."

"Felix?" Fox moved closer and peered at the man. "Good God, it *is* you! We thought you were dead."

"Fox." Mr. Felix reached to grasp Fox's arm. "You can warn him. You can get there in time."

"Get where?"

"Bridgemoor," Lucy replied. "Simon left for Essex this afternoon with Isabella Montelucci."

"Yes, the auction." Fox turned back to Mr. Felix, who appeared to be fading. "Is it LaRue? We know he is alive, that he may be in England. Is LaRue going to the auction?"

"Mr. Foxworth, Isabella *is* Antoine LaRue," Lucy said.

"What?" Both Gin and Fox stared at her.

"You heard me. She *is* LaRue, she is already at the auction, and Simon is with her. We must hurry."

"Let me call a physician for Felix, then I will be off."

"*You* will be off?" Gin propped her hands on her hips. "What about us?"

"Are you mad?" he scoffed as he pulled the bell to summon a servant. "It is no place for women."

"We are going with you, Mr. Foxworth," Lucy said, aligning with Gin. "If nothing else, I can play the deceived wife who tracked her husband and his paramour to their trysting place."

"No, it's too dangerous."

Lucy folded her arms. "You really do not have a choice. If you leave without us, we will simply follow."

"We are not useless ninnies," Gin added. "We can help."

"And there is no time for arguing," Lucy said.

"Fine!" Fox threw up his hands. "Dev will kill me if anything happens to you, madam, but never let that deter you."

"We won't," Gin said, as the servant entered in response to his master's call.

"Send for the physician and put Mr. Felix in the guest room," Fox ordered. The servant immediately nodded and left the room, calling to his associates for assistance.

"We can take my coach," Lucy said. "It's waiting outside."

"I am not yet ready." Fox went to a cabinet and withdrew his box of pistols. He checked and loaded each one, then tucked them into his coat and turned back to the ladies, picking up his silver-topped cane. "Now we are ready to leave." He glanced at Gin. "Miss Matthews, I still believe it would be better if you waited here."

"I disagree."

"I am traveling with fools." He lurched out of the room as fast as his limp would take him.

Gin followed, and Lucy matched her stride to Gin's. "Does your godmother know where you are?"

"I doubt it. As soon as I saw that fellow jump into your coach, I called a hack and followed."

Lucy shook her head. "She will be frantic, Gin. Though I appreciate your concern, you should not have done anything so rash."

"I thought you were in danger. What else could I do?" They stepped into the foyer and saw the door open and the hack driver standing outside on the step.

Fox glowered at her. "Miss Matthews, I believe this is your driver."

"Yes, it is. He needs to be paid." She patted him on the arm. "And you know I don't have enough money with me tonight."

"Of course not." Gritting his teeth, he dug for his purse. "Both of you get into the carriage. At this rate, we will be lucky if we arrive before dawn."

"As long as Simon is still alive at dawn." Lucy gave him an urgent look, then swept her skirts aside and marched past the hack driver toward her coach.

"Don't worry," Gin said as she slipped past Fox and after Lucy. "We won't leave without you."

Isabella's dinner party was a strange affair indeed.

All of the guests were men. There were seven of them—some from various cultures, and all extremely wealthy. He had no doubt he was looking at England's most powerful enemies, or at least their representatives.

Isabella presided at one end of the table, as if she were the lady of the manor, and he sat at the other. The conversation that flowed seemed somewhat awkward, though civilized. After several courses of soups, fowl, puddings, and the like, he should have been stuffed beyond the limits of his waistcoat. But he ate sparingly, certain that at some point in the evening he would need to move quickly, and an overfull belly would not be an asset.

Finally, close to ten o'clock, the extensive meal ended.

"Since I am the only woman here," Isabella said as the last platters were cleared away, "I will not retire to the drawing room while you gentlemen enjoy your port and cigars. I encourage you to follow your normal habits despite my presence."

There was an immediate denial from all the

men at the table that anyone would smoke in the presence of a lady, and Isabella laughed. "Very well, my friends. But I do encourage you to enjoy your port." She signaled to a servant, a fellow he had never seen before, who stepped forward with a decanter. "This was my late husband's favorite type of port, and I brought it with me this evening to share with all of you. Please, *signori,* drink and enjoy in honor of my dear, departed husband Antonio."

Simon's instincts went on instant alert. The name Antonio and a wine Isabella had brought herself. . .

One of Antoine LaRue's favorite methods of assassination had been poison.

He glanced around the table, wondering if one of these men was LaRue. Or was it the servant?

None of the footmen who had served them this evening had looked familiar, but he knew they were supposed to be fellow agents of the Crown, sent to assist him this evening. How difficult would it be for LaRue to slip in and take the place of a servant with no one the wiser?

He glanced at his pocket watch. If this was indeed the auction, then Isabella would have to act soon.

Perhaps that is what she was doing.

The servant made his way around the table, pouring some of the beverage for each man. Some of them toasted Isabella and drank deeply.

Some of them sniffed at the wine before sipping tentatively.

The servant poured him the last glass in the bottle. He swirled it around in his goblet, wondering how he would rid himself of the liquor without Isabella seeing it. He glanced down at the other end of the table. Isabella was watching the other men with a mad light in her eyes, her lips parted in a smile of sheer, wicked delight.

The fellow next to him—Spanish, perhaps— had drained his glass and now sat back, staring into the sky with a vacant expression on his face. He licked his lips repeatedly.

He cast another look at Isabella. She was watching him, her smile disturbing and lovely at the same time. He raised his glass in salute to her, then made to sip it. She turned away as the guest to her left demanded her attention, his red face and jerky movements indicating intoxication. Simon lowered the glass just below the line of the tablecloth and tipped half the ruby liquid onto the floor.

He nearly winced as it hit his dark blue Turkish carpet. Damned expensive rug, ruined.

With a swift move that made him both a master thief and swordsman, he pulled the glass back into sight, just as Isabella looked at him again. He grinned and saluted her with the half-empty glass. Her small smile of satisfaction confirmed his suspicions.

The wine had to be poisoned.

He placed his glass back on the table, very near the Spaniard's. That gentleman stared at him for a long, disquieting moment, his pupils so large they dominated his entire eye, just like an owl's. Then his head slowly lolled in the other direction, and he gaped at the burning candles on the table.

Keeping his eye on Isabella, who was distracted by the loud Russian beside her, Simon switched the glasses around. Now the partially filled goblet sat before the Spaniard, while the empty one sat at Simon's place.

"I say there," an English fellow called, his voice hoarse. "When do we get on with business?"

"Are all of you ready?" Isabella asked. A chorus of shouted approval made her chuckle. "Then let us retire to the drawing room and move on to the true reason you have all gathered here this evening."

As they rose from the table, Simon assisted the Spaniard.

"I cannot feel my tongue," the foreign man said. He stuck it out at Simon. "Is it still there?"

"It is," Simon reassured him. The two men moved into the drawing room, the Spanish fellow feeling his tongue with his fingers.

Inside the drawing room, the chairs had been laid out in a circle around a table. On the table rested a common wooden box that a man might use to hold important papers.

"Everyone be seated," she called out, watching

as the men, all carrying satchels of different sizes and colors, settled themselves somewhat awkwardly in the chairs. Simon lowered the Spaniard into a seat and moved toward Isabella. She stroked a hand over his cheek. "Ah, *amore mio*," she purred. "How do you feel?"

He didn't dare glance at the Spaniard. "My tongue has fallen out," he slurred.

Isabella chuckled and patted his arm. "No, it has not. Now sit here, near me." She indicated a chair right next to her, and he sank into it, trying to stare vacantly as others had.

"Gentlemen," she said, raising her voice to project to the whole room. "I know why you are all here. I have the merchandise you want to purchase." She flipped open the box and withdrew a roll of documents. "Here is the list of every English spy currently residing in France, and some of the ones still hiding in England. Have you all brought your bids for this lovely item?"

A general assent filled the room, and the men patted their satchels.

"Good," she purred. "Before we begin, I would like to thank our host, Lord Devingham, for use of his superb house." A rumble of thanks rippled around the room and a smattering of applause, all except the loud Russian, who seemed strangely devoted to the pattern of the wallpaper.

"Now, we will get started." She smiled around at all the guests. "I assume you have all come with your bids converted into gold and jewels as asked. My associates will come around to each of you to verify this."

Michael Standish and the three ruffians he'd seen at Ravenforth Abbey came into the room. They moved from man to man, examining the bags. Standish cast Simon a speculative glance, and Simon stared blankly at him as if he didn't recognize the man. With a smirk at Simon's condition, Standish continued with his examination, then looked at Isabella and nodded.

"Va bene," she said. "I am so glad you are all gentlemen of your word. Unfortunately for you, however, I am no gentleman." She reached into her reticule and produced a small vial, which she held up so all could see it. "My dear friends, your wine has been poisoned. And this is the only antidote. If you want this cure, you will quietly hand over your satchels to my men, and that will determine if you live or die."

When Lucy, Fox, and Gin arrived at Bridgemoor just after midnight, they found no servants to greet them. The front hall was eerily silent as the trio crept through the house and up the stairs to the first floor. Finding the dining room empty, they moved toward the drawing room.

"Thank you all so much for your cooperation," Isabella said, the sound carrying easily into the hallway. *"Mille grazie."*

"Isabella," Simon said, and Lucy's knees went liquid with relief at hearing his voice. "What poison?"

The Italian woman chuckled. "Deadly nightshade, dear Simon. I am so sorry that you were included in this, but what else could I do?"

"She has poisoned them," Fox whispered to his companions. "Probably in the food at dinner, or wine."

"You cannot just leave us like this," Simon said, his tone weakening. "That is murder."

"You are quite right." Isabella held up the vial again. "There is only enough of this for one dose. May the strongest man win!" With these words, she tossed the vial into the middle of the room. Instantly, those guests not stupefied by the poison dove for the container of liquid, pushing each other aside in a desperate bid for survival.

Isabella laughed at the contest. "Michael, you and the men take the gold down to the carriage. Captain Leeford is waiting for us at Southend-on-Sea."

"Yes, my love."

Fox and the ladies scrambled away from the door and hurried down the hall into a bedroom. Keeping the door cracked open, they watched as Michael Standish and three others hauled several satchels out of the room and down the stairs. Once the men were gone, they slipped back into the hallway.

"There were supposed to be men here to help Dev," Fox whispered. "They were masquerading as footmen. Where the devil are they?"

"Isabella is alone in there with Simon," Lucy said. "This is our best chance to capture her."

"Do not be foolish," Fox snapped. "We are a cripple and two women. What do you expect to accomplish?"

"Saving Simon's life." Lucy glanced at Gin. "If there are men here, they are probably locked up somewhere, hopefully not poisoned. See if you can find them."

"Just a moment here—"

Gin gave him an exasperated look. "I can be quiet and fast, John, which is more than I can say for you right now. We are depending on you to take care of Isabella."

Fox looked startled at the use of his Christian name, but slowly nodded. "Very well."

"I'll start with the lower levels," Gin said.

Fox grabbed her arm before she could take a step. "Virginia, wait." She paused, and he pressed a swift kiss to her startled mouth. "You are an amazing woman."

She blinked in surprise, then gave him a cheeky grin. "You and I will talk about this later, John Foxworth." She hurried down the hall.

Lucy shook her head as Fox turned back to her. "I certainly hope your intentions are honorable, Mr. Foxworth. Now, are you ready to proceed?"

He gave her a grim nod, and she saw, finally, a glimpse of the man who had risked his life over and again for England. "Let the games begin."

Simon waited until the ruffians had left and until Isabella was distracted with the three fellows who were trying in vain to wrestle the vial of antidote from one man, who held it tightly in his grip but could not take the thing for fear of losing it to his competitors. When her back was to him, he leaped out of his chair and snatched the roll of papers from the table.

Isabella whirled around at the movement, her eyes widening. "*Bello mio*, what do you think to do with that?"

"Save England," he replied.

She laughed. "Foolish man. Do you really believe I would write down my most precious secrets?"

He glanced at the papers he held, then undid the ribbon tying them together. "Dressmakers' bills? What happened to the list?"

"There is no list." She snatched the papers from him and threw them into the hearth, where they burst into flame. With her other hand, she grabbed a small pistol from the box that had contained the papers, freezing him in his tracks when she brought the weapon up to point at his heart. "I just told you, dear Simon, that I do not write down my secrets."

"Your secrets? I thought they were LaRue's secrets."

"Ah." Comprehension lit her face. "I see you have secrets, too."

"What is this all about, Isabella? If there is no list, then why the auction?"

"I needed money. I will take this lovely gold, and my dear Michael and I will start a new life together somewhere else. Perhaps America."

One of the bidders shouted. They managed to liberate the vial from the fellow holding on to it, but it had gone flying and rolled beneath a sofa. Four men scrambled on hands and knees after it.

"Amusing, are they not?" Isabella said.

Just then the door to the drawing room burst open, and Lucy ran into the room. "Simon, Isabella *is* Antoine LaRue!"

With those words, the whole scheme made sense. He kicked out, surprising Isabella and sending the pistol skidding across the floor. Isabella gave a cry of rage and shoved Simon toward the still-bickering gentlemen, then ran for the door. Lucy leaped in her path, and the two women both crashed to the floor.

Simon untangled himself from the squabbling, shoving bidders, and scrambled for the pistol. He leaped to his feet with the weapon in his hand just as Isabella regained her footing. With a malicious smile, she pulled a knife from a sheath on her ankle, grabbed Lucy, who was climbing to her feet, and held the blade to her throat just as Simon raised the gun.

"Put down the pistol," Isabella demanded. "Your wife has been a thorn in my side for some time now, and it would not be a hardship for me to kill her."

Simon looked at Lucy. Her eyes were wide with fear, but she shook her head, silently telling him not to lay down his weapon. How had she known about Isabella, or that he needed help? And even then, she had come herself. Foolish, wonderful woman. As he stared into her eyes, he saw a wife loving and loyal beyond imagination, and he knew he could not take the chance of losing her. Even to save England.

He laid the pistol on the floor.

"Simon, no!" Lucy cried. She could not believe he had done that, just surrendered without fighting . . . for her.

He had told her he was falling in love with her, and now she finally realized what that meant.

Isabella grinned and began backing toward the door, dragging Lucy with her. Lucy sagged in Isabella's arms, dragging her feet on the floor, making herself a deadweight and therefore harder to pull along. Perhaps she could slow Isabella down, buy time for Fox to lead the other agents to the rescue. Or maybe the right diversion would give Simon the chance to grab the gun while Isabella was trying to open the door. . .

Lucy looked at her husband. He stood stiffly, his mouth a grim line, his eyes hard and narrowed. He curled his hands into fists and opened them again. She could tell he was impatient, frustrated; she could read him so well, knew his every mood.

Knew *him* better than she'd imagined.

Their eyes met. With razorlike steel pressed to her throat, she did not know how this tableau would end. She didn't want discord to be his last memory of her, not when she'd only just realized how foolish she had been. He had lied to her for good reason, both for her safety and the security of their country, and she had been too hurt to see clearly what he was doing. He *was* the man she had married—and more. The man who had claimed her heart.

She mouthed the words "I love you," hoping against hope that it was not the last time she would ever say it.

Suddenly Fox and Gin came up behind Isabella. As Fox jerked Isabella's knife hand in one direction, Gin yanked Lucy in the other. With a scream of rage, Isabella tried to bring the knife down toward Lucy. Sharp pain sliced across Lucy's shoulder as Gin finally pulled her free of the Italian woman's grip, and she landed on her knees with a harsh gasp, clamping a hand to her throbbing shoulder.

Isabella turned her fury on Fox, kicking him

in his bad knee. As he went down with a roar of agony, she raked the knife toward his throat. Gin screamed and wrenched Isabella's wrist, turning the weapon away from Fox. At the same time, Simon dove for the pistol on the floor, rolled to his feet with it in his hand, and fired.

Isabella jerked. Blood bloomed on her chest, soaking through her expensive silk evening dress. Then she crashed to the floor, dead with one shot.

Silence settled over the room except for the scuffling of those bidders who had not yet been overtaken by the deathly sleep induced by the poison.

Simon hurried to Lucy's side and pulled her hand away from the oozing wound. "How bad is it?"

"Not fatal." She gave him a reassuring smile.

He pulled out a handkerchief and pressed it against her shoulder. "Hold this here to stop the bleeding." She placed her fingers over the rapidly staining linen, and Simon kissed her with sweet desperation, his hands trembling as he cupped her face. "Did you mean what you said to me, Lucy?"

"Yes." Aglow with certainty despite the pain of her wound, she touched his lips with a trembling hand. "I love you."

"Enough of that now," Fox said, hissing with pain as Gin helped him to his feet. "There is work to be done yet, Dev."

Simon gazed into Lucy's eyes. "Will you be all right for a moment?"

She laid her hand over his. "I am fine."

"Very well." He gave her another quick kiss, then stood. "Fox, what happened to the rest of the men who were here to help me?"

"They were locked in the wine cellar," Gin said, kneeling beside Lucy to ease her gently from her knees to a sitting position. "I let them out, and they ran after the men with the bags."

"She must not have known who they really were," Fox said, "or else she would have killed them." He indicated the three bidders who were still conscious and trying without success to obtain the vial from under the sofa. "What do we do about them? There is only one antidote."

"*Atropa belladonna*, Fox." At his friend's blank look, Simon clarified, "Deadly nightshade. It's an herb that was named, ironically, for the habit of Italian women using the extract in their eyes to dilate their pupils. The antidote for it is opium. Laudanum should do the trick."

Fox just stared at him. "You spend too much time in that bloody greenhouse."

Simon shrugged. "A man must have a hobby."

Chapter 21

Being loved for oneself is truly the greatest contentment a man can know.

The journals of Simon, Lord Devingham,
on the ultimate happiness

They stayed at Bridgemoor, though Lucy swore she would have the drawing room redecorated at the first opportunity. Simon had carried her upstairs to bed (despite her protests that she could walk) and summoned a physician, who treated both Lucy's wound and the poisoned dinner guests.

"The house seems so quiet," Lucy said, as Simon entered the bedroom.

He looked as if he expected her to be near to death, but her welcoming smile seemed to convince him otherwise. He shut the door behind him. "Marbury's men apprehended Isabella's accomplices and marched them off to the magistrate for questioning. I do believe they resented being locked in the wine cellar." He perched on the edge of the bed and took her hand in his, grinning wickedly. "I must say, I enjoyed watching Standish being bound and marched away."

"Dreadful man. What about Gin?"

"Tucked safely in her room. With us here, she is properly chaperoned and will suffer no damage to her reputation."

Lucy raised her brows. "Even with Mr. Foxworth staying here as well?"

"Fox will behave himself."

"His intentions had best be honorable," she warned, "or else he will discover my wrath."

Simon chuckled. "More deadly than the wrath of Plath."

"Indeed. He kissed her, Simon. I saw it."

"His philandering days are long over, my sweet. If anything, I believe this courtship will turn Society on its ear."

"She will put him through his paces, have no doubt of that." She chuckled, then grew serious. "And . . . Isabella?"

"She's gone, too." He bent his head to press his lips to her fingers in a passionate gesture. "You will never know the hell I faced, seeing you that close to dying. Never do that to me again."

"My love," she murmured, stroking his hair. "I

felt the same way when I saw you put down your weapon."

"I could not let her hurt you." One warm tear fell on the back of her hand, and he turned moist eyes to meet hers. "You mean the world to me, Lucy. I love you so very much, and I would sacrifice anything to save you."

"I love you, too. Completely. And I believe I finally understand why you do what you do." She sniffed, fighting the tears that welled in her own eyes. "Someone has to stop people like Isabella, don't they? And that is what you do. Who you are."

"It is the right thing to do."

"Yes." She caressed his cheek, smiling. "And you are a man who always does the right thing."

"I try. When I lied to you . . ."

"Hush." She placed a finger over his lips. "It was necessary. I understand that now. I believe in you, Simon. Just please don't send me back to Devingham. Not unless you come with me."

He pulled her hand away from his mouth. "You will never leave my side."

Her lips parted in a mischievous smile. "You do not appear to be at my side right now, husband."

His eyes lit, but then his brow creased with concern. "I do not want to hurt you."

She held out her good arm. "What hurts, my love, is your absence."

He hesitated. "Such activity will jostle your shoulder."

"Then you will simply have to be careful, won't you?" She trailed her fingers along his thigh. "Make love to me, Simon. It has been way too long."

"You tempt me sorely, wife."

She gave him a slow, teasing grin. "Is it working?"

"Too well."

"Then come to bed, husband." She pulled back the coverlet in invitation. "You are all I need to forget the troubles of this night."

"Are you certain?" He stood and shrugged out of his coat, but his expression remained concerned. "I thought you wanted to become better acquainted without physical passion interfering."

"I know everything that is important," she said, climbing to her knees with the awkwardness of a wounded shoulder. "I know that you are a man of honor, that you love me, that I can trust you with my life. And if my life, well, then, why not my heart?"

"Your heart is the most precious thing in the world to me." He stepped closer to the bed and pulled her into his arms. "I vow to take care of it for the rest of our lives."

"I will never lie to you, Simon. I love you. I want you to make love to me. I want us to be close again."

Hunger blazed across his face and lit his eyes. "That is my fondest wish."

"Then what are you waiting for?" An impish

curve to her lips, she tugged at his cravat, undoing his valet's fashionable knot.

"Plath was very proud of that knot," he commented, as she tossed the wrinkled neckcloth to the floor.

"A pox on Plath." She pulled his shirttails out of his waistband. "I want you naked."

"You're a saucy bit of goods, aren't you?"

"I'm a demanding wife, Simon. Do get used to it."

"I plan to." He lifted her off the bed, surprising a squeal from her. Setting her on her feet, he pulled the nightdress off, careful of her wounded shoulder, and left her standing naked before him. "I am a demanding husband, my love. Get used to it."

She grinned at him. "I already am."

His expression grew serious as he cupped the fullness of her breasts in his hands. "You are the most beautiful woman in the world to me. And lavender—" He sniffed at her hair. "Lavender has come to be an aphrodisiac."

"Simon," she breathed, her eyes sliding closed as the magic of his touch set her flesh aflame.

"My sweet Lucy." He guided her so that she sat down on the edge of the bed. Quickly, he removed his boots and the rest of his clothing.

Lucy couldn't stop the sound of approval that escaped her at the sight of his readiness for her, and she reached out and stroked gentle fingers along his erection. He hissed out a breath and held on to her good shoulder, caressing her hair with his other hand as she continued to fondle him.

The more aroused he got, the more excited she got. She watched his face, sweeping her hand up and down his hard shaft, marveling at the magnetism between them. After long moments, he opened his eyes, looking down on her with the fierceness of the warrior she knew him to be. He helped her lie back on the bed, then lifted her knees in the crooks of his arms and slid inside her.

It was like coming home. He fit inside her as if molded especially for her, and she gripped the covers in white-knuckled fingers, closing her eyes as her body hummed with growing tension.

When the pleasure hit, they gave themselves to it, accepting at last the bond that held them both willing captives to love.

Later that night as they lay in each other's arms, Lucy snuggled closer to Simon. "Promise me you will never lie to me again," she murmured. "Even for my own safety."

"Never for the rest of our lives." He pressed a soft kiss to her temple. "Do you believe me?"

"Always."

Two days later, Lucy marched up the stairs of the Nelson residence, a footman in tow carrying Arminda's box. She knocked, but when the butler attempted to deny her entrance, she rushed past him. "My apologies, but I must see Mrs. Nelson on a matter of the utmost importance."

"Madame is having breakfast," the butler said. "But—"

"Direct me to the breakfast room."

"To your left," the elderly servant stammered. Then he scurried after her. "Wait! She is not receiving visitors!"

"She will receive me." Lucy strode into the breakfast room to find Mrs. Nelson enjoying a breakfast of bread, jam, and chocolate.

The lady's face creased in anger as she saw Lucy. "What are you doing here? Leave my house at once!"

"Not yet." Lucy gestured to the footman, who placed the box on the table next to the lady's breakfast. "Mrs. Nelson, this box was left to you by your mother."

"I do not want it!" She cast the carved wooden box a look of loathing. "It used to sit on her bureau. Take it away."

"I cannot do that. I swore a promise to your mother on her deathbed that I would see this delivered to you."

"I do not want it."

"That is not my concern," Lucy said. "Mrs. Nelson, your mother spoke of you often. Even after you left her house, she always knew where you were and secretly watched to be certain of your safety."

"I'm surprised she did not come forth," she scoffed.

"She knew you were trying to get away from her wild way of life," Lucy said. "She stayed away, just like you wanted. Never got to see your wedding or see her grandchildren born. And now she never will. The least you can do is accept this legacy she left you."

Mrs. Nelson's eyes widened. "She knew where I was?"

"Yes. And when she could, she helped through a third party. An unexpected inheritance or a bonus for good work done when you worked in a dressmaker's shop."

"I never imagined she would look for me. Or that she would care."

"She cared very much, enough to leave you to your own life as you so clearly wanted. Before she died, it was her fondest wish to be able to present this box to you herself. Instead, she entrusted the task to me when her health proved too difficult."

Mrs. Nelson ran a finger along the carving at the top of the box. "You are very kind to do this for a dying woman."

"She was my friend," Lucy said. "Mrs. Nelson, the last words you and your mother exchanged were in anger, and now that can never change. You must accept who she was, not who you wished she could be." She laid her hand over Mrs. Nelson's for a brief moment. "Maybe the box holds good memories for you."

"I doubt it." But she pulled the box toward her and fiddled with the latch. Finally, she unfastened it.

Lucy began to back away. "I will leave you to your privacy," she said.

"No, don't." Mrs. Nelson gave her a small smile. "You worked so hard to see that this got to me that I want you to see what's inside." Decisively, she flipped the latch and opened the lid.

"What is it?" Lucy asked.

"Letters." She lifted them out, all in bundles tied with ribbon. "Letters from her to me. Never posted." She choked on the last words, emotion finally getting the better of her.

"She never forgot you," Lucy said. "And now you will get to know the real Arminda by reading these letters. Maybe someday you can forgive her."

"Thank you," Mrs. Nelson rasped, her eyes misting. "Thank you for making me listen."

"Try to keep in mind that she had very honorable reasons for what she did," Lucy murmured. "But through it all she never stopped loving you."

Mrs. Nelson managed a smile. "I think, Lady

Devingham, that this is the first time I can believe that."

"Love can stand the test of time," Lucy said. She gestured at the box. "You have the proof."

When Lucy returned home, she found Simon waiting for her. "You, madam, are supposed to be in your sickbed."

"You did not think so at Bridgemoor." With an impish grin, Lucy handed her bonnet and reticule to her maid.

He gave a sigh and took her uninjured arm. "You are a wicked piece of goods, Lady Devingham," he murmured, steering her into the morning room and away from prying ears.

"You had your task to complete, and I had mine." Lucy caressed his cheek. "Mrs. Nelson has accepted her legacy."

"And you?" He caught her hand and pressed a kiss to the palm. "Have you accepted your lot in life?"

"To live with you as your wife and mother of your children, to stand beside you and continue to love you no matter what the future brings?"

"That is what I meant, yes."

She laughed and curved her body into his. "Most definitely, my love. Just try and stop me."

He hugged her close. "And incur the wrath of Lucy? Never."